Brink Fishing

A Mystery Novel

by

Leelon Edwards

AUTHOR PROOF

34/100
LE

©Copywrite 2021 by Leelon Edwards. All rights reserved.

No part of this publication may be reproduced, or transmitted in any form or by any means, electronic, mechanical, photocopy, recording, or otherwise, without written permission from the publisher. For information regarding permission, contact Ride-the-wind Publishing at LeelonEdwards@gmail.com

Disclaimer:
All characters and events in this book are fiction. Any similarity to real persons, living or dead, is coincidental. Resemblances may be intentional but are not malicious. Places, boats and things described in this book are sometimes real and intended to provide a real sense of place where the characters interact in locations familiar to the reader. Any location identified can be considered an endorsement by the author who encourages the reader to patronize these places of business and proprietorships to fully experience the Florida Gulf Coast.

Sharp hooks and tight lines are tactics.
Persistence and patience is a strategy.

I learned that from an excellent fisherman…
My dad!

This book is dedicated to his continued belief in me and persistent but gentle nudges to do the work, be persistent, then be patient.

Contact:
LeelonEdwards@gmail.com

Visit my webpage at
www.leelonedwards.com
or
friend me on Facebook!

Chapter 1

The corpse rolled gently in the waves as the first rays of sun glimmered off the quartz-white sands of Shell Island. The beach was pink in the early light, washed in a slowly ascending tide and reflected in clear gulf waters. The ghost crabs had found him already. Now the blue crabs were tiptoeing sideways along the shallow sand where the waves sloshed off the taut skin.

In the distance, a four-wheeled vehicle approached, maneuvering up and down the wide beach at a measured pace. The turtle patrol is always the first to run the eight-mile stretch looking for crawls as they diligently search for the marks in the sand made by a mother turtle where she left the ocean to dig a nest and lay her eggs the previous night.

Drew got the call about 7:20 as he finished his coffee and the headlines. The turtle patrol had contacted the office a little after 6:00. Drew was lucky that the office had waited this long to call. Typically, he would be in the boat by 7:30, so the only surprise was being dispatched to the beach rather than offshore or some remote bay location with a funny name like Blind Alligator Bayou or an unpronounceable Chatot Indian name like Choctawhatchee.

Drew's Florida Fish and Wildlife Conservation Commission vessel was docked behind the house, a twenty-four foot center console with twin Yamaha 250s. No stereo, no plush rear seating - all those accoutrements were removed from the former drug dealer's hull. Once the envy of contraband couriers, now a gray and green workboat, reassigned to a less stressful existence with someone who can appreciate her capability and the irony that such a prize is now relegated to law enforcement.

He left the empty coffee cup and the morning news on the deck table and walked down to the dock. While the step back into law enforcement was a bit anticlimactic, Drew found it easy to appreciate the commute. Less than ten years ago, his commute was a full pack, M4A1 and a long trek in the dust and sand of Afghanistan. From that perspective, the walk from the deck to the dock can't really be considered a commute, but compared to an extended drive south on I-95 at 0700, it was a pleasant reminder that his transfer to the Gulf Coast was not a bad thing.

The house was salvaged from Hurricane Opal in '95 and several storms before that. While that reduced the number of potential buyers, it was specifically the reason he selected it. A survivor. Not just of one storm, but many. Its simplicity is a testament to old Florida and to the fishermen that worked these waters. All that remains in the area of these intrepid pioneers is a small contingent of their offspring. This house was built by one of those that knew the stakes and paid the ante. Drew counted himself among them. She stands today because of that tentative contract with the sea. It's not really a contract, it's more like an accord, and one that can become null and void without notice.

Drew dutifully slipped on his Personal Floatation device, or PFD, keyed the VHF radio, and let the FWC office know he was away from the dock. He idled out to the channel markers. The morning included a light breeze that still carried the salty smell of May even though June had just arrived. There was a cool crispness that would soon give way to a thick humid midday as the sun made its way over the water. Bright yellow day lilies were looking into the morning sun for the promise of an afternoon thunderstorm. The Gulf Coast delivers excellent reasons to be deliberate on such a morning.

"Good morning, Mr. Whear," Drew said over the idling engines.

An older man looked up from beneath a broad hat. He was standing hip deep near the channel marker. His skin was dark brown and the lines on his forehead deepened as he raised one hand in sort of a wave but more to block the sun. He lowered the top water lure he was about to cast.

"You know I was just about to catch that redfish you spooked," the old man stated with a matter-of-fact attitude.

"So you have already caught your limit this morning?" Drew asked.

"Had two tickling my toes, they was so close, but I needed the gold spoon to make 'em bite. You know I prefer the top water, so I just let them swim on past."

"Top water is more fun if you can find them shallow," Drew said, then noticed that he had cut the top water lure off and was tying on a gold spoon.

"Sometimes you're out here just for fun, but sometimes you needs to eat," he said, looking up at the rod tip to make sure it was not tangled. "The missus said I needed to bring home dinner when I left about dawn. You know at my age," he continued, "it's a good start when you wake up early in the morning." He stopped for a moment and looked up. "You know, I guess it's a good start just to keep waking up."

He was a legend in the area and carried with him the soul of all fishermen... independent, resolute, and thankful for every hour he was blessed to spend out on the bay. His face wrinkled all the way down his cheek when he smiled, but there, in his squinty eyes, was a sparkle of anticipation that the next big redfish would be hooked with just one more cast.

He chuckled and said, "So get on outta here. I gotta bring home dinner."

Drew waved and slowly pushed the throttles to clear the markers, then pressed them to the stops, leaving him to walk the shallow grass flats.

Trimming up just a bit, Drew felt that slow crescendo of power as the hull rides up on plane. A quick adjustment of the trim tabs set the boat level and he backed off the throttle for the cruise down St. Andrew Bay and out the pass into the Gulf of Mexico.

Just off the green buoy, there was a congregation of seabirds diving and dipping on a school of small baitfish. Predators in the early morning, taking their measure of sustenance from a school of bait driven to the surface by another predator. The minnows were balled up and rippling the surface. School behavior. The prey responded to a threat from below by grouping together and moving to the surface, and were now exploited by predators from above. Drew thought for a moment about slowing just for the opportunity to watch the spectacle, but that was not what he was here for. He headed on out the pass.

During the summer season, finding an event on the beach is quite easy. Determined gawkers rapidly shroud the scene. Even on an island, a morning throng had gathered and identified Drew's destination. On arrival, Drew anchored into the small surf then waded ashore. The crowd was already animated as Drew approached.

"Was he murdered?"

"Looks like a shark got him."

"Need any help?"

"Think he's been dead long?"

Without answering any of the inquiries, Drew motioned for the crowd to make some room as another boat approached. Just offshore, a 22-foot Boston Whaler Outrage with NMF in dark blue block letters on the stern turned toward the beach. The boat nosed into the beach to allow Dr. Haymer of the National Marine Fisheries to step onto the sand; then the handler backed off shore to anchor nearby.

"What do you think, Drew?" he asked, walking at a brisk pace to the scene.

"He's dead, but I just got here," Drew replied.

No formalities required for old friends. MacKenzie Haymer, known as Mack, and Drew were fraternity brothers at Auburn University. While Drew could not muster any interest in attending more school, Mack finished his bachelor's then went straight into a PhD program. He wanted a job on the Gulf Coast and was willing to stay in school until he got it.

"So let's take a look," and he waded into the clear water as a wave gently lifted the corpse and set it back down askew. Drew directed the crowd to move on while Mack conducted the initial inspection, then he cleared some space on one side. Looking up he asked, "Where is Christi?"

Drew glanced down the beach to see her torso in motion as she jogged to the site with a sealed Pelican case and a bottle of water. Mack was typically accompanied by studious, note-taking, observer-types with the pasty look of a library dweller; but this was a long-legged woman with a swimmer's build. She had lean muscular legs in bike shorts that were soaked after wading ashore and light brown hair pulled back beneath a Corona visor. The Auburn Tigers t-shirt was only partially wet and her yellow bathing suit top was tied above the collar.

Drew extended his hand as she approached. "Drew Phillips," he said, as she grabbed his hand firmly.

"Christi Miller. Nice to meet you, sir," she quickly responded, not even breathing hard.

"Sir is not required, not if you're working with Mack. We've known each other too long."

Drew thought Mack was attending to the inspection but he approached from behind and piped in, "That's right. It would be unseemly for a man of his campus repute to be referred to as *sir*."

She smiled, a genuine smile that said she was satisfied with her current pursuits. In law enforcement, it's a pleasure to see all that reflected back in a smile, particularly one associated with a pretty face. Christi was here as a colleague and interested in what she could learn from Mack.

"So is it a dolphin?" she asked.

"Yep, *TURSIOPS TRUNCATUS*, probably about three, maybe four years old. Come look," Mack replied.

Christi set the case on a step of sand at water's edge then joined Mack at the carcass. She grabbed a pectoral fin to roll the dolphin slightly on its side.

"What happened?" she asked.

"I think that's why Drew wanted us to join him. It appears anything but natural," Mack told her.

It was the first time Drew had actually taken a close look at the dead mammal but the turtle patrol had given him a head's up. That's exactly why he wanted Mack to take a look and asked the office to call him.

Mack started in, "See here, the body is virtually intact." Then he pointed to the usual scars and scrapes expected of a young male. "No noticeable bruises or contusions, but here, right side of his head, it's completely mangled. Teeth are missing, his eye and part of the maxilla are gone."

"It looks like his tongue blew up," Christi noted. "Could a shark have taken a bite like that?"

"I don't think so; it's inconsistent with any natural causes. Could be post-mortem damage by sharks or other fish, but I don't think so."

Mack put his finger down into the edge of its mouth and scared away an assertive little blue crab, then pulled back a flap of skin. "See right here, some of his teeth were forced into the upper jowl."

"So what do you think?" Drew asked.

"I'd like to take him back to the office, if that's all right?"

Christi was trying her best to be stalwart and detached, but she didn't have the armor of years and it was beginning to show. She turned away and walked to the water bottle she left on the beach.

"That's fine with me Mack. I'll need some good photos and a copy of your report."

"No problem …so what do you think of Christi?" Mack whispered, turning to look where she stood facing the other direction.

"Seems nice enough. She new?"

"Summer help. Auburn fisheries."

"Could do worse than that."

"Christi, can you bring the camera and the recorder?" Mack yelled. "Not at all like my usual summer help," he said looking up with a knowing grin.

She picked up the yellow case, took a short sip of water, and then walked toward Mack. In a glance, Drew could see her uneasiness had passed and she was ready to deal with mechanics of the job. Tough, but still holding onto that empathy and a desire for the world to be a more conscious of the sea and her inhabitants.

"Let's get some of the details documented before we try to get him into the boat," Mack said as she approached.

The beachcombers gawked but the uniform convinced them to keep their distance. Like a roadside fender-bender, there was no show anymore, just people doing their job. Drew stood back to look over the area and let them have some space.

Drew was thinking as they wrapped up, where do you find clues for a job like this one? No footprints, no tire tracks, no getaway boat, no fingerprints. It's a federal offense just to feed or harass dolphin; why would someone intentionally try to hurt one? Maybe Mack and Christi could help with the investigation. Drew looked back as they started putting things away. He hoped so, because it looked like this dolphin was murdered.

Chapter 2

Mack called three days later. Drew could stop by to pick up the report and he had all the pictures anyone might need.

"Can you email a copy?" Drew asked.

"You got it. I'll send it now, but I was hoping we could discuss it. Can you meet for a beer later?"

"4:30, J. Michaels."

"You got it ...and hey, don't be surprised if Christi comes too. She seems to have a personal interest in this one."

"You sure she's up to bad jokes and seeing *Doctor* Haymer in his true habitat, surrounded by cold beer and women in tight shirts?"

"She had me figured out at the interview. Besides, you know that Mrs. *Doctor* Haymer would have me rolling in the surf and eaten by crabs if I so much as left a furtive glance unreported. Besides, remember Debbie Miller?"

"Nickname Boom-boom? Sigma Kap, and reportedly your…"

"That's the one," he interrupted. "Christi is her baby sister. Debbie called back in January hoping I might help her get a co-op spot this summer. Debbie still thinks I pulled strings, but Christi did it all on her own." Drew's email announced the receipt of Mack's report. There was nearly enough time to go through it before meeting him.

"So I'll see you there," Drew said hanging up and opening the file.

The autopsy was graphic. The photos were not tagged yet and each page had a DRAFT watermark, but after scanning the summary, it was all but obvious. There was nothing wrong with this animal until someone fed it an incendiary device.

Drew changed out of uniform at the office then rechecked tomorrow's schedule before leaving. He could feel the Captain's eyes as he strolled past in shorts and flip-flops with sunglasses hanging from a light blue cord. He thought Drew should put in an extra hour or two if he really wants some upward mobility. Drew usually does, but it starts at sunup when he pulls away from the dock while the boss is still smacking that alarm clock for fifteen more minutes.

Drew turned onto Thomas Drive out of the Naval Support Activity where the office is located, near the Coast Guard Station. During the off-season it is no more than a ten-minute drive to J. Michaels, but schools in Alabama were out and the tourists had begun to arrive. The minivan that passed was loaded with colorful kayaks strapped to the roof, three bikes hanging off the bumper, and three heads over the backseat looking for the beach. Drew thought that he could smell the coconut-pineapple suntan lotion mom was slathering on pink skin and rubbing into anxious, unappreciative faces.

J. Michaels is no different from any other local food establishment except that the management knows that it's the locals that keep their doors open long after the summer season ends. The vintage surfboards in the rafters set a beach boy theme while the rare and antique shotguns randomly displayed speak to a redneck code that thrives from Nashville down I-65. Stepping in the door, the regulars are easy to spot.

Christi wore khaki shorts and a bright blue tank. Her hair was pulled back and her yellow bathing suit top was still tied at her neck. Mack was waving Drew over as if he hadn't seen them. He waved with a practiced nonchalance but knowing that everybody in the place had turned to see Mack's geeky salutations.

There was Mack standing and waving both hands like an airline attendant vectoring Drew into a post on the B concourse, third table to the left and next to the window. The curled unkempt hair, the round, wire-frame glasses, and the three pens in his shirt pocket-- it's all part of the packaging. Mack could never shrug off any of the 'nerd' monikers so he rolls with it. The PhD he gets to use behind his name is enough absolution and his ante to a lifetime of fish related research. At 30, he still has the face of a graduate student. Must be the stress level. Beers arrived as Drew pulled up a chair. Christi smiled as Mack picked up the tall, cold mug and passed it to him.

"He's been telling you stories, hasn't he?" Drew said to her with mock sincerity, "They're lies, every one of them!"

"How do you know what he's been telling me?" Christi answered with a feigned innocence.

"I think it's better to assume a defensive posture; then I'm in a better position to negotiate."

"That sounds too safe to be your standard approach ...*Killer*," she shot back.

"He always starts with some of the more outrageous. They were sunning beside the lake and I didn't actually take their bathing suit tops; I was bringing them back."

"But who paid the kid that ran off with them?" she asked.

Drew looked at the frosty glass and decided it was a judicious time to take a wistful sip and assume offense.

"Did Mack tell you about when he was caught on the third floor of the Sigma Kap dormitory wearing a fluffy pink robe and…"

"Okay, okay, that was nearly ten years ago," Mack interrupted. "Besides, we have business to discuss and this lady here wants your order.

Drew conceded gracefully and turned to the waitress. "I'll have a dozen raw, the smoked fish dip, and the next round."

"A dozen baked," Christi replied without looking at the menu. She smiled at Drew and said, "Had my first dozen during Spring Break my junior year; now I can't get enough."

"So did you get to read my report? " Mack asked. "It's mostly Christi's work actually. These days I just get a chop at things as they go by."

Drew explained that he had reviewed the summary and the photos but hadn't finished the text. Truth was he scanned it all the way through but didn't want to let them know that it included some scientific language that he didn't understand.

Christi chimed in, "Somebody killed that dolphin." Her tone included some malice. "We think a small device exploded at the right mandible with enough force to severely injure the animal, not fatally, but enough …enough that it simply beached itself."

Mack went on to explain in a more scientific context that other mammals beach themselves when severely injured. They simply find someplace to die.

"It's a horrible way to go," Christi added. "Mammals continue to breathe but they don't have the wherewithal to fight the sharks. This one probably bled to death. It could never eat again."

There was no soft tone. Some empathy, but Christi's voice had an edge to it.

"These are intelligent, air-breathing creatures more closely related to you and me than a fish. They have a very sophisticated bio-sonar that they use to forage and to communicate. Some research even indicates that they can connect to autistic children in ways we don't understand. I guess you can tell it really upsets me to think somebody did this on purpose."

"Who would want to hurt a dolphin?" she asked. The question was not empirical; it was a statement of disbelief.

Chapter 3

Drew took a sip of beer and tried to think of ways to make this conversation less difficult. Her passion was more than enough to propel the topic, but Drew knew there was no simple answer.

Her voice was raised and the statements were more than just factual. They were personal. The question and commentary was directed at Drew. He was law enforcement, he should know who would want to harm a dolphin.

"You know sometimes we have to protect the animal population from human stupidity," Drew replied. "I once ticketed a boater in the gulf holding his kid over the gunwale of his rental boat with a frozen cigar minnow in his hand. He was trying to get the dolphin to jump out and get the fish like they do at the marine parks. He had that glazed over *'what-are-you-talking-about'* look when I told him that these are wild dolphin and could take the kid's arm off to get that fish."

The stories abound of a short period when feeding dolphin off the coast of Panama City Beach was considered a tourist right of passage. It was a 'must do' excursion with a local captain that could guarantee dolphin sightings, as though it were something rare here on the Gulf of Mexico. Feeding the dolphin was no stranger than feeding rainbow trout in the pond behind the mountain restaurant or squirrels at a bird feeder.

"I gave another ticket to a guy in a rental pontoon with a package of hot dogs. He was genuinely pissed that the dolphin wouldn't come eat so he could show off for his girlfriend. The empty bucket of margarita mix got him into even more trouble when he claimed that she drank it all. I suspect he had a bad night."

Mack was looking around for the waitress and waving an empty glass. Christi seemed amused but countered.

"This wasn't stupid. This was intentional. Who would do such a thing?"

She stared at Drew, knowing he should have an answer. He reached for several possibilities while taking in her deep grey-blue eyes and a look of more than casual interest in finding a murderer.

Drew thought to offer spearfishermen but that would likely have been a 12-gage bang stick or a barb-tipped shaft. Shrimpers maybe? No. They could be net fishing at night but FWC has not reported much of that in the gulf. According to the late shift and aerial surveillance, shrimpers are working the bay. He thought for another minute, looking for a phrase and for the right way to start this complicated discussion.

"You know, the world has changed for what used to be the most pleasant and desirable jobs in the south," he said.

Christi glanced up with a look that said *don't change the subject.* She took her first sip of beer as Drew's eyes confirmed that he was still on topic.

"Who wouldn't have wanted to be a charter boat captain in the '60s? Get up early, crank the boat and head out the pass at dawn, catch fish and come home with a boatload of happy fishing buddies. Big tips to the young deckhands, a couple nice snapper for the captain to take home." Drew lifted his hands lightheartedly, "and you get to do it again tomorrow!" Lowering his hands and shaking his head, he continued, "That way of life is simply disappearing."

Christi looked up again as though Drew was reminiscing and not answering her question. At one point in the past, Drew had considered charter fishing as a profession. Be your own boss, fish everyday, nice boat and sunsets. All sportsmen get the idea at one time or other.

Drew explained how boat maintenance is expensive. A deep-water boat slip is required for most of the full-time captains. Just like a store entrance, a marina slip with a high traffic count is a big cost of doing business.

Then there is the cost of fuel. Diesel is two, maybe three times what it was just a year ago, so charter rates have to go up. Again, just the cost of doing business.

"So you are saying the commercial fishermen are to blame?"

"Not necessarily but when those happy bubbas come down from Anyplace, Georgia, once or twice a year and pay a thousand, or maybe two thousand dollars, they want to go catch fish."

"And so they should," Christi added, providing him a chance to reassemble thoughts and sip a beer. "My dad used to bring me here as a kid and I loved to fish off the pier. It was a special time when I got to go fishing with my dad."

Drew nodded to a local that waved on his way to the back and noticed several other fishermen gathering for libation after another day on the water. Right after he passed, he felt a sharp kick to the back of his chair. Drew had just set his beer back on the coaster or it would have been all over Christi. Drew jerked around catching his chair before it upended several tables.

"Oh, 'scuse me officer! I'm afraid I lost my balance as I spotted this lovely young lady." The local tipped his ball cap to Christi then proceeded to join the others at a table toward the back.

Drew put his hand on the table about to stand when he felt Mack's hand on his shoulder. "Let it go," he said, watching the captain of *Reel Fun* shrug and hold his hands out, palms up, approaching the table of charter captains and crew. They were looking at him and glancing back to see if Drew was going to stand.

Drew looked at Mack and then back at a couple of captains he knew at the table. They looked and laughed at the arriving captain but they kept glancing back at Drew's table with a wary eye. Drew may not be one to hold a grudge but they knew he was taking names.

Lowering his voice and picking up his beer, Drew leaned toward Christi so she would know he intended to tone the discussion down a bit. "What I was pointing out is that the law steps in under the guidance of the National Marine Fisheries. The law restricts the number of fish and the size that these captains can keep in the interest of saving the fishery. While saving a resource is a noble cause, it doesn't help these guys make a living," he said nodding toward the table in the back.

"But they don't have a living if we can't keep the fishery from collapsing," Christi said. Her voice had energy and a matter-of-fact tone but it was still a bit too prominent even for a loud oyster bar. "Look what happened to the cod in New England, the salmon in Oregon. Look what we did to the whales!"

"Of course, in the long term, you're right," Drew agreed. "But these guys make their living when their patrons catch fish. Long term studies and objectives won't buy fuel or pay the mortgage."

Christi looked down thinking about the reports and studies that she might read weekly plus all the textbooks and classes on species and phyla and fish physiology. They were her business but they did not affect her paycheck.

"These captains are the front line of law enforcement." Drew added. "I'm not there to tell the guy from Birmingham with three-too-many beers that he only gets to keep two red snapper and they have to throw the big one he just caught back over the side," Drew said and pointed up at the captains. "They have to do it, and they have to do it without a fuss."

It was obvious that Christi was listening, even if she did not entirely agree.

"In order to save the industry, we've put these guys on life support and fed them salty bitter medicine. I can't imagine somebody making a successful living while paying for fuel, dock space, and service and trying to keep customers satisfied with fewer and fewer fish. These guys are brink fishing the edge of an economic tragedy. How long would you want to continue working if every year they cut your pay then required you to work harder?"

Drew let the question hang for just a moment. Long enough for her to know that he was heading toward the question but still working on that answer.

"It's my job to enforce those laws," Drew said and took a sip of beer then looked down for a second, "but I understand what it has done to their way of life."

He glanced back at the table of professional fishermen behind her laughing loudly at something one of them had said. "See that guy behind you on the right?" and he looked toward the table behind her. She turned slightly to see three guys at a table near the wall behind her.

"The guy on the left is a charter captain, the kid in the middle is his deckhand, and the guy on the right is a captain that currently doesn't have a boat. The reason he doesn't have a boat is because it was repossessed this past winter. Last season was one of the worst in recent memory. When the fall season ends, most of these guys get other jobs or head south and operate in the keys or West Palm. There simply isn't enough work here."

"The other captain, the one that kicked my chair, he operates the *Reel Fun*. He docks at Captain Andersons and seems to be keeping his head above water. He tells me that loyal customers he's had for years, who would charter two or three times a summer, now just go once. For those customers, fishing doesn't just mean going out there drinking some beer and slapping buddies on the back; it means coming back with fish."

Mack was becoming more insistent about that second round and finally got the waitress' attention by standing with an empty beer glass held high waving with three fingers pointing at it. Mack can be anything but discreet.

"Then there's the weather!" Drew said. "Rough seas and thunderstorms cancel trips. All it takes is Jim what's-his-name on the Weather Channel to show a radar reflection in the gulf with some red in it and customers call to cancel. You can imagine what a hurricane in the Caribbean does. It can wreck the charter business for weeks."

While Christi remained considerate of Drew's rambling, she bluntly stated the obvious. "So what does that have to do with a murdered dolphin?"

"Sorry," Drew said, looking up and seeing that she was still intently interested and hadn't veered from the original topic. "It's predator or prey. The dolphin is just another predator eating away at the charter captain's way of life."

"How's that?"

"They eat the fish that the charter boats catch."

"Of course they do," Christi said, as though he was being facetious.

"No, I mean they eat their catch. Ask around, talk to fishermen, or we'll go fishing one afternoon and I'll show you. Considering all that they have to deal with, the dolphin is probably the recipient of a lot of anger. I would bet that less than half of the undersized catch the charter boats return to the water ever make it back to the bottom. The dolphin eat them on the way down."

Drew and Christi's eyes were still locked as she absorbed the data dump he offered. She was unconvinced but not fully willing to dismiss the conjecture. From Drew's perspective, it was the best he had to offer and probably a bit more than he should have.

"So who has the baked?" the waitress spouted, arriving with beers and a platter of food. Drew pointed at Christi, and a plate of hot oysters landed with melted cheese and the aroma that reminded him of all the reasons he chose to live near the ocean. Drew looked at Mack as he dashed some Crystal sauce into a shell of chilled oyster, then reached over to an empty table nearby for a sleeve of abandoned saltines. He was about to ask Mack what he had wanted to discuss. Then it occurred to him.

Drew looked over just as Mack slurped up the first oyster. Mack grinned knowing that Drew had just answered his own question before he even asked. Drew picked up the second beer and raised it slightly in his direction then took a sip knowing that Mack's conversation had just concluded. Christi's passion said all that he needed to discuss.

The table in the back was getting loud and some of the captains were nodding and pointing. Drew was staring past them and out into the clear blue; temporarily lost while absorbing the fundamentals of Christi's inquiry. A noise from the kitchen brought him back, he looked away and shook his head. Christi stayed lost in a baked oyster she moved around the shell with the edge of a cracker.

"Hey, I need your help next week," Mack said spewing cracker crumbs. "I'm supposed to speak at a fishing meeting; in fact, I'm hosting it. Think you can help me get some of the nerd-speak out of my talk? I mean, seeing as how you get along so well with the captains and all...."

Christi looked up and smiled. It was time to change the topic but Drew knew the results of her simple question could lead to a bigger concern. More dolphin deaths could spin into a real problem for a tourist community. If a fisherman was involved, it could start a spiral that wouldn't stop. The vortex could swallow the sportsman and the commercial fleet. In a series of bad decisions, it could take the whole industry like a goliath grouper inhales its dinner.

"I'll be glad to take a look at it," Drew replied.

Chapter 4

The shrimp boats were still trawling the bay and there was a dark gray edge to the morning when Drew backed away from the dock. Off to the east, the clouds reflected the orange of the sun that had not yet made it above the tree line. The same color stained the water behind him as he headed toward the pass for his assigned patrol.

Just off Buena Vista Point, a lone fisherman waded well off the beach and cast a top water lure toward the change in water depth. Drew recognized the broad hat and lean silhouette against the yellow reflection and slowed to wave. Usually he waved back, but sometimes he was too intent on the slight variations in the water; a fin above the waterline, a swirl, a school of ten or twelve finger mullet, or the flickering silver of small pinfish feeding in the eel grass. Sometimes that moment was not to be disturbed and today was that sort of day. The man had fished these waters for over 60 years. As long as he could fish, there would be food on his table. His remaining days were measured in changes of the tide and mornings when he could fish a top-water lure for fun.

The crabber-dude was pulling traps along Alligator Point. Drew would often stop and talk to his high school buddy, Arlin Finch, while he pulled traps and sorted the catch, but there wasn't time today. After the discussion last night, he needed to spend some time offshore. Christi was versed in the physiology. She had the knowledge to see that there was clearly human intervention, but she did not have the time on the water. While they could consider the dialog as an opportunity to discuss business with colleagues, it was quite clear to Drew that he was not paying enough attention. He needed to survey the broad spectrum of anglers and those that made their living from the sea.

The conversation was changing. Drew felt that change more than it was obvious. The discussion about fishing and preserving the species had started civilly but now it was reacting to additional constraints and outside impetus. That happens when incomes were threatened.

Drew had learned there are really only two responses to a threat that deeply intrinsic. One approach was to school and run like baitfish. The predator would slowly reduce the grouping, but the best defense was working together to find protection in numbers. The other approach was to turn and attack. When the prey was no longer satisfied with protection in numbers, there was always a group ready to turn and fight. The fishermen were balled up and the attack on their incomes made it very real. Drew needed to be closer to that possibility before he could understand it. Someone needed to know before they committed to that last turn.

###

Drew's boat and uniform project an enforcement presence in the field. Today he just needed to feel it. He needed to feel the slow swell, needed to hear the VHF chatter, needed to see where the boats were headed and when. He needed to feel the ocean and take in what she could tell him by being out past the sight of land.

Drew needed to be out where it's predator or prey. The ocean is such a simple existence; run or attack, assemble or disburse, eat or be eaten. It's all there in the salt water from the smallest to the largest creatures on earth. Answers would come by just being there.

Drew stopped to watch as the charter boats pulled alongside the bait barge anchored just inside Sandy Point. This is the last point of land between safe dockage in Grand Lagoon and the pass that leads into the Gulf of Mexico. All boats entering the Gulf pass Sandy Point. For that very reason, the bait barge anchors just inside where the deep-water permits access by the large charter boats. They would stop here on their way to pick up bait and from here, Drew could see the fleet. The usual string of oddly named vessels pulled alongside and passed a net to the young attendant. Larry had half a day's work under his belt at dawn having already received a supply of live minnows, blue runners, and mullet from the bait netters that work the night. By noon he would close up shop so he could be back on station before three the next morning.

Cap'n Law, Aegeus, and *Kelley Girl* arrived early and were pulling away as Drew maneuvered along the deep water next to shore, far enough to be clear of the captains' maneuvering dance but close enough to see who was dancing. *Reel Fun, CatNround,* and several other boats jockeyed for position next. Most of the boats picked up cigar minnows so they could skip the ritual of catching them at buoys just outside the pass. Several picked up big trolling baits. *Reel Fun* picked up a net full of expensive blue runners, probably for some amberjack after they had their snapper quota in the box.

Drew moved to a position just outside the rocks at the state park and monitored the radar to see where the crews were headed. The jetty that marked the entrance to St. Andrew Bay also afforded the only concealment to be found on the huge green gulf. All Gulf-bound anglers would pass through these rocky portals. He knew several would be fishing to the south but only the full-day charters would be headed that direction. The rest would head southwest or west to visit GPS numbers that had been productive in previous excursions. By 7:30, he was headed southwest too. He rode the slow swell and listened to the clear gulf water, the gulls, and the VHF chatter. He heard no clear answers but he knew this is where he would find them.

###

Drew was not offshore to check catch limits and licenses. Since there is only one pass in and out, it is much easier to do that chore at the end of the day. Drew slowed as he passed the bridge span reefs about 10 miles offshore. A quick run south and west would also give him a chance to note who and how many had staked out a section of the ocean to fish. It was also good to show the gray and green so the anglers would know that enforcement was offshore.

Drew pulled the throttles back about 14 miles out when there were no boats to be seen except on the radar. He had one GPS number nearby that he could check, so he turned on the depth sounder and slowed over the top. The screen painted a red show of bait near the surface with some pelagic fish in the mid-water. The bottom marked a bottom structure well in dark green but there was not much to on the screen except for what was likely to be a huge goliath grouper, the size of a small sedan, hovering just off the bottom.

Looking over the side, the water was clear and shafts of light from the bright morning sun speared down into the green-blue. No jellyfish to speak of in the main column. Drew saw several large schools of cigar minnows on the surface on the cruise out, a good sign that the bait was migrating. There was a group of birds to the east feeding on another school, or perhaps some anchovies or herring.

The VHF radio blasted Channel 16 and Channel 79, which most of the charter captains monitor, so Drew could listen to the banter. It was the usual truncated code that they use to avoid specifically telling the network their precise coordinates. It sounded like a typical sort of day.

"Hey Charlie, just put a big 'who' in the box!"

The response was garbled. Drew switched the radar to a wider range but there were too many options both east and west to guess who was responding.

"Caught 'em on the way out headed south, got another twenty minutes before we're on the first stop."

Another squawk and muddled response with clicks and noise.

"Finest kind. Will let you know when we get back."

Drew could think of many places he might prefer to be this morning, but this ranked high on a rather short list. As he listened to the radio conversations, he watched the cumulous clouds already building north over land. He watched a flight of birds crash into a school of bait that tracked wildly across the surface in orderly vectors while bonito or mackerel ripped through their ranks. His sunglasses turned the bright rays of reflected sunlight into long patterns and streaks of white on blue. It wasn't until nearly ten o'clock that he got a break.

"Hey Wayne, was that you?"

"Yeah, just doing some dolphin training."

"Ok. Sounded like maybe you were having engine problems again."

"Naw, naw, got that fixed, not backfiring anymore. Couldn't stand it myself so I know the customers didn't like it."

"Was that another one?

"Yep, Toby got 'em on the run. Don't need to be feedin' 'em these."

"Yeah, I gotcha, standin' by."

Reel Fun was to the west. Drew saw him headed that way out of the pass. Several boats showed up on radar. He called in his change in position to dispatch and pushed the throttle up to head a little south of their location so it wouldn't look like the boat was headed straight for them. As the boat stepped up on plane, flying fish scattered and skipped across the surface airborne until slipping back into the water.

There were three charter boats to the northwest as Drew headed toward the *Jubilee* just to their south and east. He came off plane nearby and contacted the captain by radio. The captain said that he was about to be headed back, four-hour trip followed by another this afternoon. Drew told him he wasn't there for an inspection but could he discuss whether he had been seeing any dolphin?

"Naw, ain't caught any dolphin, but then we's bottom fishing." The captain thought Drew was referring to the fish, also known as mahi-mahi, not the mammal.

"Sorry, Cap'n. I meant bottlenose dolphin …porpoise. Having any trouble with them eating your throwbacks?"

"Oh yeah, nothing has made it back to the bottom today. They's all out here with us. I hear it's not so bad to the south, but there's lots of Flippers out here today. "

His use of the term 'Flipper' was in reference to the '60s television series. It was a popular drama series about a dolphin in the Florida Keys. Drew could not remember it, but his dad says he remembers that it was one of only a few shows worth watching back when television was black and white.

"Haven't had much trouble today with them taking them off the line on the way up but then we haven't caught many of any size. Mostly beeliners and porgies and a few snappers."

"Thanks captain, that's what I've heard as well. I hear some of the fleet have been trying some homemade abatement techniques."

"Yuh'know I can't say I know anything about baitin' techniques."

"Sorry, Captain. I said 'abatement. Those are methods of keeping dolphin from eating the by-catch."

"Ohhh, I see, 'baitment. Yeah, I did hear some fellas have been looking into a sonar kind of noisemaker. Probably make a lot of money, course that's if there was any money left in this business. Can't say as I would pay mor'n a hunnert dollars for some electronic contraption, but then some of them big boys would."

"What about other methods?" Drew asked.

"What other methods?"

"I mean have you heard of anyone using poison or explosives or ..."

"Oh, yeah, yeah, I see what'cha mean. I guess there was a couple boys I heard were going to try shockin' em using a probe out each side of the stern with a switch hooked to a second generator. I heard some guys were trying cherry bombs but there's no way the customers would put up with that for long. Now some of them monkey-boats have come up with some interesting methods…."

Monkey-boat was a derogatory term assigned to all non-professional fishermen, anglers, divers, boats in general that are operated by anyone other than a trained captain. It has become more of a colloquial term not unlike 'cracker' or 'redneck'. It doesn't have to be a pejorative, but it can be. Drew tends to ignore it. It was not worth the effort to try and find a less derogatory term.

"Thanks Cap…" Drew started to say but he cut Drew off. The keyed microphone caused a loud 'sqwaak' feedback and static on the speaker.

"You know I think it be right good to come up with something that didn't hurt the buggers but make 'em stand off a bit. You know, for their own safety. Maybe just put one on every charter boat." Sqwaak!… "Ah…. but then it'd probably come out like one of those bladder stickers where they just tell us we gotta have one and we go spend more money."

"Well I appre….." Sqwaak! He did it again. "Sometimes you wonder if the government is just going tell us there ain't any fish out here and we need to get a job at the mall." Sqwaak! "You know I just couldn't work a job indoors like that, well maybe at the bookstore. But then there ain't many bookstores left, you know. I just don't think…"

Drew cranked the volume down and started a log entry. He could hear him going on for another several minutes. He turned it back up when the feedback went silent.

"Well, I guess I better ring the bell and head on back in to get another batch," he said, and the bell nearby sounded just as he finished up. The anglers along the side of the boat started reeling up.

"Thanks for your help, Cap'n. You have a good day fishing," Drew said.

"No problem there, son. We'll see you back inside." Then he added, "and I always have a good day fishing."

Drew pulled just east of him as the *Jubilee* sped up to his slow return speed and followed alongside. He knew what Drew was up to but it wasn't discussed. Drew used his radar shadow to get a bit closer to the charter fishermen north of him, toward the beach. As the *Jubilee* approached his closest point to the other boats, Drew put his log back in the hatch below, pushed the throttles and the vessel jumped up on plane. Turning to starboard, he made a circle around the *Jubilee's* stern and headed directly toward the remaining two charter boats. As he rapidly approached, the radio squawked.

"Best cut it out, Wayne. I'm betting that's 'The Man' at 110 degrees."

"Got it. Thanks, Bubba."

Drew watched a small eruption in the water aft of the closest boat. Could have been a fish jump or a ray but it was suspicious. He was still too far away to hear anything but the visual was enough to engage and see what he could learn.

Pulling alongside the *Reel Fun*, Captain Wayne yelled from the flybridge.

"What do you want? You ain't mad at me about kicking your chair are ya?"

"No, Cap'n. Just checking on conditions out here."

"Well check 'em out and move on. I got paying customers."

"Jubilee tells me that the dolphins are particularly bad in this area. You having the same trouble?" Drew was looking at him, but thanks to his dark Costa Del Mar's, he was eyeing the back deck to see what might have been left lying around.

"Oh yeah. Lots of trouble with them eating the profit right off the back of my boat. Toby can't get the fish in fast enough. If they stay in the water for just seconds, a dolphin will take the good half and leave nothing but the head."

Drew could see six or eight fin's rolling in the vicinity aft of the boat as they spoke. Dolphins are opportunistic but they will only stay in the area if the food source is lucrative. It probably meant *Reel Fun* was having a good day.

"So you want to check my fish or what?" Wayne said with some derision.

"No, just trying to chase down a problem."

"Well, get on outta here then, I got work to do." Wayne looked at his bottom machine and pushed the throttle on the port side in reverse. The maneuver pushed the stern away and at the same time put his bow nearly on top of Drew's position. Drew backed down sharply on both engines and maneuvered back along side, a bit closer this time and yelled up at him.

"Word is you came up with a way to stop the dolphin from getting your fish?"

"Don't know whatcha mean," he shouted back.

"Are you doing something that keeps the dolphin backed off?"

"Well you won't let me shoot 'em," he said staring down without cracking a smile.

"So what are you doing?"

"Nothing illegal."

"I'll need to stop by and talk to you about that."

"I'm sure you will. Now let me fish. Toby! Reel 'em up, we're going to move back over there."

Captain Wayne pushed one throttle forward and one aft and the boat turned in place, its stern slowly moving toward Drew's starboard side. Drew pushed both throttles forward and jumped up on plane producing a wake that was abnormal for a routine departure. Captain Wayne's maneuver was provocative so Drew didn't give it another thought.

There was no sense in pushing it any further. Drew throttled up and moved away, then turned hard to port and came back alongside keeping the *Reel Fun* fifty feet to his port. He heard one of the patrons yell, "fish on!" Drew watched Toby move to that side with his gaff at the ready. On the flybridge, Captain Wayne wasn't watching his patron or looking for the fish to show in the stern; he was still watching Drew's departure.

As Drew sped west toward the other fishing vessel, he heard the VHF on his working channel. He slowed and responded do the call. It was the office dispatcher. A local parasail outfit had just called in. There was another dead dolphin off the county pier.

Chapter 5

Drew arrived on scene just after another FWC vessel found the corpse floating about a half mile south of the county pier. He pulled alongside and listened while his lieutenant in the other vessel reported back to FWC dispatch. Drew could see the county pier and the tall condominiums that rose straight up from the beach on the east side. The condos continued for miles along the shore standing 22 stories tall on the white sand; the heart of the tourist trade. The parasail outfit had provided GPS coordinates and the drift was easy enough to estimate. Two small sharks swam away as Drew approached, but it was easy to see that several large predators had already started the natural process.

Drew was glad that he had eaten a sandwich underway. The animal was swollen to nearly twice its normal size and major portions were completely removed. Drew wanted to phone Mack but that sort of command decision would be up to the lieutenant.

"This look anything like the one you worked last week?" the lieutenant yelled over the sound of outboard motors.

"Let me pull around to the other side. I'll have to see the area around its mouth. May be too far gone already." Drew thought that the lieutenant looked a little pasty and nauseous, but then the smell could do that.

Drew maneuvered aft of the lieutenant's haze-gray, rigid-hull inflatable boat and put the dolphin downwind on the port side.

"Whew, bad idea," Drew said. "I'm going to try bow-on and see if I can keep my lunch. Can you get a boat hook on that pectoral fin and pull it over a bit?" he shouted across to the lieutenant.

He looked over at Drew with a jaundice eye. "With that smell, I'm not sure I have one that's long enough," he replied, but he was rooting around below the gunwale. The sides of a rigid-hull inflatable are large flexible tubes so the gunwale, or gunnel, is rounded with little storage space.

Lieutenant Bannacer was new to the office. He transferred from the Pensacola area some weeks ago. He was selected for promotion after helping with a somewhat sensitive oil spill issue along the shores of Pensacola Naval Air Station. While the issue may have been sensitive, Bannacer was not. The guys at the office recognized the type. He was a showboat; there for the camera, out front and aggressive. He would make certain that the captain could see he was an enforcer.

Experienced field investigators knew to watch the showboat with one eye half closed and the other aware of the periphery. Sometimes they are entertaining. They push hard. They screw up. Then they crash and burn an otherwise promising career. Others are dangerous. They push hard. They screw up. Then they do everything possible to make sure the error is pinned on someone else. This one got promoted. Drew squinted one eye.

Drew typically did not give much credence to the rumor mill. Bannacer will get the chance to show that he can work like the rest of the field team or prove that he is what they say. Three chances like everybody else.

When Bannacer pulled the fin, the mammal rolled to the side and pressed up against the inflatable. From there Drew had a good view of the right side of the dolphin. It was obvious again with this victim; most of the right side was missing from the mouth back. He took out his cell phone and got two photographs before the swells prevented the lieutenant from holding the pectoral fin.

"Do I have to get it again?" he shouted, but there was no need.

"Don't bother, lieutenant. This one is considerably worse. The entire side is missing. Some of the damage may be from sharks but I don't know. Okay if I send these photos to Dr. Haymer at Marine Fisheries and get his opinion?"

"Yeah, yeah, do that. What do you think we should we do with this?" He asked, backing away from the bloated and pungent remains. "Think we can just let the sharks have it?"

"I'll ask him."

"Did you see that fin to starboard?" Bannacer said, pointing over Drew's right shoulder. "If he wants him, he can have him!"

Drew looked back after locating Mack's number on his cell phone. He was right. The hammerhead was completely undisturbed by the FWC boats. He could easily be 12 feet long or more. The dorsal fin was still protruding out of the water as Drew looked back, but was slowly sinking below the surface like a periscope.

Drew pressed the call button to Mack's cell and backed away.

"Hey, Drew, what's up?"

"I got another one Mack."

"Dolphin?"

"Yeah, but this one is much worse. It looks like he swallowed the thing before it detonated. I just sent you some pictures."

"Aw, crap!" he said and Drew heard a female voice nearby ask what was the matter. "So, guess where I am headed?"

"I don't know. Flamingo Joe's for a smoked tuna sandwich?" Drew said, but had to stifle that feeling again as the smell of a saltwater death drifted past.

"We're on our way now to another one."

"What do you mean?"

"I mean we got a call from the White Sands Motel where a dolphin beached itself. This one is still alive. Motel guests are holding it at waters edge."

Several oaths came to mind immediately that Drew choked back under another stifling whiff of the current problem. "Okay, I'll call the office and get someone headed that way. I'm down off the pier, so I'll be awhile."

Mack explained that the Gulf Marine Park veterinarian was to meet them at the motel. If the dolphin could be saved, they have a quarantine capability and a rescue facility.

"Call me if I can help," Drew said meaning it personally and professionally. "Hey Mack," he added almost as a second thought, "I assume Christi is with you."

"Oh yeah, she's driving. I closed my eyes when she blew through the red light on the curve at Thomas Drive."

Drew heard her in the background, "You drive like an old man. I want to save this one!"

"So if we make it to the scene alive, I'll call you later."

"Mack, what should I do with this one?"

"I don't need to see that one, Drew. Like you said, it appears the dolphin ingested the explosive. I hate to say it, but it's probably best to let the ocean take care of it. Take it offshore so it doesn't float up on the beach. The mayor will have a conniption if another shows up during peak season."

"Got it. The lieutenant is here with me. I'm sure he will be stopping by your site. You'll probably need some help with crowd control."

"Did you see that?" the lieutenant said loudly, pointing toward the carcass.

"Alright, we'll talk later," Mack said, hanging up.

"That shark swam up and rolled onto its side and ripped a big hunk off. I saw both sides of his head clear the water. He practically pulled the dolphin underwater until a piece ripped off. Look, I was holding that fin with the boat hook a minute ago and now it's nearly gone."

"He can have it."

"Is that what the Marine Fisheries guy said?"

"Yeah, that and he needs some help with another one that beached near the White Sands motel."

"So what next, Phillips?" Bannacer asked.

"He wants us to pull this one offshore so that it doesn't end up on the beach and become a tourist problem. If you'll help me get a line around the tail, I'll pull him out."

"After seeing that shark, I'm not sure I want to put my hand in there. Besides, one of us needs to help them at White Sands. Think I'll head that way. Call me on the net when you start back and I'll meet you at the office."

"Who said I was headed back to the office?" Drew said, but it was too late. The lieutenant was already pushing the throttle and the boat wheeled rapidly around toward the beach.

"Okay, that's one," Drew said aloud. Just like a showboat. No doubt, he wanted in on any rescue attempt.

Drew put a loop around the dead dolphin's tail and about thirty feet of towline and began the trek offshore. He needed some time to think. The slog offshore at slow speed gave him that time.

Someone was killing these creatures using a vicious method. It's unlikely that dolphin in the wild would eat dead fish; it is simply not part of their normal diet. They eat live fish. For this dolphin to have ingested the explosive, it must have been inside a fish or attached to it somehow.

Mentally, Drew drifted off to West Bay, an undeveloped body of water surrounded by timberland that feeds into St Andrews Bay, where he had watched a mother dolphin teaching her young calf to corral mullet into the shallows. They would maneuver the school into a pocket of shallow water, then catch them as the school scattered. It was inevitable that the prey returned to a depth where they weren't in danger of becoming food for a mother osprey teaching her young fledgling. Predators teaching predators.

He reflected on the natural process and the irony of predatory behavior from two different directions: one from the environment that you live in, the water; the other from a completely different environment, the air. The prey maintains a constant vigil and learns survival techniques to avoid the inevitable. Drew wondered if the prey was taught or if it was simply instinctive to swim in schools and run to shallow water.

The boat began to rock with a slight unintentional course change and it brought him back to the task at hand. Drew arrived at the theory that someone is intentionally putting an explosive in live fish, maybe in bait or perhaps in a fish that was caught and then released with the explosive attached. Live fish. Releasing them with a device specifically designed to injure or kill dolphin.

"Who would do that?" Drew asked aloud. "It's despicable and cruel but it would probably do something just like what we've seen." The slow drone of the motor and the slap of waves against the hull eliminated the sound of his voice altogether.

The seas were building a bit with a slight chop from the southeast wind. Thunderstorms were mushrooming off to the northwest. Drew thought about what he saw approaching the *Reel Fun*. Small splashes off the stern like little explosions. He thought about Christi and her passion when she asked the same question that first time at J. Michaels.

"Who would do that?"

Chapter 6

"Okay folks, stand back and let these people through!" the sheriff officer barked.

Mack, Christi, and the Gulf Marine Park veterinarian, Dr. Harrison, made their way through the parting crowd that gathered on the beach behind the White Sands motel. The midday sun radiated light and heat off the sand and the smell of coconut sunscreen barely pierced the sultry, thick scent of saltwater. The deputy sheriff in uniform looked bizarre on the sandy water's edge with arms outstretched in a community of umbrellas, coconut-scented lotions, and the sounds of country, hip-hop, and beach tunes all mixed as a single sound and disbursed by an occasional salty breeze. His green and gray wool pants and patent leather shoes did not fit in among the bathing suits and sparsely dressed tourists but they offered an authority that was needed. Christi thought it was a good thing that he remembered his hat in this hot sun, but when she passed to his left, she felt sorry for him. His light complexion coupled with the heat was already problematic.

Christi moved into the water placed a wet towel over the dolphin's torso to keep it damp and protected from the blistering sun. Mack and Dr. Harrison went to the head and thanked the two young men that had stayed with the mammal and kept the crowd from getting too close.

"Did you try to move him?" Dr. Harrison asked.

The two looked at each other with a guilty look, then one of the young men responded, "We were going to try to get him back into deep water but the motel owner came down with a tablet and had looked it up. It said to call you and keep him calm so that's all we did. We took turns holding a towel up to block the sun and keep him wet without getting near that hole on the top that he breathes through."

"Good job guys. If you could hold that towel up for another few minutes, Dr. Haymer and I will see how he's doing."

"Think he'll be aw'ight, doc? He sure ain't slashing his tail and moving his head as much as when we first got here."

"Too soon to tell. He is considerably distressed," the doctor replied.

Christi helped them with the towels while Dr. Haymer and Dr. Harrison moved slowly into the water near the dolphin. He was still at the water's edge where the waves washed up against him.

Dr. Harrison moved closer and reached out to check the dolphin's pectorals. The dolphin moved its head and tail abruptly but not aggressively.

"He's very lethargic. Think we're too late?" Mack asked.

"His breathing is shallow; he won't last long here. We need to get him to the quarantine tank. Do you see the blood there at his mandible?

"Yes, consistent with the previous injuries we've seen. This one is not as serious but the animal is traumatized."

"I concur. I could investigate further but that can be done later. I think there's at least a fifty-fifty chance he can survive if we can treat the wound and get him out of the sun. The rescue team is on its way."

"They need to hurry," Mack said, tipping his head toward the beach walkover they had just come over. "Here comes the local news." Mack directed his eyes toward the beach walkover where the cameraman was taking off his shoes while the news lady held the camera and shot some footage of the surroundings. She wore a dark blue dress with a shock of red hair tied loosely behind her head. She kicked off her shoes like a local then zoomed in on the scene at the shoreline. The cameraman wore tennis shoes and socks with a pair of oversized jeans that could drop whenever he lifted the camera. Instead, he rolled up the legs and took a hitch on his belt before taking the camera back.

"Why don't you speak with them and I'll take over when your team arrives," Mack said.

Dr. Harrison nodded and started back to meet them near the deputy sheriff.

The lieutenant was anchoring nearby after directing some curious observers on jet-skies to keep moving on out of the area. He waded ashore and walked over to help the deputy with an ever-growing crowd of onlookers.

"Christi, can you see the mandible on this side?" Mack asked.

"Just barely, but it looks similar to the one we saw last week."

"It does. Why don't you see if you can get some photos for comparison before the rescue team gets here?"

Christi dropped the towel and ran up to get the camera.

"I don't see anything else that would cause him to beach. Do you?" Mack asked as she arrived back at the scene.

"Nothing visible, just the mandible, something internal maybe? Will he make it?"

"Vet says fifty-fifty."

Christi took the photos silently. She moved to where she could get good close-ups of the injury to the mouth then several other shots that showed that there was no other observable injury. She backed away to get some general photos of the beach area, some of the crowd, and one of Dr. Harrison speaking into a microphone held by the local TV news lady. The crowd had grown somewhat and she wondered how it was such a spectacle. Maybe it was like a wreck on the turn in a NASCAR race; it's never expected but you have to be watching or you miss the whole thing.

As she finished up, the rescue team hustled down the wooden beach walkover with a hand-held stretcher and made their way toward the crowd. Chairs had appeared on the periphery. Tourists looked on with great anticipation. An older couple sat beneath their umbrella while nearby two college boys sat on their ice chest and opened a couple of cold beers. They started cheering and yelling as the rescue team passed like it was the home team coming out after half time. Christi thought to herself that it was no wonder reality TV shows had such success early in the 21st century. She did not consider this entertainment.

Two young ladies in tiny bathing suits positioned themselves on either side of the deputy sheriff while a third took their picture with a cell phone and included the rescue team and dolphin in the background. With cheerful giggles, the photo was sent to someone and someplace north of here and posted, then they scampered around the crowd and on down the beach. The deputy never cracked a smile but just as they skipped away, the deputy staggered and dropped to one knee.

Christi set the camera back in the case and grabbed the wet towel she left at the water's edge. In this heat, she recognized the symptoms of dehydration. He was on both knees and one hand when she arrived with the cool wet towel that she placed on his neck, while removing his hat and replacing it with a section of wet towel.

"Can you hold it there while I get you some water?" she asked.

He nodded, sweat dripping off his brow and the color gone from his face. She was turning away when one of the college boys stepped forward with a cold bottle of water he pulled from the ice chest he sat on.

She took the water and smiled at him. He lifted his beer in salute and moved back to his seat on the cooler without a word.

"I guess I'll have to let them off for drunk and disorderly," the sheriff said taking the water and getting a bit of his color back as he took a small sip, then another. "Thank you ma'am! I think I nearly blew a cooling gasket."

The crowd had stepped back when the sheriff fell but the lieutenant had stepped in and continued crowd control.

"It's easy to do in this heat. I'm Christi Miller," she said, holding her hand out to assist him in getting back to his feet.

Christi watched the deputy look at his sandy right hand. She realized that he was easily twice her weight and it caught her as a bit funny. The deputy used the sandy hand to grab his hat and extended his left hand to allow Christi to assist him.

Christi smiled when she felt his enormous, sweaty left hand grab hers and pull just slightly as he rose back to his feet.

"Deputy Jason McBride," he said, standing. "Thank you, Ms Miller."

"I guess it's a good thing you didn't really need much help getting up," Christi said.

"Thank you just the same." He put his hat back on then tipped the edge in a gentleman's manner as he turned to get back to work. She headed back to gather her gear and looked back just in time to catch Jason stealing a glimpse of her departing. Smiling, she bent over to gather her stuff before Dr Haymer returned.

Mack had traded places with Dr. Harrison when the Gulf rescue team was in position. In just minutes, a tarp had been slipped beneath the dolphin and it was lifted onto the stretcher with light wet towels placed strategically over the dolphin's torso. The team hustled off the beach with Dr. Harrison following. He recruited the two rescuers to bring a pail of salt water that they could use to keep the animal wet during transit. He told them that he had four free tickets to Gulf Marine Park for their assistance. Christi took several more photos of the process then watched as the dolphin disappeared.

As the crowd disbursed, she gathered their things. The midday sun overcame the slight breeze and she no longer wanted to be there. Dr. Haymer had finished his discussion with the news lady and was walking back.

"Did you tell her?" she asked.

"No, but the word will get out. I told her there were many reasons a mammal would beach itself and it was thanks to volunteer groups like these at Gulf Marine Park that we were able to save some of them."

"Think she believed it?"

"Oh yeah, she's just here for the story. It doesn't matter which story except that she has to leave with one."

"Didn't even ask about the blood?"

"Oh yeah, got right to it, but there are lots of reasons I offered and any of them might show up on news tonight," Mack said grabbing his bag. "If you are through flirting with the deputy, let's get out of here."

She glared but knew that anything she said would just be fodder for a continuing banter, so she let it go.

The news lady was interviewing Lieutenant Bannacer as they walked past. Christi tried to see his uniform nameplate but decided not to be any more blatant. Drew would know who he was.

"The sheriff office uniforms just aren't made for this environment. Similarly, the uniform I'm wearing isn't made for a sheriff cruiser or knocking down meth labs. The Sheriff's office and the Wildlife Conservation Commission each have separate missions but in cases like these we work together ...," Christi heard as she passed the lieutenant. She was rather sure the deputy sheriff had opted out of the discussion and was already reporting in from the comfort of his air-conditioned vehicle.

"I just saw him walk back over the crosswalk," Mack said.

"Who's that?" Christi asked.

"Deputy McBride."

Christi knew that she would have to put up with him all the way back to the office unless she could find an alternate topic.

"So have you heard from Drew?"

"Not yet. Hopefully he's dragging the other one way offshore."

"What other one?"

Mack detected her immediate reaction. There was that passion again; this time it showed up as anger. Her brow furrowed, shoulders stiffened, and her eyes focused somewhere away from this beach. It would be a difficult ride back to the office.

"Sorry, forgot. That was why he called earlier. I'll tell you in the car."

They were headed up the walkover when they heard the two college boys start cheering and yelling again. Looking back, the lieutenant was running across the beach toward his vessel anchored just off shore with one hand on the butt of his pistol, the other waving dramatically at an incident.

Apparently, one of the rental jet-skis had not observed the anchor line that extended from the bow of the lieutenant's boat out ten or twelve feet then under water. The college boys were clapping and begging for a replay as one of them made hand motions describing the event. Evidently, the jet-ski had approached at speed and hit the anchor line at handlebar height. The male jet-ski driver and female passenger were launched when the jet-ski abruptly stopped. The jet-ski flipped upside down with the anchor line wrapped around the handlebars.

As designed, the jet-ski had slowed and attempted to right itself but it remained tethered by the Wildlife Officer's anchor line and was now improvising and creating an art of anchor line entanglement. Both the riders splashed down about fifteen feet farther and floundered hysterically until one of them stood up to learn that the water was just over four feet deep.

Christi glanced at the cameraman who was making similar motions to the news lady. He had captured the entire event in the background behind the lieutenant's interview. Christi shook her head and turned back toward the parking lot; the entertainment never stops.

Chapter 7

Drew arrived back at the office not long after the lieutenant. He hadn't heard about the jet-ski incident over the radio simply because he was ignoring it. He called Mack to hear about the dolphin rescue but in typical Mack fashion, it was primarily a findings report. He relayed a series of clinical statements that he would use again when he prepared his field report. Officer Rodriquez had just walked down to his boat to retrieve some personal gear when he spotted Drew's vessel rounding the point. Javier, Drew's friend and occasional boat partner, met him at the pier.

"So did you hear about the lieutenant?" Javier asked, taking the bowline.

"Don't think so. He was out there with me. We were down off the pier but he left to go to White Sands for the dolphin beaching."

"Showboat had a jet-ski hit his anchor line while he was being interviewed by the local TV station. They have the whole thing on tape and called the Captain for a statement." Javier spoke rapidly with a slight accent. He was a native Floridian but his grandparents were Cuban. He had that dark black hair and hazelnut complexion that screams Miami but had grown up in Ocala, one of the many towns of inland Florida that has a thriving ranch and equestrian culture.

"Anybody hurt?" Drew asked.

"Only pride, it appears." Javier replied, taking the stern line and securing it to the piling. "The two on the jet-ski got a scare. It launched them about 20 feet. It would have been altogether different if the anchor line had not caught the jet-ski handlebars.

"What do you mean?"

Javier shook his head and looked at the dock. "At that speed, had the line hit his neck…" Javier made a gesture with one finger of the line crossing his neck, "I would not want to have taken that call."

"Got it. Kid was lucky. What about Bannacer?"

"He arrested both of them for reckless endangerment. Tourists out of Albany, first time on a jet-ski. Video will tell us how fast he was going that close to the beach. He wasn't drinking, just stupid."

"No law against being stupid."

"If there were a law against it we'd have to build more jails. Besides, both of us would have been arrested years ago."

Laughter has no accent and Javier's laugh was infectious. It was full bodied and genuine. He retained just enough of an accent to ensure membership in one of the fastest growing cultures in Florida. It wasn't like he was trying to hide his ethnicity; in fact, he was quite proud of it. It was just that he could blend in North Florida better with a shade of redneck and hint of Ocala cowboy. He traded useful traits and personas like hats, simply another accoutrement to a complicated, compelling individual.

"Captain won't be happy about the lieutenant talking to the press. You know how he gets about that. Guess we'll have to wait until the evening news. If he looks like a hero, he'll make rank in a year. If he looks like an idiot…" Javier made the hand gestures of a jet rocketing toward the ground and blowing up on impact.

Grabbing his gear bag and work satchel, Drew stepped up on the dock.

"Think I'll make an exception and watch the news tonight! What channel did you say it was?"

"Channel 7, I think. You know, the one with the spunky little redhead. What's her name?"

"You're asking me?"

"I forget, you haven't watched TV in three years. Why is that again?"

"Afghanistan. Didn't want to see it anymore. Didn't want to hear about it. Didn't want to think anymore about the years I lost there."

"That's right. I just thought by now you'd at least watch American Idol or Dancing with the Stars. I mean sitting at home, just you and the dog."

Drew looked at him like he was an alien or someone that he had never met before. "I don't have a dog."

"I know, I know, its Channel 7, I think. Her name is Rachel. Rachel Frances or Rachel Francisco. You know, it's like two first names."

"Rachel Franco."

"Yeah, that's it. How did you know, man? How do you know if you don't watch the news?"

"Let's just say we have history."

"You got history with Rachel Franco? How is it I don't hear this before, amigo? You got history? We talking ancient history, or family history, or carnal history?"

Drew opened the back door and entered the office while Javier continued to imagine and vocalize the possibilities.

The office was moving like shift turnover. It was after five and most of the staff had already left for the day. The Captain was still in his office and so was Bryan, his assistant. Bryan picked up two pink phone messages and waved them at Drew. He was on the phone but raised his eyebrows and held both of them up as Drew strolled past.

Drew took them without looking and headed toward his cube. Javier walked behind him, ostensibly headed toward his own cube, but he passed it and stepped one cube further to where Drew was offloading his satchel and gear bag.

"So… it's a personal history, like something with pictures, romance, and a heartbreaking ending?"

Drew looked up and waved him off while he hung up his PFD and spread the two phone messages between his thumb and forefinger.

"Ironic," Drew thought.

One from Christi about an hour ago-- the other from Rachel Franco not even 20 minutes before.

# # #

Drew tried Christi's cell phone first. "Hey Christi, this is Drew. Sorry I missed your call. Give me a call back and I can meet you someplace if you would like. Call me back."

Drew left the message and looked back at the pink note. No subject, no message, just a check in the "please call" block.

Looking at the other message, he tried to decide whether to make that call now or after he left. She does not call anymore. Drew had not spoken with her in what, a year? …at least a year.

Drew was fumbling through the paperwork. It looked like he was busy but they were just motions being made while he thought about the two messages. If he called Rachel now, Javier would hear it. Drew knew he didn't need that right now but he hated to call from the new cell phone; then she would have the number.

Drew didn't say anything but his actions said something altogether different. He may have gotten over the fact that they were once a couple but he wasn't comfortable with it either.

"Amigo, if you aren't talking then I'm leaving," Javier said waving as he walked past the entrance to Drew's cube. "See you tomorrow. Buenos Noches."

"G'night," he said in response, but he was still evaluating the pink note.

Drew picked up the phone and dialed the number for Rachel without thinking about it anymore.

"Rachel? Hey, this is Drew."

"Hi, Drew! Thanks for calling me back. It's been a long time."

She was overselling. It was in her voice. She wanted something.

"I'm sorry to call you at work."

No she wasn't. Drew was a resource. A resource with history.

"But I just can't seem to get that lieutenant to return my call and hoped maybe you could help."

"Sorry. You know I'm not permitted to speak with the press without going through media relations."

"I know, I know. I just have this story we're running at six and I can't seem to get a statement from anyone there at your office."

"Phillips, you still here?" the Captain's voice boomed over the cube farm from his office door.

"Hang on," Drew said to Rachel cupping his hand over the phone.

"Right here, Captain," he replied, standing so the captain could see his head.

"My office," the Captain, said closing the door and picking the phone back up to his ear.

"Rachel, I gotta go," Drew told her while sitting back down. "Captain wants me in his office."

"Okay, just tell that Lieutenant Barrancas to call me please. Just tell him I want to know how to pronounce his name."

"It's Bannacer. Ban-uh-sir."

"Of course it is. Just be a darling and ask him to call me. Good talking to you, Drew."

He was saying that it was good to talk to her too when he heard the dial tone. It wasn't. But that's what's left of the 'history,' a cordial, overly sweet tone with a 'good to talk to you' added on the end. It's like eating the middle of an Oreo and throwing the rest away. It's too sweet and completely unnatural.

Drew stood up and could see the Captain still on the phone. Walking to his office, his cell phone played a familiar ringtone that was probably Mack. He pulled it out of his pocket just as the Captain motioned that he should come in and sit in one of the chairs to his left. The call was from Christi and he clicked it off just before opening the door.

The Captain continued his conversation with his superiors in Tallahassee and pointed to a chair.

Drew opened the message app and sent Christi a quick text, "N Capt ofc, will call if I survive."

The captain hung up, made a note on his pad to the right, then looked toward Drew and folded his hands in front of him.

"Drew, what can you tell me about Lieutenant Bannacer?" he asked, leaning back and clicking his ink pen on the desktop.

"Not much, Captain. Today is the first day we've worked together since he arrived. Seems to be on a fast track, good field knowledge and assertive. Can't say I've had much of an opportunity to assess his leadership with the team," Drew said, holding back his thoughts about the shark. Maybe he had a Pensacola Bay job instead of one that took him out into the gulf.

"Does that mean he's an asshole?" The Captain was not one to dance around nuance.

"Too early to say. I hear he's a showboat but then most lieutenants are if they want to get promoted. Okay if I get back to you on that in a month?"

"Yes, but make it two weeks. Make an appointment with Bryan after hours-- like today. What is it, 5:00 or 5:15?" It wasn't a question for Drew. It gave him time to look at his watch and prep for the real reason he called him in. It was nearly 5:30.

"I want to watch the news in thirty minutes. You have a good reputation with the field teams and I need to know if Bannacer is going to make it on my team or if he's a maverick. I only need one maverick in the shop and you have that slot locked down," he looked up at Drew as he grabbed the door to his office and looked back.

"That'll be all."

Drew knew that meant he intended to see whether Bannacer made them look good today on Channel 7 and he was excused. Drew opened the door and closed it as he left. The Captain stood up and opened a cabinet that held a nineteen-inch TV. He had the remote and was pushing buttons and cussing when Drew got back to his cube.

Drew saw that Lieutenant Bannacer was leaving when the front door opened.

"Lieutenant!" he said loudly and Bannacer turned around with his hand on the open door.

"What is it? I got to go."

Arriving at the door Drew said in a normal voice, "That lady from the TV news left a message that she wants you to call."

"Where'd you hear that?" His gruff tone was condescending but Drew just took it as an excuse that he was in a hurry. News would be on in just a few minutes.

"Bryan, the Captain's assistant, had a phone message."

"I saw it."

"G'night then," Drew said turning and headed back to his desk.

He didn't say anything. Drew heard the door close behind him.

Drew pressed the 'call back' button to return Christi's call. She answered as he grabbed his gear bag.

"Hey, I'm headed to Christo's to catch the news. You want to meet me there?"

"Is that the bar at the gas station?" Christi asked. "I don't usually like that kind of…"

"I know, but it has a TV and we can get there before the news comes on in ten minutes." Drew hustled out the door still talking. "There are TVs at several other local spots but you can't hear them. Maybe we can go over to J Michaels and gets some oysters after the news. What do you say?"

"I'll meet you there," she said.

"If you get there before I do, ask BJ to put one of the TVs on Channel 7." Drew hung up without the niceties. He couldn't make it in ten minutes but he could get close.

# # #

"Thanks BJ," Drew said, banging the door against the cigarette butt can with smoke drifting out of the top that was positioned too close to the front door.

"No problem, Drew, Two?"

"Do you want a draft?" he asked Christi who had already arrived and was sitting at the bar near the TV with the local news on instead of a sports channel.

"No, just water."

"Just one and a water with ice."

Drew pulled up the barstool next to Christi and heard the reporter say, "Up next, a beached dolphin is rescued plus video of a jet-ski accident just off Thomas Drive. Stay tuned."

"So this is what you wanted to watch?" Christi asked.

"Yeah. I hear you were there, so was my lieutenant."

"I've had about enough of this today, I'm going to go," she said, leaning forward to get off the barstool.

"No, no, stay. Maybe we can learn something. I'm making some progress but it's slow."

"That's why I called you," Christi said, and she looked over at Drew. "It's too slow." Her eyes were red like she had been crying but her jaw was wired tight.

"I want this to stop. You have to catch them." She had raised her voice. BJ looked back toward Drew and he waved that everything was okay.

"I want to catch them," he replied earnestly. "We have people on the ground asking questions. I've spent time on the water. We just don't have much to go on yet. It's not like I can use fingerprints."

"So what do you need?" Christi asked exasperated, her hands in the air. "This could go on for weeks and there will be more dead dolphin. What do you need to stop this?" Again her passion spoke in a voice above the normal bar room murmur.

BJ showed up with a draft and a glass of ice water. She asked if they needed anything else but Drew knew it was to see about reducing the decibel level. Christi was angry. She was mad but she wasn't mad at Drew Phillips. She was mad at the helpless pace of a slow investigation with no leads, no arrests, no change at all. The lack of progress was infuriating almost a week later and the raw edges were showing.

"Okay." Drew said. "Let's watch this story; then we can turn it off and step out onto the patio and talk." Christo's is a small sports bar with the typical dark interior but it has a patio area where patrons can sit outside, and on nice afternoons you could call this a gentle braking spot in an otherwise reckless week.

She didn't reply. The news was coming back on. "A dolphin beached itself off Thomas Drive today. The dolphin rescue team at Gulf Marine Park responded. Rachel Franco was there and files this report."

Rachel was always so natural in front of the television camera. Drew tried to ignore those characteristics that he knew too well and listen to the story, but she was another reason he never watched TV. Maybe the real reason but he continued to say it was Afghanistan hoping that one day he would believe it as well.

The events of the afternoon unfolded on camera. Drew closely watched the segment with Dr. Harrison while Christi fiddled with the straw in her water glass. She looked up when Mack came on to see how he would look with his nerdy presence and academic responses. After watching the rescue team carry the dolphin away Drew knew what was eating at Christi. It would be a long time before Dr. Harrison knew whether Gulf would be successful getting the dolphin rehabilitated and if it would ever be returned to the Gulf.

"Hey, at least he survived," Drew responded as the story wrapped up.

"That's good, but not enough. We have to stop them," Christi replied. She was terse and unable to conceal the torment the dolphin injuries were causing. Drew could tell it was best that he remain silent.

The video of the jet-ski accident was edited, but the cameraman had captured the essentials of a dramatic event. As expected, but to Christi's lament, it was entertaining. It was just inches from catastrophic and a handlebar away from disaster, but Americans love to see it. The lieutenant did not crash and burn in his interview. While the Captain would chastise him for speaking to the reporter, he probably wouldn't be shipped off for making the office look bad. As some of the other footage was used in wrapping up the discourse, Drew spotted folks on the beach that were unexpected.

"Christi, look! That's Chuck Whear. He's the deckhand on *Aegeus*. What's he doing there? And there-- that's Dr. Bentley, isn't it, the founder of the environmental action group, Protect and Preserve? Did you see any of them while you were there?"

"I wasn't looking. I thought they were all tourists. Most of them were."

"You're probably right. Maybe I'm just seeing tourists that resemble those folks. What would they be doing there?"

"Wait." Christi said. "I have pictures." Her words were the first she had spoken with any enthusiasm. "I took photos of the area a couple of times during the rescue. We can check those if you think it's important."

"I don't know if it's important or not, but it is odd. Maybe there's something here that we aren't seeing."

"The camera is at the office. Mack, I mean Dr. Haymer, gave me a key. We could go now."

"Maybe nothing, but if that is who I think it was, it may be our first break."

Chapter 8

Christi opened the metal doors that served as an entrance into the Marine Fisheries laboratory offices. There was a large, dimly lit saltwater aquarium just inside the door, so she grabbed Drew's hand and held it until she found the light switch and the fluorescent lights flickered on. It was a somewhat typical under-whelming government facility with sound panels hung over painted concrete block walls in the green hue of old elementary schools. The only adornments were framed photos hung neatly along each sound panel of fish and invertebrates along with species posters browning at the edges.

"I'll go get the camera from the lab. Why don't you go in there and turn on the computer," Christi said pointing toward a dark room to the right.

Drew flipped the light switch and a well-appointed conference room appeared with an overhead projector, rack-mounted computer in the back to the left, and a large table for meetings and discussions. There was a similar set up at the FWC office; he managed to figure out the remotes and what to turn on before Christi returned with the camera.

Gone was the sour demeanor that showed up at the bar. There was quickness in her step in getting it all set up.

"I'm going to download all the pictures to our shared drive, then we can look at them here. We've used this screen to consult on necropsy and analyses with other labs so I'm sure we can zoom in on any face in the crowd."

Drew sat at the table in front of the large screen and thought about why someone from the fishing community would show up during the middle of the afternoon for a dolphin beaching. For that matter, why would someone from the environmental action group show up at all. This certainly wasn't new. It also wasn't altogether unusual. Somebody knew something. Maybe somebody had suspicions. Maybe somebody wanted 'eyes' in position to see who else had showed up. At some point Drew started working it aloud, talking from the front table as if he were the analyst postulating on events and possibilities. Christi listened while the photos were downloading.

"If I were the Charter Boat Captains Association, this is a threat. The public would see dolphin killings by the fishing industry in a very unfavorable light. At this point in their existence, public support is one thing they can't afford to lose."

"Then again, if I were the head of an environmental action group, this is an opportunity. I certainly would want to see first hand what was happening to the dolphin but I would also want to be prepared to use that against a well organized fishing organization that enjoys a favorable public opinion."

"Why does the public like the Charter Boat Captains Association? Fishing is a part of Florida and St. Andrews history since it began. The apostles of Jesus were fishermen. Because fishermen just want to work. Who would be opposed to men that want to keep working, men who do not want to be at the welfare line, who just wanted to make a living the same way fishermen have for centuries?"

He paused for the moment as if to reflect, then started back as if to refute the previous statements.

"Why does Protect and Preserve remain in an unfavorable public light? It's not that they don't like the cause of protecting the fishery. It's just that their cause intentionally intends to restrict these fishermen from making a living. It is inherent in their objective to preserve the species and protect the resource. Their cause is just but the result is an injured party. Men who have fished and provided for their family for years need to find another job. Men like the apostles John and James that have to go find another way of earning a living. Protect and Preserve seems to have a public relations problem."

"What am I missing?" Drew asked. "I have to be missing something."

The lights dimmed as the screen presented a series of thumbnail prints.

"Sorry to interrupt, Drew. Here is what I got today."

Christi flipped through the graphic part of the dolphin injuries rather quickly, and then stopped where she had begun taking photographs of the surrounding area.

"So that's looking east. There is the motel and this one is looking west down the beach." Christi worked it like a vacation slide show.

"That is Dr. Harrison, the veterinarian at Gulf Marine Park. He's the one that called in the rescue squad. At that point he gave the dolphin fifty-fifty odds of survival. He said that they have taken some with less, and some of those pulled through."

"Here's one where the news media is arriving. Dr. Haymer and I stayed with the dolphin until the rescue team arrived. After that Dr. Haymer went up to talk to them."

"So here are the crowd shots. I only took a few. Here's the rescue team on the beach and Dr. Haymer talking to the media. The rescue team moving the dolphin onto the gurney then another shot of Dr. Haymer as the team is leaving. That's it. I didn't get a shot of your lieutenant but he was there along with the deputy sheriff you could see in the crowd shots.

"So let's go back to Dr. Harrison talking to Rachel."

"Who's that? You mean the news lady?" Christi asked, flipping back through the slides quickly. "This one?"

"Yeah, that one," Drew said.

Rachel was standing barefoot interviewing the veterinarian. Her red hair pulled back and the microphone held up to Dr. Harrison like a personal object she was sharing.

"Nothing here except Dr. Harrison and the media," Christi said. "These are old tourists and over here a couple of college guys. Ready for the next one?"

"There is the deputy sheriff. Can you zoom to the upper left?" he asked. "Right there. I think that is Chuck Whear. Can you see him on the next picture?

Christi moved to the next picture and zoomed in some.

"There." he said. "He's wearing sunglasses but that has to be Chuck Whear. Can you print that? Christi didn't respond but a little window appeared that said it had been sent to the printer.

"Now go to the last crowd shot."

Christi moved past the next photo and then zoomed to the left on the one after.

"See the guy in the straw hat right at the edge of the picture? That's Dr. Bentley. Wait. I recognize the guy next to him, do you? Who is that?"

She zoomed in closer and Drew looked at it a minute. The photo was good. He just couldn't place the man standing there next to Dr. Bentley.

"That's the lawyer," Drew said, when the brain cells aligned. "He's that guy that they used for the spill. What's his name? It's uhh...."

"I don't know," she replied. "I don't even remember seeing him today."

"It's Gharty or Garskie, something like that." Drew looked down and closed his eyes. When his hand landed on the table, he just shook his head and looked at her. "It'll come to me. Let me get that picture too."

Christi's phone rang on the table next to her. She looked at it then clicked it off.

"Need to take that?" Drew asked.

"I probably should," she stood up and walked toward the door to the conference room. "Hi Jason. Sorry I missed your call earlier. What's up?"

It's Gardey, ...Harold Gardey, that's his name," Drew shouted as she left.

Her voice disappeared as she walked out of the room into the main offices.

Drew looked at the picture of Dr. Bentley on the screen. He started thinking about what to do with the pictures. There was nothing incriminating about standing on the beach watching a dolphin rescue. It's a public beach. It's just odd. Drew was thinking that maybe they finally got a break, but was it just an anomaly? A coincidence? His gut said otherwise.

Drew had been in situations before that required him to count on a hunch that was less documented. He had that feeling. It wasn't an eminent threat or premonition. It was just a feeling. Experience has taught him to trust that intuition.

"Who's Jason?" he wondered.

Christi returned with the photos and her phone in her pocket. She gave the copies to Drew and started shutting things down.

As she turned off the light to the conference room and walked toward the exit, Christi said, "That was Jason McBride, he was the Deputy Sheriff on the beach today. He just told me that Protect and Preserve has called for a demonstration Thursday. After that dolphin story on Channel 7 this evening they have gotten a huge sympathetic response from the public. He thinks they are going to try to use this injured dolphin to bend the public sentiment a bit."

"Did he say where?" Drew asked.

"St. Andrews Marina."

"Great. Right where the fishing fleet docks. That probably means the Charter Boat Captains Association will have a contingent on hand …and the media will be there."

Christi quietly gathered her things, then walked back to where Drew was sitting.

"You mean Rachel?" she asked.

The question hung in the acoustic tiles. There among the fish photos and old posters was a question Drew couldn't answer. A simple 'yes' would not be enough.

Christi grabbed his hand and turned out the lights. Drew suppressed an urge to pull his hand back. Rachel used to do that. She would grab his hand as if it belonged to her. There was still a dim light on in the aquarium but the foyer was dark. As they walked out the door and into the warm summer evening, he let the urge melt away. Drew left the question hanging back there in the dark.

Chapter 9

Drew awoke in a cold sweat. He could hear the dream reverberate through his semi-conscious brain, remembering every detail. He remembered many of those things he tried so desperately to forget. The sun was bright and warm but the salty gulf breeze kept the temperature from climbing. Drew closed his eyes to reduce the glare and the dreams ...the dreams started over again.

"Hey Drew, watch out for snipers on the rooftops ahead!" the platoon sergeant shouted. Ahead of his position, Drew could see flat-roofed adobe structures. Drew's platoon walked along a wall that ran adjacent to the road, or at least what there was left of the wall. The prospect of a roadside mine was less likely along the well-traveled path. The squad was assigned to assist a convoy headed south and east into Helmand Province. The 101st needed these supplies.

"Hey, when is that convoy supposed to..."

The conversation was never completed. A single shot stopped the monologue in mid-sentence. The sergeant asking a benign question became a nightmare Drew would revisit as often as he would wonder if there was anything that he could have done about it. The platoon sergeant was a casualty on a very dangerous street in a very dangerous locale. It could have been anybody. Drew could handle the fear, the irritation, the uneasy edge of conflict but random events are hard to assimilate. The indiscriminate and casual happenstance is chaos that no planning or training can overcome. Drew never liked it and despised how it arbitrarily stripped control of any situation. It happens that way because it happens that way and...

KAH-Boom!

A roadside bomb exploded just 500 yards from our coordinates and the squad jumped to a prone position. The dust blew up and out then slowly settled on a vehicle upside down and burning.

"Drew, take your squad forward two klicks," the lieutenant shouted. "Make sure the route out of town stays clear. I'll backtrack to the convoy."

The lieutenant didn't wait for confirmation of his orders. He turned and scrambled onto the road and waved to a team on the opposite side that would follow him back.

"We're headed east toward the river," Drew yelled back to the squad anchored against the wall. "Move out!"

The squad moved with caution onto the roadway and started east. Eyes were wary and guns were ready. The area east of the city to the river was a known ambush point.

We had advanced two kilometers east when we could see the convoy approaching but there was very little cover

"Take position," the corporal shouted. "Convoy is in sight."

"Let's get this convoy across the river and go home!" Drew shouted. The corporal slipped up alongside and asked, "Where?"

The squad assumed defensive positions behind damaged trucks and in bomb craters along the highway and waited for the trucks.

"So whatta ya think, Staff Sergeant?" The corporal asked. "They gonna let us alone?"

"I don't think so, Travis. Something doesn't feel right." Drew said.

Drew always had a sense for the situation. Call it a gut feeling or instinct. Today would be another time that Drew was glad that he paid attention to the perceptions when he felt them. Travis saw Drew jump and followed him into the dry wadi alongside the road.

KAH-Boom!

The earth shook from the explosion and one of the medium-wheeled tactical vehicles in the convoy tipped over onto the side of the road.

The radio squawked and the crew scrambled out of the felled vehicle before it exploded in an orange fireball. Vehicles behind screeched to a dusty halt while those ahead proceeded hastily along the planned route.

KAH-Boom... BOOM!

The second one exploded on our position. They were waiting for us. Waiting to intercept the next major convoy headed into the Helmand Province and unbridled mayhem.

"Staff Sergeant, they took out the lead..."

Drew jumped before he finished and headed toward the bombed unit. Most of the shell-shocked team followed. Despite the risk there were few options. There might be multiple bombs but Drew's reasoning, flawed or not, was that there wouldn't be multiple bombs in a single location.

BOOM.

The blast was behind us, close to where we had been along the wall. We were headed toward the convoy and ....

KAH-Boom.

This one was to the side as we dodged vehicles full of men and gear stopped in the middle of the ambush zone.

"Bring up that personnel carrier; let's get this out of the road!" Drew shouted.

The crew of the armored personnel carrier were reluctant to participate still clinging to buddies that were no longer part of the battle or being attended to by the corpsman.

"Push it to the side and let's get this convoy moving!" Drew said. "We're targets! So move it!"

Once the road was cleared, the convoy began streaming past the damaged vehicles while we stood aside. Where they were headed was best driven in daylight and they knew it.

Drew felt it again. He grabbed the corporal and dove into the ditch adjacent to our fallback route.

KAH-BOOM.

The blast hit our squad from an abandoned hulk of a burned out vehicle nearby. It was designed to be a clean-up device; kill anyone left standing.

The corpsman was busy with the injured in the main thoroughfare. Drew and the corporal looked for members of the squad injured near the road. We found two of the guys wandering nearby but they couldn't hear. Drew motioned for them to follow. Those that got full exposure to the IED were dead. Two others could be saved if we could stop the bleeding. The corpsman shouted to hold this and Travis jumped to take his place pressing a saturated gauze on Juan's chest. Fred was bleeding out and the corpsman wrapped a tourniquet around his thigh. Drew kneeled and spoke to Fred. "Hang in there. We got you." We could save them if we could just stop....

KAH-BOOM.

Drew awoke again in a full sweat. He was at home in his chair out back. There was no desert, but the sun was hot and the sweat was real. There was no wadi and no convoy. There was only a green backyard. There was a barbeque grill to his left and a raised herb garden. The umbrella and patio table served as a bunker and he was comfortable.

Drew closed his eyes again, this time determined not to fall back asleep. He could hear a blue jay in the tree to his left and the whistle of an osprey out on the water. He heard an outboard motor moving west to east out on the bay. A rainstorm was approaching and he could feel the slight rustle of the wind and the coolness that preceded the rain.

Keee-acka-boom!

Drew dove beneath the patio table.

The lightning was authentic and surprisingly close. The sound was altogether different, he could hear the charged particles crackling through the air before the report.

With full mental faculties and a sense of urgency, Drew grabbed his phone and the book he had been reading and headed for the house. The rain followed with a thorough, immediate drenching. He made it to the porch mostly dry.

Drew looked out over the backyard and could not see the bay. The wall of rain was so complete that even the obvious was lost in a shade of wet gray. It was a rain that washed away the vivid memories of Afghanistan, leaving them as gray and colorless as the summer downpour.

Just inside the porch, he stood looking out into the thunderstorm. The fury, the passing melee, the cleansing, the sultry wet air that swallowed the afternoon; it was a Florida summer ritual.

A bright light illuminated all the surrounding area like a wake-up call from the Almighty with the screeching sound of a raptor racing to the ground.

Drew dove to the floor just inside the screened-in porch where he counted the moments until the thunder arrived.

BOOM!

The thunder followed the lightning with a delayed, yet predictable report. Three counts, so it was less than a mile away. Lighting was an indiscriminate force with deadly power. He knew it was simply a natural cooling process. Warm moist air meets cool dry air, negatively charged earth, positively charged air, electrons traveling up and back down in a burst of lightning and a report that transported his thoughts back to the loss of comrades, uncontrollable anger, and a mindset as negative as electrons from the ground. Drew could no longer appreciated the sound and fury of a summer thunderstorm. That love was lost to a memory… and it was a memory tied to anger, fear, and death.

While the thunderstorm would always be a part of the heat transfer process of a complex global environment, it was a regular reminder of a past that Drew intended to forget. He had survived that post-traumatic period; in fact, he got off easy, but it had cost him more than a year. He would never again enjoy a summer storm, with its rage and passion, the unpredictable streak of hot-white lightning, the resulting blast of thunder that exploded, then rolled across the bay and into the distance.

Sheets of rain were now blowing like sails ripped from their halyards and whipping across the yard untethered. Raindrops in torrents raced sideways, then disappeared like a school of minnows chased by a threat behind them.

Drew closed his eyes when another streak of bright lightning chased charged particles crackling toward earth. That sound, that unpredictable, raw and unharnessed energy he once loved was no longer the same. It was now a sound that sparked torment, …and that bothered him. He could remember when he loved that sound, it was a marvel, a natural wonder; but now he was irritated that it could evoke such a visceral, subconscious anguish that was barely in his control. The trade space between that very real pain and his fascination with nature's process was a breach Drew would not likely reconcile.

Drew never liked the fact that he was unable to fully control that feeling. He once marveled at these indiscriminate occurrences. Now that feeling is one of discomfort that he can't shake.

The school of raindrops slowed and swam slowly down in rivulets of leaves and grass toward the bay. The torment was gone. The afternoon would return with a steamy wet air that would resolve to a cooling breeze coming in off the bay by evening.

Knowing that would happen, Drew stepped off the adrenalin-driven surge of memories and feelings and fears that he had so successfully suppressed for years. He took a deep breath and thought back to that rainy cold day when he was helped off the medevac flight in Germany. He wasn't home but there were no bombs, no sounds of rifle fire, trucks and helicopters. He remembered the training, deep breaths, control your thoughts, be here, you're not there, you have control, trust those feelings, it will be okay.

He set his phone and book on the end table and slid into the couch to let his gaze drift out past the dock and across the bay into the late afternoon shadows and spears of light escaping from the gray clouds.

Chapter 10

Drew heard the phone ringing somewhere.

It was getting dark and he had fallen back asleep on the couch. He shook his head to reorient. It was nearly 7:30. He clicked the receive button just before the voice mail picked up.

"Drew? Hey, this is Christi. Can you come meet me at Schooners?"

"Sure. Is there a problem? Should I hurry?"

"No… not really. I'm with Jason. It's nothing really. I just don't want to be here anymore and I don't want to drive. I'll tell you about it when you get here. We're in the back next to the bar."

She clicked off. Drew thought about it for about three seconds. He splashed some water on his face at the sink and swished a slug of mouthwash. He grabbed a bottle of water out of the refrigerator on his way out the door.

He started the truck and sat in the driveway. He told himself not to call her back. It doesn't matter what's wrong; she just doesn't want to drive; don't make a big deal of it. But she's with Jason, what if…?

When he turned onto Thomas Drive, possible concerns had grown disproportionately but he was able to rein it back in before crossing the bridge over Grand Lagoon. By the time he walked through the front door he was ready for anything-- a drunk date, a bar fight, a broken heart or a crime scene. Bring it on.

While Drew stood at the entrance surveying the after work crowd, the hostess asked if he needed a table. Drew said he was just here to meet someone.

"She's in the back, at a table to the left. She asked us to keep an eye out for you." The hostess pointed out onto the deck through the rear doors toward the beach.

Schooners is one of the last beachfront bars that transforms into a beach front restaurant then back into a late night club. The service is fair, the food leans toward predictable, but there are few places Drew would rather spend an afternoon and evening, during the offseason anyway. Drew walked past the long wooden bar and onto the deck out back. The bar was still full of locals that had stayed after happy hour. Most were still enjoying the light banter or getting a bite to eat before heading home. Christi spotted Drew and waved before he saw her.

No obvious sign of malevolence, no broken bottles, or weepy girl tears, but he still approached cautiously.

Christi stood up as Drew moved toward the table. They met about two tables away and she embraced him like someone she hadn't seen in awhile.

"I've had a little too much to drink. He has too, but I don't want to make a scene out of it," she whispered in his ear. With her back to the table, she took both of Drew's hands and mouthed, "Help me," while backing up.

She backed toward the table where she sat with Jason and two other friends. Drew surmised that they were also from the sheriff's department.

"Jason, have you met Drew?' Christi asked. "This is my friend from the Florida Wildlife Commission that I was telling you about."

Drew leaned forward to shake the hand that was offered slowly. He was looking at Drew like someone he should recognize. Drew suspected it was just latency in cognition because they had not met before.

He introduced his friend to the right and she introduced the next guy over. Drew let his guard down; just drinks after work that turned into a gathering. There doesn't appear to be anything wrong here. That gave him a moment to second-guess. Drew knew he should never second-guess.

"Pull up a chair, Drew." Jason responded. "She did mention your name earlier, just before Fred and John left. I'm afraid you just missed the party; we're all that's left of the sheriff contingent anyway. Christi joined us to make it a special occasion." He hoisted his beer bottle and tipped it in her direction.

"What can I get you?" the waitress said leaning over Drew's shoulder. Christi turned from the water and looked back.

"I'll have a draft beer, something light, ok?" Drew looked at Christi and she waved off.

"I'll bring you some water," the waitress said.

Jason turned to his two friends and asked, "Did you see that clip with the tourists on the jet ski? That was hilarious!" he said laughing. "You know she saved me that day," Jason said, pointing at Christi then repeated a story that had been told several times already.

Christi looked toward Drew and leaned over. "He's been really nice all evening but I wasn't comfortable not knowing any of the others. Thanks for coming." Christi looked back out toward the water over the beach. "I remember being here. It was only a year or two ago, with some sorority sisters."

Her eyes looked out over the dunes as she reflected.

"Something tells me you're drifting someplace way out there," Drew said.

Jason told a joke that his friends were laughing about but Christi had mentally stepped away and her thoughts were elsewhere. Drew could tell there was something else on her mind. Something that made her call him.

The waitress set a beer and a glass of water on the table nearby then disappeared in the crowd. Drew reached for the beer and looked around. The evening dinner crowd was just arriving. It was not like him to be here when the venue changed into an evening dinner crowd. He picked up the water and leaned toward Christi still staring out over the sea oats.

Drew quietly leaned over further and waved the glass of water in front of her unfocused eyes staring across the dune.

"I'm so sorry," Christi said. "I was drifting off someplace. What did you say?"

He looked at her, grinning.

"What's so funny?" she asked defensively.

"Nothing," Drew said, laughing. "I had just mentioned that you were drifting way off someplace."

"Oh… I was, …sorry, but no place in particular. It's just so beautiful and I was remembering when I was here before. It was Spring Break, not last year maybe the year before. It seems like such a long time ago…it's just a couple of years, but a long time ago."

Drew leaned against the piling and looked up as she continued.

"I think changes are about to start happening fast in my life," she said to the sand, then turned toward Drew. "In another few months I'll be finished at Auburn and trying to figure out what to do with a diploma and a degree in a field with very limited employment opportunity."

About that time, Jason's two friends stood to leave. Drew and Christi waved as Jason stood to exchange pleasantries. He turned back and pulled his chair back up to the table.

There was a redhead being seated at the next table over. In a glance, Christi recognized her and leaned over toward Drew. She held her hand up to her mouth and signaled for Drew to lean forward.

"Isn't that Rachel?" Christi asked, already knowing that it was.

He glanced that direction and, of course, it was Rachel. She looked every bit as striking as she did on television. She was dressed for dinner and seated too close for Drew's preferences.

"Ohh," Drew heard Christi say with her hand at her mouth, "and she's with the show-off lieutenant that helped you with crowd control on the beach the other day," she said to Jason.

Jason lifted both arms and stretched so he could make an unobtrusive look behind him. Drew looked over as Bannacer sat down in the seat opposite Rachel.

Lieutenant Bannacer was just another face in the crowd, but Rachel did command an audience. Drew noticed that many of the other tables had observed their arrival and were sharing similar mouth-to-ear conversations. Rachel had a look that bespoke confidence and she carried herself like a celebrity. Just a little haughty, but Drew knew that was a defense mechanism for someone as visibly about town and the face of the local news. Christi continued to look. Rachel was used to it. She was pretty and Christi was not alone in recognizing that characteristic. Her brilliant red hair was a striking contrast to her slightly tanned face. Rachel had an incredibly made-for-TV look and she wore it like a woman on a mission. *What is she doing with Bannacer?* Drew thought.

On the other side of the bar Drew heard, "Rachel, over here. ...Rachel! So good to see you!"

Rachel looked in that direction and Jason looked up with a mock snarl. The voice ignored all those at tables on either side and instead made an overt display of arriving at her tableside to press cheeks. His tumbler dangled precariously from one arm as he maneuvered through the chairs. A large unlit cigar was wedged between two fingers at the rim of the tumbler. All the patrons he passed were aware that they could be anointed at any moment with some flavor of fine Kentucky bourbon and ice dripped over a Dominican Churchill cigar with a Connecticut wrapper.

Christi giggled when his posterior was thrust toward Jason. It was the only position that the man could assume if he wanted to superficially hug Rachel while she intentionally remained seated. It was one of those great-uncle hugs, a little more hug than should be expected or deserved. Jason moved his chair closer to the table and bumped the man's butt intentionally. It moved without so much as a 'pardon me,' and the banter continued.

"Ah, yes. Mr. Bannacer," we heard the man say. "I believe we had some business when you were stationed in Pensacola. Did I hear you transferred to our fair city?"

Drew looked over to see Bannacer reach up and shake hands. The man's posterior was still immediately behind Jason's head and it appeared that Jason was about to make a scene.

"Well, at least something made you laugh," Jason said. "What if I poured this beer down his trousers?" Jason said, holding his beer bottle over to that side as if the man's leg may receive a beer soaking with the slightest bump.

The man stood up and shuffled around then began making arm gestures to emphasize points of his conversation. Jason started over-emphasizing the same gestures and the couple at the table behind Christi started laughing. By the time the man had completed his conversation, Jason had an audience. He was clearly overacting and his movements were exaggerated but they were the same mannerisms. His representation was of a more severely inebriated, pompous jerk.

When the laughter got a bit louder, the man turned briefly to see what was funny and Jason sat motionless as if nothing had taken place at all.

With a nearly empty glass still dangling out in front of his trajectory and the unlit cigar still smashed between two fingers, the man moved away from Rachel's table. After he passed, the audience offered a brief applause. Jason stood up and bowed. Christi took a second look at the man as he passed by. It was the man in the photograph that Drew recognized-- the lawyer. The man glanced back and shrugged. He rattled the ice in his glass in the direction of the bar and the attentive bartender started assembling the ingredients for his next absolution.

"That was funny," Christi said.

"I despise that guy," Jason said with a smile that seemed to disagree with his statement, "but I'm glad it made you laugh."

"Who is it?"

"That is the renowned Harold Gardey, lawyer, bachelor-at-large, guardian of the environment, and world-class shyster, but that, of course, is my opinion," Jason said. "I haven't figured out all the buttons yet, but someday he's going to get his …and I hope I can be there to help."

Jason and Drew turned and observed as the man mingled between patrons then disappeared into the bar crowd. Jason's disdain was not something ethereal; in a glance, Drew knew it was personal. Drew was surprised that he hadn't recognized him. On the other hand, it was interesting that Jason had.

Now that Drew had a chance to view Gardey with more than a disproportionately enlarged beach photo, he could see the markers. His eyebrows were dark and bushy with a hint of gray and several long unruly strays sticking out or curling up over his eyes. His forehead was a distinctly lined interlude between his eyes and the shock of dark hair, also graying, but distinguishing in a mature sort of way. He had that full head of hair that every television evangelist wants and a loose sort of flowing jaunt of pretentious audacity.

Christi looked over when Rachel stood up. Rachel glared at Bannacer and he slowly stood up as well, holding onto the napkin from his lap. She picked up her purse, and then turned to plant a solid, open-palm slap across Bannacer's right cheek.

Bannacer appeared ready to lift his arm and swing but caught himself and managed to maneuver that arm to the back of his head as though the blow had affected his neck.

Rachel glared. Her look was one of derision.

"There was no call for that," Bannacer said.

He was a bit too loud, which meant he was embarrassed.

"Excuse me, Mister Bannacer, I'll be leaving now. There will be no need to call again. I will not answer," Rachel said, attempting to walk past him on the side of the table.

Bannacer stood next to his chair but it blocked her route out. She looked to the other side and made a move to exit the other way, right past Jason's chair.

Bannacer stepped forward and grabbed Rachel's arm firmly.

She turned then stepped forward directly in Bannacer's face.

"I said, excuse me, Lieutenant Bannacer. Release my arm or I will call the authorities."

Jason and Drew stood up simultaneously.

Bannacer looked over and saw Drew. He looked at Jason, then at Rachel, as he released her arm.

Rachel did not say anything. She simply turned and left.

Bannacer set his napkin on the table, finished his drink, and turned to leave without a word. Christi broke the silence by excusing herself to the ladies' room.

Jason turned to Drew and said, "I have no idea what that was all about, do you?"

Drew shook his head and watched Bannacer look for his dignity and the waitress.

"So where did she go?" Jason asked.

"Don't know."

The band started playing in the main dining area and they sat back down. The music replaced the sound of clinking silver on porcelain plates but it was a bit loud for normal conversation.

Jason knew that it was time to leave when Christi returned to the table. Drew was still thinking about Rachel and Bannacer. For Jason, the afternoon had turned into evening and the happy hour had turned into a slight headache.

"So should we get something to eat?" Jason asked looking at Christi.

"Another time," she replied.

"Yeah, me too. I'm thinking it is about that time." Jason grabbed his beer bottle. "...To chance meetings," he said, raising it eye level.

Christi picked up her glass of water and clinked the side of the beer mug. "And special occasions," she said, with eyes that could melt the awkwardness. She turned toward Drew and did the same.

Christi took a sip then set it down ...but Jason caught her eyes as she looked up. He wasn't a Deputy Sheriff here. He was just a guy, a big confident guy that was interesting and interested.

"So what is that look?" he asked.

"It's nothing. Just a notion I'll keep to myself," she answered, smiling up at him.

Drew took a sip of beer and asked, "So does that mean you're headed out?"

He looked over at Drew and replied, "Yeah, I think I need to take it in. My shift starts early tomorrow. Good to meet you."

"So, Miss Miller, something tells me that I picked the right place," Jason said pushing his seat back and standing up.

"This has been great, Jason. Thank you," she said, while tasting the bitter little white lie as a harsh aftertaste to an otherwise pleasant afternoon.

Jason leaned over and said, "Your help on the beach was an act of kindness. I should have recognized dehydration earlier but then, if I had, we wouldn't be here. Thanks for coming and let's do it again."

Jason leaned over and kissed her on the check as she demurely looked to one side.

That's awkward, Drew thought. He felt a little like a big brother instead of a knight rescuing the fair damsel.

Jason picked up the black folder the waitress had left then pointed at Drew as he departed to pay the tab, including his beer.

Christi seemed uncomfortable. She looked out over the gulf with a wayward glance and Drew wondered if that was the cost of caring about dolphin or a deputy. There was crime that gripped her psyche and sucked a bit of pleasure out of a delightful afternoon as thoroughly as a summer thunderstorm.

"So you called. Do you need a ride home?" Drew asked, breaking the silence.

She looked back at him.

"Yes. But I wanted to apologize for being so mean last night," she said.

She looked up with a sincere but hesitant expression. "I simply couldn't let it go and it made me so angry. You are the only one helping to solve the case…and I've let it get so… so, personal.

She looked down at the decking, gathering her thoughts and continued.

"You know, I just want the killing to stop, but it always seems to come back to something important to me… something I want. Not that two dead and one injured dolphin aren't important to other people, but I've always been prone to that level of passion. I've been inconsiderate and pushy and I'm sorry."

There was a tear welling up in her eye and Drew couldn't stop it. He took the hand that wiped the tear away and held it in his. "Being guilty of passion is something this world could use a bit more of," Drew said.

"I want to help," she said, looking back up. "I want to help you solve this. What can I do?"

Her apology was sincere and her resolve was visible. He had no idea what she could do. Pretentious busy work would not suffice but he was certain she could help.

The band started playing an upbeat rendition of Van Zandt's "Alive" instead of a classic Buffett tune one might have expected.

"There's something else," Christi said. The tears were gone but she didn't pull her hand back.

"Rachel was in the ladies' room when I went in there. She was visibly upset."

Drew looked at her anticipating the worst. Rachel could go either way if she were to start talking about their time together.

"She said Bannacer was an insensitive twit. Well, she called him some other things too."

"Did she say why she slapped him?"

"Yes, but I'm not telling you."

"Why's that?"

"Because she asked me not to; but she made it clear that she would have preferred to kick him in the nuts."

"Oh, then he did make her mad. She has a way of bringing out the worst in some men." Drew knew that he probably shouldn't have brought that up but it was too late. Christi let it go but that didn't mean it was gone.

"She said to tell you to check into Bannacer's record while he was working in Pensacola."

"Did she say why?"

"Something about the oil spill. Something Bannacer did something after the oil spill. She said that you'll find it interesting.

"She didn't say what?"

"No, she didn't. She seemed to know that you would follow-up."

She was right. She knew him well enough to know he would have to look into it. Drew thought it was a bit ironic that she could still manipulate him with what she didn't say.

"She also said that the dolphin killings are related to oil leases that are scheduled next month."

"Did she say that?"

"Yes. Then she asked me to see if Bannacer was gone."

"Anything else."

"Yes, but it was just girl talk," she replied with a knowing smile.

Great, Drew thought. *That means I'll never know.*

"Let's get out of here," Drew said, standing up and taking her hand.

A large cigar appeared in their path to the door. The cigar was still captured by two fingers that also held a glass tumbler half-full of ice and a trifle caramel liquid.

Harold Gardey was still holding court. Bannacer was standing next to him at the bar.

Drew could feel Bannacer's eyes on his back as they pressed past them without a glance.

As they walked through the front door, a voice from the hostess station said, "Excuse me, sir, Ms. Franco left this for you."

Drew looked at her as though she were speaking in a foreign language, "Ms. Franco left this for me?" he repeated, taking the napkin from the girl's hand.

"So, what is it?" Christi asked.

"I have no idea."

Drew opened the door to his truck for Christi, then opened the napkin under the street light before getting in on the driver's side.

On the napkin, Rachel had written, "Drew. Sorry not to even speak. Lt. Bannacer was not as much help as I thought he might be. I think he was trying a bit too hard when he let it slip that the dolphin killings are part of an oil company ploy to draw attention from the oil leases next month. I'm not sure how he would know. I can also tell you that he is an egotist, a bore, a fool, and he is certainly no gentleman. Love, Rachel.

p.s. Glad to see that you still have impeccable taste in women."

Drew handed the napkin to Christi.

Her smile was worth the embarrassment when she read the last line.

Christi looked up and asked, "So does this mean we have a clue?"

"It's more than we had before. It also means I have some follow-up to do." Drew thought that the timing was good. The captain had wanted him to do that anyway.

Drew pulled onto Thomas Drive and looked over at Christi staring out the window. Things were changing fast. It looked like this evening was a step in a different direction. She had broken through uncertainty and was no longer apologizing. Her focus was on the dolphin and that was not going to change until the case was resolved. Earlier, she stood on the perimeter and spoke to those who were in the business of solving crime. After tonight, Christi was part of the solution. She knew that she could contribute and that was transformative.

Drew didn't say anything until she looked over at him. It looked like she wanted to ask something, but Drew blurted out the obvious.

"So where do you live?"

Chapter 11

News of the demonstration went viral, locally anyway. Regular updates from Gulf Marine Park with photographs of the injured dolphin were posted to social media sites. A webcam was established so the public could routinely check on the dolphin's status. In the background, a poster encouraged viewers to make donations for the dolphin's continuous, round-the-clock care by texting or by calling a 1-800 number.

Drew spent the morning at his office going over the pictures Christi had given him, then reviewing them again. Why was Chuck Whear on the beach? What would Dr. Bentley and his lawyer have to gain by being there with a dolphin that had survived a murder attempt? Dolphins don't sue people.

Drew made a call to a fellow officer in Pensacola that he knew personally and professionally, hoping that he might steer him in the right direction for some info on Lt. Bannacer. He was on patrol and Drew realized that was probably good. Drew left his cell number so that he could be somewhere other than the office when his friend called back.

Drew searched the Charter Boat Captain's Association website. There was nothing there. The usual political bent, a familiar face and a commentary with a 'Contact Us' button, and the web page front matter that makes you at least want to look a bit further. There was a list of the typical officers of a typical association, many of them fishermen and captains' names that he recognized. Drew printed a copy along with the "mission statement" page and added it to the small assembly of information in the folder.

The Protect and Preserve website was set up in nearly the same manner, some pretty pictures of marine life and tranquil estuaries with links to the various initiatives. Under the Gulf Marine Sanctuary link was a map of the region where they hoped to eliminate all activities except ship transportation so that it could become a preserve for marine species. Drew was interested to learn that it was not just conservation, there was a protectionist notion as well. That's where the environmental activists would be found. The mission statement was the predictable rhetoric except that it was written by a famous actor. Other recognizable celebrities with thumbnail photos were linked to the page below and on the sidebar. The 'Contact Us' included a list of officers and sponsors. Drew noticed that their sponsors included the infamous British oil company logo along with several other prominent north Florida conglomerates that spanned from Jacksonville to the east and Pensacola to the west. He printed a copy of the page along with the mission statement for the record and added it to the folder.

Drew kept at it until the slow drum of the demonstration in the afternoon and the need to get out of the office took precedence.

When Drew stepped out back, Javier was walking up the dock. Drew's thoughts were elsewhere and he leaned against the wooden railing, looking down along the waterline. He really didn't see Javier until he slapped him on the back with a loud "Compadre" that shook him from the place where his thoughts had drifted.

"So where were you off to?" Javier asked. "It didn't look like you were even in this hemisphere."

"I don't know," Drew replied. "I just can't seem to find firm footing on this dolphin case. I spent all morning poring over the websites and documents I could find on the Charter Boat Captains Association and Protect and Preserve. I got nothin'."

Drew held the photos that he had been working with all morning in his hands. Javier snatched them and leaned over the rail in the same position he had found Drew, head down, elbows on the rail and a dour look of dismay.

"So," he said curtly, "in this hand it appears we have a member of the Whear family, and in this hand, we have some guy in a big hat and his strait-laced brother-in-law or maybe his accountant.

"That is Dr. Bentley," Drew said, pointing to the man with the big hat. "The other guy is the lawyer, Harold Gardey. Harold represents…."

"Oh yeah, I recognize Harry!" Javier said. "He made some money on the oil spill. Several good friends of mine cashed a check thanks to him."

Drew knew that Harold had been heavily engaged in the oil spill litigation in the months following the event. Once the visuals made it to CNN, the lawyers and assorted predators rapidly assembled and began a slow spiral around the entire gulf region. The scent of culpability must be close to that of blood in the water. Once the cut was made, it didn't matter whether it was because of responsibility or guilt; the feeding frenzy was quick, thorough, and expensive.

"So nothing on Protect and Preserve, nothing on the Charter Boat Captains Association. That can only mean one thing," Javier stated.

He looked over at Drew, handing the pictures back.

"It must be him," he said, pointing at Harold Gardey.

"So why do you say that?" Drew asked.

"Because he's a lawyer… and he's only in it for the money." Javier said walking toward the office. "He's pure predatory behavior personified."

Drew looked toward him with the photos in hand as he opened the door to go in. Javier looked back at Drew's quizzical expression and said, "Don't you get it? He doesn't care. All the guys I know that worked with him on the oil spill thing said that's why they chose him. He's only in it for the money and he's good at it. It's never personal; it's just what he does."

The door closed behind him. Drew leaned forward on the rail and looked down the dock. Too simple, but it was worth a look.

Drew went back in and phoned his office.

"Gardey, Renquin, Borski, and McClain. How may I direct your call?"

"Mr. Gardey's office please."

The switch was immediate and the phone began to ring with no further conversation.

"Mr. Gardey's office. May I ask who's calling please?"

"Good morning. This is Officer Phillips at the local Florida Fish and Wildlife Conservation Commission. I would like to make an appointment with Mr. Gardey."

"Officer Phillips, will this be a personal or professional visit?"

"It will be a professional call. I need to ask some questions regarding Mr. Gardey's involvement with the organization Protect and Preserve," Drew replied so that he would know this was not a billable visit.

"I can take a message, Mr. Phillips, and have Mr. Gardey return your call. His calendar is quite full but I'm sure he will want to make time for law enforcement."

Drew thanked the woman and left his office number. Knowing that it is nearly impossible to get him at the office, Drew left his personal cell phone number as well. After ringing off, he questioned whether that was such a good idea but, too late now.

By mid-afternoon, the captain heard about the pending demonstration from headquarters in Tallahassee through official channels. Law enforcement saw this as a provocation. Protect and Preserve could easily have chosen a location that did not implicate the commercial fishermen but instead chose to have the demonstration essentially in the fishermen's backyard.

Drew was assigned to be at the docks. A bit later, the captain assigned Javier also. They were to arrive by boat and be in the vicinity, but not to engage. This was police jurisdiction and FWC was instructed to remain in the boat unless specifically requested to assist. On the other hand, if a boat was involved, then FWC would be there to help.

Drew and Javier arrived about three and docked at the marina store. They stepped inside to see the lovely Jeanette who ran the small store and managed the marina slips. She also kept an ear close to the ground and knew everything about the goings on in the small water town. She knew who was out shrimping and when the long line boats would be heading out. She knew the former mayor who lived in the nearby condominiums. She also knew he was trying different boats and thinking about buying a trawler. She knew the wives of the fishermen that stayed on the boat and she knew the mistresses that came and went. Between Jeanette and the 'Shrimp Lady' who sold fresh shrimp from the pontoon boat docked at the corner, there wasn't much that escaped without notice.

"So, Jeanette, what do you hear?" Javier asked.

"You guys don't want to know what I hear. You just want to know about the fish and tree-huggers infesting my space."

"Don't hold back," Javier said, tongue-in-cheek. "We want to know how you really feel."

Jeanette did not need much provocation.

"You know I don't like it when something messes with my routine. I like the quiet gossip and the occasional crimes of passion."

She picked up a cup of coffee that had long since cooled. It consisted more of milk and sugar than the black over-cooked syrup from lunch that was still sitting on the burner.

"Some decadence, some debauchery, some clueless tourists and the occasional domestic dispute; just add tequila and pour it in a hot tub of 98% salty humidity and you have my Florida marina. Just the way I like it."

She took a sip like it was fresh made and set the cup back on a trivet atop a stack of newspapers and old magazines.

"Most everyone here just wants to fish or have a job that lasts longer than the weekend. We don't have much space available for save-the-planet types. Even the occasional fire-and-brimstone evangelist can't handle the heat here for long."

"So, do you think it's going to be a problem?"

She leaned on the counter with both elbows accentuating two flattering personal assets and cocked her head a little to one side.

"Not at all," she stated with authority. "I told all the commercial guys to go home... go see their wives. I hired extra security to patrol the docks."

"You think they took your suggestion?" Javier asked.

Jeanette looked over at Drew with the look of incredulity. It was a look that said, "Where'd you get this guy?" She turned to grab an electronic cigarette she had hidden behind the stack of newspaper and magazines. She took a quick draw and turned sideways to exhale past the Florida trinkets.

"Look, they know I see everything that comes and goes. They know that I know." She lifted her hand and placed four fingers in the cleavage of her breast.

"I'm mother superior to everything from here to that sign where the concrete ends," she said, pointing at the sign where the road ends and the marina starts. "Plus most of Bay Drive, at least to Uncle Ernie's. Even the things I don't know, they think I know. So yeah, they went home."

Drew stepped up to the counter with a bottle of water and looked at Javier.

"Satisfied?" Drew asked.

"Sounds like we just need to worry about the basin. The charter boats should be coming in over there in the next hour or two."

"You're right. You need to be in the basin near the charter boats. That's where the show will be," Jeanette said, taking another draw and turning to put the electronic cigarette back where it was before.

Drew pulled some cash out of his pocket and handed it toward Jeanette.

"Don't worry about it," she insisted. "Just cruise through occasionally this evening would you? I couldn't get off-duty law enforcement this evening so I had to get rent-a cop."

"You got it," he replied, opening the door. Javier stepped out and walked toward the crew of people making signs beneath the covered pavilion. Drew stepped back in long enough to retrieve his sunglasses from a semi-permanent position on his chest and put them back on.

"Drew!" Jeanette called just as he was about to open the door again. "I saw Ol' Man Whear this morning. He stopped in for a new Zara Spook."

The red and white Zara Spook is a long time favorite of top water fishermen. While there are lots of new shiny, sparkle-and-flash lures, the old timers know that consistency counts for something.

"What did he say?"

"Well you can guess what he thinks about these environmental action groups, but he's worried. There are a lot of fishermen that can't just quit and find new work. This is what they do. This is what they know how to do. I think he's concerned that one of these firebrand environmentalists could say the wrong thing or step just over that invisible line. If they do somebody will get hurt."

Drew nodded and opened the door, "Me too."

"Hey, stop by again. I'll buy you a cup of coffee."

Her coffee? Drew thought.

She was a very attractive woman just a few years ahead of Drew in high school. Time in the sun had given her a coffee and cream-colored skin. Unfortunately, that delicious tan does not age well. On the other hand, she was a rock solid Florida girl that knew her way through the dark shoals and shallow reefs. She wore confidence like other women wear eye shadow, and it is a pleasant, comfortable shade.

"Looking good, as always, Ms Jeanette. Keep it up," Drew said, putting his hat on and stepping out.

"You keep it up too!" she teased, with undertones that could stop a swordfishing long-liner from leaving the dock.

Chapter 12

Javier and Drew assumed a position just off the boat launch when the parade of seventy, maybe a hundred, demonstrators supporting 'Protect and Preserve' assembled under the marina pavilion. The original plan was to stop the march at the Shrimp Boat parking lot north of the yacht basin, but the owners would not grant them permission. It was tourist season, so the denial wasn't entirely without merit. The Shrimp Boat is a restaurant from a bygone era that was rebuilt as an attractive series of fashionable seafood dives on the main street through the heart of old St. Andrew's. The protest would march right past the charter fleet docked in the yacht basin adjacent to the Shrimp Boat. These commercial fishermen are fresh seafood suppliers to the restaurants and several markets in the vicinity. They are also customers of high-traffic slip rental locations. As a result, plans had to be changed to continue the march from there up the road to a church parking lot where the rally would be held right on the U.S. highway that follows the coastline. The police were setting up detours and roadblocks to route commuters through the back streets.

Protect and Preserve had outfitted the group quickly with signs and banners. Activists flitted here and there to organize the assembling crowd handing out dolphin toys and streamers. The group assembled under the pavilion on the marina where an occasional speaker squelched the music with a rallying cry followed by a chant and raucous cheer. A large screen to one side showed the live stream on Facebook Live. Right on schedule, one of the leaders stormed the stage and took up the Protect and Preserve banner then marched from the podium to the chorus of Melissa Etheridge's "I need to wake up." The crowd melted in behind her. Turning the corner the protest coalesced into a vocal movement and the organizers cranked up the speakers belting out John Lennon's "Power to the People."

Out front were several distinguished members of Protect and Preserve; faces that were often in the news or seen as leaders in local environmental programs. Prominently carrying a large picture of the injured dolphin was Harold Gardey. He was in a suit despite the warm summer day and clearly a motivator in the throng of protestors. He was known to be passionate about gulf concerns and backed a number of causes against polluters and exploiters of Florida's somewhat convoluted and arguably ambiguous environmental regulation. Harold was head of the local Sierra Club and a well-positioned defender of Mother Nature herself, not to mention all those that funded her causes.

Behind him were board members and sponsors of the organization along with several recognizable endowment leaders. The press keyed in on Mara Hadley, internationally known designer of ladies' accessories. She was a leader and patron of the local chapter and living, at least part of the year, in a nearby village. The presence of Dr. Tom Bentley, as one of the original founders and renowned biologist and protectionist, was obligatory. They were followed by the rank and file supporters of Protect and Preserve, including a large contingent of high school and college students, but otherwise a general mix of the local population. The turnout would likely have been better if it had not been on a Thursday afternoon. The city council would not abide a weekend event that could interrupt the flow of tourists coming from the beach. This was still prime season and those customers and their spending were the life-blood of the town.

A police car blocked traffic at the corner as the protest walked past, but the officer stayed in his air-conditioned vehicle. Another blocked the boat ramp with lights flashing, much to the dismay of several boat owners lined up to back down the ramp and wrap up a day on the water. Because of the rather insistent ramp users, the officer leaned against the side of the car with his sunglasses in place so he could still hear the radio and read the crowd.

Drew slowly motored past the pier and around the docks into the yacht basin where several of the charter boats were already docked. It was nearly five and the charter boats that were booked today had recently returned. There were only three that Drew saw come in, but all the boats were manned or appeared to be.

"That's odd," he thought, but then again, these are the front lines. A presence is required in light of recent events.

Those that had caught fish had laid them out on the boardwalk for pictures in a usual manner. The anglers were gathering their gear or huddled around the stern of the boats while pictures were taken; a typical mêlée that followed a day of deep-sea fishing. Wives and children were arriving to see the catch. Buddies toasted successful days and hoisted slimy fish for cell phone photos directly uploaded to social media.

The news media had set up beside the road just past the yacht basin. The vans were parked, antennas were already up, and they were standing by to broadcast live. The media knew that this would be the point where the two factions met. They also knew that the location was all for their benefit; both sides of the story wanted to ensure media attention and coverage.

From the boat, Drew could see Rachel standing up front beside the van primping in the side mirror. He remembered telling her that he despised what she did for a living. That was a fight to remember. Drew was certain that he could have taken the high ground but instead he equated her work to that of the first profession, a news prostitute. Her desire to be in the limelight, right out front and in your face, was tangible. It was part of her make up and it never went away, even on quiet nights at home. It all had to be sensational. She had to be seen at Starbucks in the morning looking perfect. Lunch was a business opportunity. Drinks after work needed to be at an acceptable location where she could observe the shakers when they shook and the movers when they moved. Even steaks on the grill needed some special sauce or flair, preferably from the Food Network. The same translated to the bedroom.

"Drew, when are you going to tell your good friend Javier about your history with that *chica caliente* Rachel, eh?" Javier said.

"Nothing to say, amigo. More than a year ago now."

"She's still not married?"

"Not too many can keep up with her. She's engaged to her profession," Drew said, looking at her and the bright yellow sundress that she wore. "Besides, you know Selena would have you turned into fish bait if she knew you were talking like that."

"Carumba! ... a man can look, eh?" Javier liked to think he had a romance that was turning into something even more with a nightclub singer on the beach. Her name really was Selena, and she could do a spectacular impression of the late Selena Perez. He had as good a shot as any but Drew suspected she just enjoyed the comfort of law enforcement close by. A talented lady with her looks had a lot of choices... come to think of it, so did Rachel.

"Here they come," Javier said. "The police just blocked the road at 14th Street next to Hunt's Oyster Bar. I'm going to move over to the bulkhead next to the boat taxi."

Javier pulled alongside the bulkhead just as a sheriff's car pulled into position with the vehicle facing toward the road. His presence was highly visible despite the darkened windows but he was prepared for a hasty exit if necessary.

When the northbound side of St Andrew Boulevard was blocked, there was no more traffic. The motorists would be upset but it would likely be less than thirty minutes, Drew thought. Besides, the locals know the side streets. Okay, so maybe it takes an hour, given the news media and the fact that every business in town wanted the publicity.

Javier was watching Rachel as she moved into position in front of the van where the camera could see both the charter fleet and the protesting marchers as they came around the corner. There was Harold Gardey waving his sign with both hands. The fish were no longer displayed on the dock and the anglers divided their catch and headed quickly for their cars. Drew was thinking that it really should make quite a news story as metaphorically two armies passed side by side.

A deep voice came from above and to the left. "Hey, just thought I'd let you know I was asked to stand by in case you or the police needed any help."

The Deputy Sheriff had stepped out of his air-conditioned vehicle and was standing on the boardwalk to the left. Because of the dead low tide, Drew looked toward his voice and saw the stripe on his uniform trousers about knee level. He squatted lower just as Drew looked up.

"Not our jurisdiction down here either," he said, "but I can call in help if we need it. Just thought I'd let you know."

"Thanks," Drew replied. "I think our bosses must have collaborated on this plan. We're just to show the colors unless it gets out of hand."

Looking up into the sun, it was bright even with sunglasses, so Drew stepped back where he could see that the deputy was a stout fellow and young. The stiff dark hat and sunglasses gave him a rather imposing look even though it didn't fit the voice. For the sheriff's department it must be a defense mechanism taught early in the training phase. The more imposing, rugged, don't-mess-with-me exterior persona, the less likely confrontational people will choose that option.

"I'm Drew Phillips, and this is my partner, Javier Rodriquez," Drew said extending his hand up to where he could reach it.

"We've met, just not professionally," he said shaking Drew's hand with a firm grip, then Javier's. Familiar face, but he couldn't place it.

"Jason McBride."

The name went through the soft wiring of brain cells then across a specific synapse and clicked. It surprised Drew that it took that long, but then the uniform and sunglasses changed his appearance considerably.

"I'm supposed to stay in the car but wanted you to know I'm available if needed. Hope not."

"Me too, but glad to have you standing by," Drew said.

"Did you see that?" Jason said, pointing toward the street.

In a flash, something small came over the sidewalk from the stern of the *Aegeus* to the right. It was almost like confetti but it got Drew's attention. Immediately after that, silvery confetti flew from the stern of another boat, then another.

"Javier, look at this. What is that?" Drew asked.

Javier turned to look toward the street and saw something fly from the stern of the boat nearby.

"Is it ice maybe?" Javier asked. "It's not very big."

"Can you see if the police have noticed?" Drew asked Jason.

He stood up and looked out past the charter boats to the corner. "He's out in front of the traffic; if he noticed, it's not setting off alarm bells."

Drew spotted one of the deckhands on the boardwalk take a bag from his pocket and toss the contents out across the road, then step back aboard. Several others did the same.

"It looks like fish... very small bait fish," Drew said, as several handfuls sailed over the crowd on the boardwalk and landed in the street.

"You mean small like mullet or small like menhaden?" Javier asked

"Small like menhaden, only smaller... maybe glass minnows."

Harold had stopped at the corner and waited for the straggling troupe of demonstrators to catch up. He would want to make sure the media saw them not as a small contingent of straggling do-gooders but an enthusiastic parade of passionate environmentalists.

Javier said, "I'll go look."

"No-- direct orders from the Captain. We stay in the boat."

"I can look," Jason said, walking forward. "If it's fish, I'll give you a thumbs up."

A seagull swooped down over the street, picked up something, and flew off.

"They are fish," Drew said to himself, watching Jason arrive at the street curb. The thumbs up sign confirmed his speculation.

"Rain minnows. There could be hundreds of them on the street," Drew said to Javier. "Oh boy, standby. That is what Jeanette was talking about."

"What do you mean?"

"Remember? That's where the show will be. That's what she said."

"Not really, no… but if you say so."

Another seagull swooped, followed by four more.

Harold and the demonstrators had reached marching strength and the full contingent had turned the corner toward the media. Cameras were live, the reporters positioned strategically in the foreground. Jason walked back to his vehicle. The charter boat crews were aboard their vessels and out of the way of those marching and chanting in the road.

Another swoop of six or eight seagulls dove in front of the crowd. In only seconds, seagulls appeared from all directions. The seagulls hovered, then dropped in front of the marching crowd to retrieve a small fish, then retreated. The demonstrators were defiant as the numbers of feeding birds grew. They marched in lock step in front of the *Aegeus* at the front end of the row of charter boats. Seagulls flew in from the bay over the charter fleet and plunged into the street, diving in front of the marchers only steps away. Some of the gulls stayed in the street and moved aside; others burst between the oncoming demonstrators. The sound of feeding gulls mixed with protest chants was a cacophony of noise, like something aboriginal with a vocal rhythm accompanied by the continuous hawk and caw of seabirds. The gulls flew low along the sidewalk and snatched minnows, then lifted off through the marchers only to turn and dive into the gap it just created with wings and calls, moving people out of the way.

The demonstrators' lines began to falter before the leaders made it past the last charter boat. The seagulls still came. There were seagulls standing on the opposite side of the road ready to dash between feet to pick up a minnow. Others hovered and dove straight through the crowd like catching bait behind a shrimper. One of the ladies on the front lines yelled and stopped in the middle of the street when a seagull defecated on takeoff, and it landed across her cheek and shoulder. Marchers behind her stopped abruptly, then marched around her. The back lines were moving to the side of the street, no longer waving their signs for the media but waving them fiercely to swat at the seagulls diving for minnows and bursting out of the crowd in front of them.

Harold rallied the troops to form behind him but only half of the squad reassembled for the march to the media. Many were wiping bird feces from their clothes, and others simply turned around and started the trek back to the marina where they left their car.

Harold Gardey and maybe two dozen made it to where Rachel was standing to ask questions in rapid succession. Harold was rattled and it showed later on TV. He was trying to ignore the seagulls and focus on the purpose of their demonstration. This was about the dolphin recuperating from a vicious attack, the need for vigilance and protection of the species. Who could protect these mammals from attacks, from pollution, from the deadly diseases? Statistics indicate dolphin mortality is higher than ever seen in our history.

He spoke well and with conviction. Unfortunately, regardless of his delivery and the message, the story was already broadcast. Drew could already see it unfolding. Seagulls Attack Environmentalists! The wire would pick it up and so would the Today Show. Al Roker would talk about it during the weather segment, something about raining seagulls. Jimmy Kimmel would make a joke about nature taking sides. A link to the video would show up on YouTube and social media would take it from there. The irony of an environmental demonstration fragmented by nature itself would carry it to the top twenty-five or maybe the NY Times top ten.

Harold Gardey and his fervent supporters, including Dr. Bentley and Mara Hadley, stayed with him as he moved toward the other news media van. Their clothing was noticeably peppered with black and white spots from seagull droppings that detracted seriously from their on-screen appearance. Even from Drew's vantage point in the boat, it looked as though Mother Nature had anointed them in a most distasteful manner. A group of twenty besieged marchers moved up the sidewalk as planned and headed toward the church for the rally. The sponsors faded into the crowd.

In just minutes, the seagulls had cleared the road and the charter boats had begun their boat wash down. The wash would be a little more thorough than usual since the seagulls did not take sides. Their boats were targeted with equal precision, but the crew watched the spectacle from the covered fly bridge or from beneath the deck overhang and were personally spared the indiscriminate onslaught. Several had pictures that were, no doubt, being uploaded to social media and distributed widely to friends and other fishing buddies.

"I better call the captain," Drew said to Javier.

"Yeah. Better do that. Tell him not to miss the 6 o'clock news and that we're going to need some overtime to wash the boat."

Drew smiled back and pushed the call button. There would be no overtime.

"I guess we got lucky that the uniforms were spared."

"I guess *you* got lucky," Javier replied, turning around to show where a long white stripe started at his left shoulder.

When the call was answered Drew heard, "Officer Phillips, this is Bryan. Please hold for the captain."

In just moments, the captain picked up. "Drew, I caught the end of the live broadcast. Tell me what happened."

Drew explained that they had seen the minnows come from the charter boats but did not have eyes on who threw them because of their vantage point in the boat behind them. The seagulls simply responded predictably. And, of course, they didn't care that food happened to be located right in front of the Protect and Preserve group.

"...and the TV cameras," the captain added.

"So, should we follow-up?" Drew asked.

"Anybody hurt?"

"Some pride was damaged but other than that it's just a cleanup."

"What about the police? Are they looking into it?"

"I don't think I've seen an officer out of his cruiser. Have you, Javier?"

He shook his head and looked back to see Rachel doing some candid interviews. She was desperately trying to get someone from the charter boats to talk to her, but to no avail. The crews simply kept working the boat clean up under the watchful eye of each captain sitting on the fly bridge talking on the phone.

"Nothing that we can tell."

"Come on home then. We'll stay clear unless someone asks."

"Got it. We'll cruise the marina then head in."

Drew pushed the end button and Javier looked around from in front of the console.

"So we're off the hook?" he asked.

"Cap'n said to bring it home."

"One more chance to walk up there and introduce me to your 'history'," Javier teased, walking back around the console. "You're afraid she would immediately fall for my *piel bronceada* and the irresistible Caribbean accent."

"Nope, not afraid, but you should be."

Drew started the outboards and put one in reverse to back away from the bulkhead. Once clear, he put the other in forward to spin the bow around then headed out of the basin.

"Let's cruise the marina like Jeanette asked. We can still be at the pier before dark. You supposed to see Selena tonight?"

"Of course! What about you?"

Drew didn't answer. He thought that he might call Christi, but probably won't, not after seeing Jason again. Drew wasn't surprised, but what were the odds? Besides he's more her age, Drew thought. Even though it was just eight years past, college was a lifetime ago.

"After my time in Afghanistan, I suppose it was."

"Talking to yourself again, my friend?"

Drew ignored the question.

They cruised slowly out of the basin then around the docks without a lot of banter. As they finished the circuit and came away from the boat ramp, Drew spotted a lone fisherman.

Walking out from shore next to the yacht basin channel was Mr. Whear. Old straw wide-brimmed hat permanently perched on his head and a brand new red and white Zara Spook on the end of his fishing rod. Drew pulled the throttle back well before coming alongside.

"So, Mr. Whear, did you watch the show?"

"What show's that, Drew?"

"The Protect and Preserve show right down Main Street."

"Naw. I just woke up and figured I could get a few casts in before dark. But I hear that the seagulls won!" he said, smiling, but still walking slowly out toward the change in water depth and shuffling his feet.

"I suppose by anybody's rules, they did."

Mr. Whear looked up and stopped his slow trudge through soft wet sand. He smiled and looked at each of us then back at Drew to say, "You know, when you choose to play in our backyard, you're going to have to play by our rules."

Mr. Whear tipped his hat and continued walking. Drew pushed into forward and idled on past him.

"Interesting," Drew thought to himself, and wondered whether that meant there were rules ...or are they more like guidelines?

Chapter 13

Drew arrived at the office of Gardey, Renquin, Borski, and McClain a little early. Punctuality is a courtesy that most southerners still recognize as respectful. For Drew it is a compulsory refinement; early by fifteen means you are on time, on time means you're late. Gardey had agreed to meet Drew just after his last appointment of the day. Drew was guessing that he wouldn't remember his face from Schooners but he was ready with a quip and the name of a close relation in case he did.

Drew was looking through the assortment of magazines and found an old *Florida Sportsman*. Gardey's assistant was packing up for the day and asked if he needed anything.

"Mr. Gardey typically keeps a strict schedule," she said. "I expect he'll be with you very shortly."

The door opened just minutes later and Drew watched as Harold Gardey slapped the shoulder of Chuck Whear then shook his hand. Gardey stepped over to the desk and handed his assistant a check, then turned for a moment to see something she had prepared.

Chuck froze when he saw Drew sitting there. He reacted worse than if he had been caught with undersized snapper in the boat. Law enforcement officers learn the different looks from working in the field. The guilty look is extremely recognizable by action and expression.

Tossing the magazine back on the table, Drew stood and walked toward Chuck with his hand extended.

Gathering his wits about him, Chuck said, "What're you doing here?"

"Good to see you too, Chuck," Drew answered. Chuck has always been a bit reckless with his no-nonsense demeanor. "Not catching many here," Drew added.

"Not today, personal business. But we've been loading up on good snapper down to the south but it's a long ride. Our really good customers will cover it but most of the routine charters won't pay for a ten or twelve-hour trip."

"Officer Phillips," Harold Gardey said loudly, stepping over to our conversation. "Of course you and Mr. Whear are acquainted, both sides of the same profession."

He put his hand on the shoulders of both men as he stepped up.

"Chuck, I'm sure you have places to be. Officer Phillips and I have a matter to discuss. I have already booked our next visit, so Pam will give you a reminder call a couple of days in advance."

Chuck knew that he had just been dismissed.

Drew reached a bit saying, "Chuck, I saw that you were on the beach when they rescued that dolphin a week or so ago. Do you think I could stop by the boat and talk to you about it?"

Chuck looked at Mr. Gardey like he was looking for guidance. He knew Drew wasn't asking. It's another southern courtesy to ask. Receiving no input from Gardey at all, he looked back at Drew.

"Yeah, what about it? We was jus' watching. We didn't have a charter that afternoon and I heard 'bout it on the VHF radio and drove out to see. Those fellas at Gulf sure got a way of snatching 'em up. It was pretty impressive."

"So you don't mind if I stop by one afternoon that you aren't out fishing?"

"Naw, I don't mind so long as my uncle's okay with it."

His uncle owns the boat where he works as a deckhand. He's also head of the Charter Boat Captains Association. He operates out of the yacht basin in St. Andrew. Ol'Man Whear is his father. Chuck's father used to work the business but got into operating the crew boats to the offshore rigs in Louisiana. Fishing just wasn't steady enough.

He stepped away and waved as he pulled his ball cap out of his left rear pocket, put it on backwards, then turned to leave.

"He's a good kid," Harold Gardey stated as he turned toward his office. "Had to help him through of a couple bad choices he made a few years back, but he seems to be staying on top of things."

Gardey leaned back through the door as Drew stepped into his office and said, "Pam, I'll lock things up after we're done, so you don't have to stay."

His assistant recognized that she had just been dismissed, as well.

"So how can I help you Officer Phillips?" Gardey asked. He pushed the office door closed as Pam left with her belongings. He extended his hand toward two chairs that looked out over a picturesque bayou filled with sailboats at anchor that were visible through the mix of palm trees and stately oaks loaded with Spanish moss. Drew took a seat while Gardey stood at the window looking out.

"Mr. Gardey, I'm looking into the Protect and Preserve organization and I understand that you serve on its board of directors."

Gardey turned from the window and looked at Drew curiously.

"So, this investigation is about a charitable organization I'm associated with?"

"No, I can't say that, Mr. Gardey." Drew replied. "I'm simply following up with both the Charter Boat Captain's Association and Protect and Preserve in an effort to be thorough. Can you tell me if there is anyone in the organization that you think would be capable of deliberately killing dolphin?"

Gardey's dark silhouette blocked the sun streaming in from the large window as he stepped toward Drew. He sat on the edge of the adjacent chair and looked at Drew sternly.

"Officer Phillips, surely that must sound as absurd to you as it is offensive to me." Gardey's voice was louder with distinct enunciation as though he were speaking so a jury could hear. "Protect and Preserve is a very sound group of professionals that would pay, and do pay, large sums of money to ensure that would not happen."

His stern look included a measure of contempt. This was something he considered personal and unexpected.

"So there isn't a zealot among the rank and file that might consider taking…let's say, extraordinary measures?"

Gardey leaned back into his chair and put his hand on his chin with one finger over his lips.

"I concede your point, Officer. We do have some very committed members but no, I can state unequivocally that I can think of no one who would willfully and maliciously do such a thing without cause."

Drew paused briefly to write his answer in his book.

"Is there any reason that you can think of that Protect and Preserve could benefit from such an occurrence?" Drew asked.

"I'm not sure I understand what you are asking Officer."

"Mr. Gardey, as you know, this community has experienced the brutal extermination of a dolphin, and now more than one. Is there any way that Protect and Preserve could benefit from such an occurrence?"

Drew could tell he didn't like that question, or maybe it was how he phrased it. Drew hit a nerve and he did not want him to see it.

"Officer, I am not sure I want to answer such a provocative question," Gardey responded. "How on earth would you think that such a clear disregard for the law and the wellbeing of the species could benefit Protect and Preserve? It is abhorrent, it cannot be condoned, and it is offensive to our very existence!"

Gardey stood and moved back toward the setting sun and stated, "I don't think I understand your premise Officer."

Drew could tell that Gardey was at that point. This is where he could break through or it all falls down.

"I mean, let's take it to an extreme." Drew said. "If all fishing were to be halted in the Gulf of Mexico, can you think of how that might benefit Protect and Preserve?"

"Yes." Gardey conceded, "in that we would no longer be overfishing the species, but that's inherent in our existence and in your premise. Protect and Preserve, ostensibly doesn't want to stop all fishing except in set aside regions of the fishery; but to take that much further I think we would have to ask the Board, and our legal council, of course."

"What about you, Mr. Gardey? Is there any way that you as a director could benefit?"

Drew looked straight at him in finishing the question. Drew needed to read his face. He wanted to see if that question caused a similar discomfort. Unfortunately, he had fully recovered. You don't get to be a successful lawyer when you sweat under pressure and Mr. Gardey was very successful.

"No, Officer, there is no benefit that I can derive nor can any of the Protect and Preserve board members."

Drew was writing his answer down and desperately trying to imagine another question that would let him dig a little deeper.

"I appreciate your time, Mr. Gardey. I think you and I know that this was simply a 't' that needed to be crossed in my report. As you can imagine, if the dolphin killing continues there could be political ramifications therefore I need to be very thorough."

"I do understand those sentiments very well and a thorough report can only help," Gardey replied.

Gardey stood and began moving slowly to open the office door as Drew finished writing. When Drew turned around, he stood in the doorway.

"Mr. Gardey, do you know a Lt. Bannacer?" He asked.

"That is a familiar name," Gardey replied, "but I can't seem to place it. Should I?"

"Someone mentioned that you had assisted him with an oil spill matter a few years back."

"Bannacer... hmm, Bannacer." He stepped over to the tablet on his desk and picked it. "That was a very busy year, or several years, I should say...and so many clients whose very livelihood were adversely affected. After flipping through several electronic pages, he stopped on one.

"I did work with an Officer Bannacer. It was in a few years ago over in Pensacola. The details are privileged, of course, but we did achieve a substantial recovery. His was an unusual case but perhaps that is why it was so lucrative."

Gardey continued to flip through pages briefly. "Was there something you wanted to ask about this case?"

"No, no. I simply wanted to know if you knew him. He recently transferred here from our office in Pensacola."

Drew walked toward the door as Gardey put the tablet back on his desk. He was lying. They were drinking together at Schooners the other night. Why would he not want to say he knew Bannacer?

"That reminds me," Drew said as an off-the-cuff remark. "I heard that they were considering some area over near Destin to offshore oil exploration. Wouldn't that just be a hard sell after all that litigation a couple years back."

Gardey didn't even look up. He walked deliberately toward the office exit.

"You haven't heard about that?" Drew asked, as the office door swung open.

"Can't say that I've kept up very well on that side of it." Gardey replied curtly, then caught himself and quipped, "On the other hand, I'm sure if they spill even so much as a thimble full I'll hear about it," and he looked up with the most genuine, fully engaged smile.

Drew was done here. Gardey wasn't willing to spar on his own time and was creating an out.

"That Chuck Whear is a piece of work. I hope you're helping him. There was a time when it looked like he could catch trouble without any bait."

Gardey stepped out the door behind Drew and moved into his reception area.

"He is a good kid, but you are right. He caught some trouble that his granddaddy knows nothing about."

Drew raised an interested eye as he walked toward the exit. "Not much gets past ol'Man Whear if it happens in St. Andrew."

"As a law officer, you know that there was a substantial list of people that got away with fraud in the period immediately following the oil spill," Gardey offered with a note of remorse. "Let's just say he wasn't one of them. He was lucky I was able to help him," Gardey said with the same plastic smile.

As Drew left the building, he thought of several other questions he should have asked. He thought that he would want to pry a little next time he talked to Chuck Whear. Looking back, Drew saw Gardey talking on his cell phone looking at him through the window beside the door.

Drew had done what he came to do. All the fish on the reef are aware that the barracuda lives there, but when the barracuda starts cruising their part of the reef, he commands their full attention.

# # #

The captain's meeting had already started when Drew slipped in the front door of the Harvest Church just off 11th Street in old St. Andrew. Drew checked his watch and he wasn't late. They must have gathered a bit early.

Capt. Whear, Chuck's uncle, waved when he saw Drew take a seat in the back. His father was seated in the pews to the right and most of the other pews were full of captains from all around the bay. The enclave also included interested family members who sat about midway back. Drew was the only law enforcement officer and used to sitting in the pew at the very back.

"Officer Phillips, thanks for coming," Capt Whear said and waved. Heads turned to see him sitting in the back. "We appreciate your being here. I apologize that we started a little early with some local business but we won't keep you long.

Drew waved at the faces that turned around to see him sitting in uniform at the rear of the church.

"As I was saying," Capt. Whear continued, "the meeting will include an open forum where we will have the chance to speak, as well as the other groups. We need a good showing though. The panel will be making decisions that affect our ability to fish and that means it affects your pay. Pass the word and let's fill the house with professional fishermen like yourselves. Bring your brother-in-law, your nephew and your granddaddy!"

Drew saw Chuck sitting next to his grandfather at the front. It looked like talking to him was going to be difficult. As the meeting droned into minutes from the last meeting and old business, Drew watched ol'Man Whear stand up and walk out the side door followed by Chuck. This looked like his chance, so Drew slipped out the front door hoping to catch Chuck.

Drew came out the front door and heard their voices before he left the top steps. Chuck's voice was raised and somewhat emphatic.

"…that's what I'm telling you, Grandpaw. I can't make a living this way. Carol Lynn, she wants new furniture and you know she wants a baby, and I just can't afford to keep working the fishing charters and make enough to do that stuff."

Rather than step into a family quarrel, Drew stayed near the front door and sat down on the top step. He couldn't hear most of ol'Man Whear's response. They must have sat down on one of the benches near the big oak.

"I got several side jobs just like you said, but none of them will get us any insurance and part time just don't pay enough."

Drew heard the ol'man say, "When I was your age…" but that was about all he heard. He knew that wasn't going anywhere. There really wasn't much here except fishing back in the 1930's.

"I know, Grandpaw. I've been working the boats with you since I was twelve. I don't know what else I can do but I'm gonna have to find out."

"You got to make those choices Chuck. Right here you know you have a place to work and fish to eat. We're family. It might not pay as much but it's as sure as the sunrise and steady as the tide."

Drew stood up and opened the church door, then shut it a bit loudly. Walking down the steps to the street, he could see them to the left and walked that direction behind the row of parked trucks and cars.

"G'nite Drew," ol'Man Whear said.

"Good evening, Mr. Whear," Drew said from the dark. "I was kind of hoping to catch you two out here. Think I could have a few words with Chuck?"

"Come on over and have a seat," Mr. Whear offered. "Mosquitos aren't too bad but this place is ate up with dark."

Drew hadn't noticed, but no streetlights illuminated the courtyard. Only some dim lights were on at the church. He walked through the trucks but didn't sit down. Instead he leaned back against the bumper of a pickup.

"Chuck, is this a good time to ask you a few questions about the dolphin?"

"No sir ...but there's not a good time, so go ahead."

He still had a bit of an attitude. Some of it was youthful defiance but some of it was probably because of the words he and his grandpaw had just finished. Chuck pulled a can of Skoal out of his rear pocket, opened it with his left hand and put a pinch in his lip.

"Drew, before you get started, Chuck ain't in any trouble, is he?" the ol' man asked.

"No, Mr. Whear, not that I know of. This is just routine follow-up on some leads associated with that dolphin that was beached."

"All right then. I'm going to go back inside. Chuck, you still going to give me a ride home?"

"Yessir."

Mr. Whear stood and walked back toward the single light glowing just outside the side door. Chuck put the lid back on his can of Skoal and returned it to his left rear pocket. His granddaddy didn't like the fact that he dipped snuff but Chuck intended to make a point of it.

"Chuck, I can make this pretty short," Drew said. "I want to know what you were doing out at the beach watching that dolphin. I don't believe you just rode out there to see it."

The dark closed in a bit as Drew confronted him. He looked down at the dirt and fiddled with his fingernails before deciding to answer.

"I owe Mr. Gardey some money, and he gets me to help him now and then."

"I know you got into some trouble after the oil spill stretching the truth on some of those invoices."

"What's that got to do with the dolphin?" he shot back.

"What kind of help does Mr. Gardey get you to do for him?"

"Well, that day, I picked him and some doctor friend up and drove them out to the beach to see that dolphin."

"What else can you tell me about Mr. Gardey and his friend?"

"I know his doctor friend is a strange bird. Never says much to me. Treats me like I'm ignorant. Now Mr. Gardey, he's always nice. Pays me pretty good… well actually, he just takes it off my bill, but I can't get that kind of hourly rate working around the marina."

"So what else does he have you do?"

"Not that much, really. I drove over to Mobile to pick up some papers. Even got to go to New Orleans once. Drove over the bridge to some warehouse in Algiers where I picked up a crate and I drove it back. "

"What was in the crate?" Drew asked.

"Don't have a clue. They loaded up in the back of my truck and I drove it back to Mr. Gardey's house that evening. He gave me a hundred dollar tip."

"Didn't it make you wonder?"

"Sure it did. Picking up a crate in some lowdown district off the Mississippi River, it'd make anybody wonder. But he don't pay me to be curious."

"Any idea what he wanted out on the beach looking at a dolphin rescue?"

"Now that was sorta strange." Chuck said looking at his hands and the dark ground between them. "He and that doctor friend stood off to the side and watched the whole thing, and then we got back in the truck and drove back. Only thing I heard Mr. Gardey say was, 'I'll bet that's going to piss off the Mayor.' The doctor friend, he never says anything. Least he never says anything I can hear, but this time I hear him say, 'I'll bet it's going to start the war.'"

Chapter 14

Mack called early the next week, this time to request some help. Mack was hosting a public hearing for proposed changes to the fisheries management plan for the Gulf Coast region. He needed someone from law enforcement to attend as an enforcement consultant should questions arise.

Payback is an understood obligation. It's more of an intrinsic aspect of friendship than a commitment. It's what friends do and Drew was certainly willing after several things Mack had done, not to mention the ongoing dolphin investigation.

He also wanted Drew to look over his presentation. As a noted marine biologist, Mack tends to go scientific and speak of studies, modes, related data, and analyses with alacrity and without any reluctance. That would simply not work with this crowd. These men fished everyday and relied more on sky conditions, current, water temperature, moon rise and personal experience.

"I know I should call through channels," Mack conceded, "but I don't want just any law enforcement. I would prefer to have you there."

"No problem," Drew said, letting him off the hook too easily. "The boss knows we're friends so just send an email and I'll work it through the office."

Drew wanted to know if Christi would be coming too. He finally decided she probably would and he didn't ask.

"Thanks, Drew. You know the climate we currently have in the fishing community; I'd just rather know you had my back."

"You think there will be a problem?"

"Not sure, but the proposed change cuts the snapper season again, so yeah. The charter guys will be there and so will the recreational fishermen. Nobody likes it."

"I'll be there," and Drew hung up. There was something in the conversation between friends that didn't require anything more. Mack was asking for help and Drew would be there to support him.

"Another cut in the season," Drew thought to himself. "This could get ugly."

Local media would be there too, so he talked to the boss about backup just in case. The boss agreed but suggested Drew contact the sheriff's department. It was their jurisdiction.

"Maybe I should just call Jason and ask him to sit with us," Drew muttered leaving his office. The National Marine Fisheries Management Group, under the Magnuson-Stevens Act, was assigned the task of managing fisheries in Federal Waters from the state limit out 200 miles. The hearings are mandated to allow public input for proposed changes in the management plan. Unfortunately, what is good for the fishery is seldom a proposal welcomed by fishermen. The level of disagreement had now reached a threshold.

Truth is, Drew told himself, if he were a fisherman by trade, he'd probably stand with them too. But that's the sportsman talking, Drew thought; the enforcement side would at least hear the argument. From the fisherman's perspective, it is really hard to imagine how they get the fish to cooperate when they do an offshore census. Drew was sure it gets all scientific and statistical, but he had enough good 'ol boy in him to be skeptical.

With hearings pending, Drew needed to do a little research. If he was to provide input from the enforcement perspective, he needed to be ready for the hearing. With the captain's permission, Drew spent the next day at the office reading.

Drew had a phone message from Harold Gardey's office and from the head of the local Charter Boat Captain's Association. Since he was to be in the office, he left messages again with both. Mack and Drew planned to meet for lunch so he could get a copy of the panel presentation. The morning went very fast.

Mack met Drew at Coram's. The diner is one of several breakfast and coffee shops along Thomas Drive with the typical bar stools and booths. This one is a 24-hour fisherman's favorite that smells like bacon and fried 'covered and smothered' hash browns. Mack's wife won't let him eat at the diner because she can't stand the fried smell and he has to watch the cholesterol. Mack, on the other hand, chooses that location at every opportunity probably for that very reason. He was on the phone and didn't see Drew walk in, so he managed to slip into the booth before Mack made some sort of a welcome scene.

"Hey, Drew," he said hanging up. "Here's my slide presentation; thanks for looking it over."

As usual, Drew felt completely inadequate to review and comment on a presentation prepared by a PhD and accomplished professional in his field, but he took it and promised to get right on it this afternoon. Drew was in the office and working the dolphin case today. He wanted Mack to know that in case Christi asked.

"So how's that going?" Mack asked. "You know Christi is going to grill me when I get back to the office."

"I'm not making much progress and she isn't going to be happy about it." Drew replied.

"I was afraid of that," he said, then ordered a cheeseburger and fries from the waitress standing quietly at the end of the table with her order pad and pen.

"Is that going to be all, sweetie?" she asked. "I know you want a piece of that key lime pie, but I'll wait until you get about half way through and remind you."

Drew ordered the tuna melt and handed Mack the folder that Drew had started.

"Now you boys just sing out if you need anything," she said, looking down and kicking aside a stray biscuit that had fallen on the slippery tile floor.

Mack flipped through the package containing photos, some notes, and his necropsy report. He stopped at the prints that Drew had made on each website.

"So what are these for?" he asked, looking over the Charter Boat Captain's Association mission statement. "Do you think they are involved?"

"I don't know," Drew said, shaking his head and somewhat disheartened. "I was just trying to second guess myself. I'm still looking for any reason why these two organizations would have a representative at the beach watching a dolphin rescue. I still haven't put anything together."

Mack flipped through the rest of the folder then back to the website screen shots.

"I see what you mean," he said still reading through the material. "Not many handles here even though the crime itself is fairly well documented."

"Have you looked into the explosive residue?" Mack asked.

"Commercial grade from China, nothing to work with...."

"What about the one they are rehabilitating? Anything from that one yet?"

"Nothing really. It's all the same. Same method, similar effect. Only the more recent one is still alive, and for that reason this whole case continues to simmer."

"Here's your cheeseburger, sweetie," the waitress said from the end of the booth. A plate landed in front of Drew then Mack, but Mack kept reading.

"Have you investigated this list of Protect and Preserve officers?" Mack asked.

"I have a call into the lawyer's office, but haven't reconnected yet."

Mack pulled a tablet from his briefcase and entered a few things while Drew started into the tuna melt.

"Check this out," Mack said, turning the tablet toward Drew. "This guy is a lawyer from Mobile that represents Alabama Drydocks and several big oil interests."

Mack pointed at one of the members of the Protect and Preserve advisory board. He turned the tablet again toward Drew and there was a brief downloaded from LexisNexis that the lawyer had written. The last page included a brief bio describing the lawyer's associations and credentials, including major clients and a relatively current photograph.

"I could tell that P&P had a much more affluent sponsorship than the charter captains. I thought it was interesting that even with that sort of funding they have a public relations problem. You know I met with Gardey, and he didn't seem to know anything about it."

Mack didn't look up. He was scanning the list of officers from the Protect and Preserve website.

"So what do you see?" Drew asked.

He kept reading.

Drew took another bite and noticed that Mack hadn't even picked up the cheeseburger yet.

"So, you see something, Mack?"

He looked up like he had been in a library or someplace way away from this little booth at the diner. He shook his head like he was coming out of a trance, then looked down at his plate and closed the folder.

"Maybe," he said, picking up the burger.

"That organization has an impressive board of directors with links all along the Gulf Coast," he said, before taking a huge bite. With some difficulty through the mouthful of burger, he said, "I'm going to ask Christi to look some of these guys up for you. The office has some on-line resources that may help. Let me know if you hear back from Gardey."

Mack remained somewhat disconnected the rest of lunch; he was trying to connect dots that appeared unrelated. Unlike the child's game where the dots are numbered and you connect them in order to see a picture, Mack had dots that weren't numbered and he was mentally trying different ways to connect them but still no picture emerged.

"I'll call you later," he said, getting up abruptly and leaving before Drew was finished.

He pushed the napkin under the edge of the plate and walked out. Drew saw him turn out of the parking lot back toward the office. He still had that contemplative look that indicated his brain was sorting elements in another dimension and probably shouldn't be driving.

The waitress walked back over with her hands on her hips.

"He always gets the pie," she said, as if Drew were supposed to have enforced that maxim.

Then she slipped both bills onto the table and picked up Mack's plate. She looked down to see that Drew was still eating then back up. Drew took the last bite of tuna melt and shrugged.

"Do you think maybe he lost something?" she asked.

"No, I think he found something," Drew replied.

Chapter 15

Drew arrived at the hearing in uniform in his FWC truck. The Captain made it clear that Drew was there for show and to help the commission panel. Other than that, he was to remain low key. He reminded Drew several times that he wanted to avoid problems with local fishermen. He was fine with letting the Marine Fisheries keep that problem and the responsibility.

Drew was a little early and the facility at the local state college was filling up fast. As expected, the media had arrived and set up live broadcasting.

The head of the local Charter Boat Captains' Association was speaking with a female reporter just outside. Drew confirmed that it was Rachel as he walked past. The lights were bright and darkened all the landscaping and building pillars behind him. Drew thought that he might pass unnoticed. Even if he hadn't, Rachel kept the interview moving and didn't miss a beat, so he might as well have.

"They pass this proposal, there will be serious repercussions in our business. You can't take weeks away from an abbreviated snapper season and not expect a problem! We already got charters booked. Those people in Alabama and Georgia don't want to come spend their money here if they can't catch snapper. Do you think they will spend the night in the beach hotels, eat at local restaurants, and take their kids to the go-cart track? Not if they don't come they won't."

He spoke well and passionately. Ol'man Whear was his father and the "Whear" name has been synonymous with fishing in this area back before the day of state and federal regulations. He was a good spokesperson because he was sincere and didn't come off as a hothead or just out to make a buck. It was his personal appeal as a man of the community. He made his living this way just like his daddy had, and his daddy before that.

Drew waved to him as he passed without being distracting. He had known him since high school. He was a decent guy, worked hard for the fishing industry in addition to owning and operating a boat of his own. He had a good reputation as a fisherman and he respected the job of enforcement which, admittedly, is a bit rare. Those that play by the rules want to know that the rules apply the same to everyone.

Another local station was set up to the right of the staircase after entering the double doors. The local sportscaster was there with the celebrity weekend angler, Matt Schmit, to provide color. The angler looked like he had just stepped out of the pages of *ProBass* Magazine. The jumpsuit, the patches, the sponsor's hat, and a pair of expensive sunglasses that hung from his neck on a lanyard advertising a popular redfish lure were all part of the persona. Drew recognized him as one of the regulars on the early Saturday Sportsman's show and a Discovery Channel featuring flats fishing in the area.

They had ambushed Dr. Tom Bentley, who was definitely out of place here. After the Protect and Preserve march in old St. Andrew, Drew was a bit surprised to see him. But then, he is a respected biologist and would certainly have something to say to this distinguished panel. Besides, he was anything but low key. He could switch from radio science host to neighborhood know-it-all in seconds, and didn't mind throwing the switch. Drew had heard him on a good tirade once when someone brought up the topic of feeding dolphins. His chameleon change was instant and he delivered an over-the-top treatise on the why's and wherefore's with statistics about mortality from boat interaction and how it was abnormal for the species to associate humans with food. Drew was sure it had merit but the tone did nothing to endear any soul to his cause.

The lighting for the local sportscaster and bass pro turned the dark corner into daylight and provided a source of heat that nobody really wanted. Dr. Bentley had entered the camp of the 'enemy.' His unwarranted confidence was bolstered by his firm belief that he was surrounded by ignorant people. It was his duty to enlighten them.

The local sportscaster was courteous but was clearly bent toward the fishermen and asked Dr. Bentley, "So, by severely reducing the catch of local anglers and charter boats, the proposed change adversely affects fishing. Can you tell us how it improves the environment?"

Dr. Bentley was a proponent of the new rule. While reinforced with a false confidence, he was without the benefit of make-up and he looked pale and sweated profusely. His balding forehead was white and reflected the bright lights. The white shirt and tie didn't do much good for his stage presence and made him look even more like a politician caught with a seventeen year old floozy that was reportedly a friend of the family. Drew didn't wait around for his response. The answers were already written and they just needed the protectionist to add credence or dissent. The media could run with it either way. As Drew left he heard, "So what is your impression of the recent Protect and Preserve march in St. Andrew? Dr. Bentley, have you angered the seagulls? Do you think Mother Nature is opposed to your cause?"

Drew might have thought that he could get over the fact that the news was already written. They just needed the footage for effect. Unfortunately, it still bugs him. He didn't want to think that viewers were being manipulated. He turned off the nightly news years ago because he couldn't abide the sensationalism. Well, he keeps telling himself that there are reasons other than Rachel not to watch the news. Even the national channels have reached out to entertain rather than inform. Nobody needs the lady with two first names to look so serious and ask inane questions. Television applies the first coat of dark brown stain to see whether blemishes show up. The blemishes become wounds or scars torn or ripped by the culture, the enemy, or bad luck. Then they move on to the next sensational object or pan to another pretty face that demands that you now refocus your attention to the new topic at hand. Drew preferred to read the news.

The hearing room was a large area that could be expanded or reduced to several rooms by unfolding flexible wall panels. A crew was already removing the last of the wall panels to make more room.

Captains and deckhands nodded as Drew walked in and scanned the room. He saw a number of sportsmen, but by far the largest of the groups represented were the charter boat captains. That was not unexpected.

With one day of research, Drew learned that the Marine Fisheries Management Group was proposing a four-week reduction of the season plus a one-inch increase in size for snapper. Additionally, they were looking at closing the grouper season for the remainder of the year. Taking snapper and grouper off the marquee of the charter boat captain was tantamount to taking bowls and spoons from the local soup kitchen.

"Drew …hey, Drew!" it was Mack calling but all Drew could see were hands aggressively waving near the head of the room. He moved in that direction knowing that Mack would prefer that he were somewhere close.

"There you are, thanks for being here! I have a place for us over here near the front," Mack said with his usual upbeat enthusiasm. He seemed happy with the turnout but a little flummoxed as well. Who wants to deliver bad news to a stakeholder group this large, particularly one with the reputation as a rowdy, kickass crowd?

They moved toward the front where the panel was being seated. The press had a section off to one side and Drew had a seat next to Mack on the other. Drew glanced around to find the exits. Plus, he needed to see who would be seated behind him. It's an old habit that's hard to shake. It probably comes from too many dark bars but Drew thought it may be hereditary. He was told that his great-grandfather was a rumrunner in his day. He liked to think some of that independent attitude still ran in his veins. It's the same stuff that continues to drive these single-minded boat captain entrepreneurs. It's the self-assured spirit of being responsible for your own destiny; and not a spirit in short supply in the fishing community. Tolerance, on the other hand, is an ingredient that is rationed to this sort and always in small quantities.

As Drew took his seat, he spotted a familiar hat and face already seated close to the exit door opposite where the throngs of people now entered. Drew gave a cursory salute to Mr. Whear and he ever-so-slightly nodded courteously in his direction.

Chapter 16

The room was full and the available standing room in the back was slowly moving forward. Drew looked over his shoulder to see two sheriff officers assume a position on either side of the main entrance doors.

Mack stood and walked over to shake hands with Dr. Bentley who had someone save him a seat at the front. Drew could see that they were cordial, both of the PhD affiliation and similar fields. Mack keeps his personal politics separate from his professional ones. Dr. Bentley, on the other hand, as a founder of the Protect and Preserve advocacy group, espoused strict controls in the belief that commercial fishing was on the verge of collapsing multiple species. When one collapses, another is affected, causing another to become a nuisance, and so on. Essentially, one collapse is causal and results in many effects throughout the ocean ecosystem. Mack shook hands again and they spoke for a moment; then he stepped back to where Drew was standing.

"Sometimes that man can be a bit difficult," he said, looking at his watch.

Drew added, "and other times he can be just bizarre."

"I guess it's time. I'll be right back after I kick this off," Mack said, leaving a notebook on his seat and pulling some papers from his pocket.

"Ladies and gentlemen, if you'll please find a seat ….," the voice boomed over the speaker system. A support person fiddled with the sound panel to the side and the noisy bustle and buzz of conversation waned.

A member of the local Chamber of Commerce introduced Dr. Haymer, head of the local National Marine Fisheries Laboratory, our host for the evening. He then introduced the Honourable Stan Northland, congressional representative who stood and waved. Each of the other members of the panel stood and waved, including the popular restaurateur and state representative plus the well-spoken leader of the Charter Boat Captain's Association, who received a raucous applause.

There was cordial applause for the other panel members but all who were present could feel the tensioning of the room. It was tight as a weighted downrigger manned first by the academics. They were versed in the language of the law and had the research to support their recommended adjustment. The professional sportsmen would man the rig next and adjust the tension based on years of hands-on experience. Finally, the panel would get to hook the fish. How they played it would determine whether it was a catch or another broken line.

Mack represented the academics. He was a brilliant researcher with the respect of the panel, the conservationists, even the protectionists, and the media. Unfortunately, his research would show that the two species had not yet reached the anticipated resurgence. The data indicated that neither species was past the danger threshold, and both species could still collapse. His data supported the proposed snapper adjustment for another year to allow the species time to recover. The grouper closure was recommended due to the lack of conclusive input and the need to avoid overfishing at this critical juncture.

Christi arrived about the time he started to speak. She brought a handful of large charts and went straight to the easel that had been set up in front of Drew. With a finesse that was not represented in his pre-meeting state, Mack moved directly from lecture to demonstration. Christi would place the appropriate chart in front, allow Mack to discuss the content, then replace the chart with the next one. The groans and sounds of restless sportsmen enduring input they didn't like grew louder as he proceeded. In a few short minutes, Mack had made his case. The applause was not enthusiastic, and included more than a few audible boos.

The head of the local preservationist group and the Charter Boat Captain's Association were each given a chance to speak next. As expected, Dr. Bentley's Protect and Preserve urged a more decisive, but provocative, approach. He was booed with considerable gusto. He accepted their displeasure with the disdain and egotistical attitude of an academic that rose above and dismissed such trivial disparity.

The head of the Charter Boat Captain's Association promoted a considerably slower and deliberate approach that reduced the effects on the livelihood of local fishermen. While he was considerate of Mack's report, he didn't believe it and stated as much. He was less considerate when addressing Dr. Bentley's approach. This was met with considerable agreement, nods, and amens from the audience.

The panel mostly listened. They asked a few questions, scribbled notes, and soaked up the dissension. Periodically, one would signal for an aide that would arrive and scribble on a small pad as the panel member cupped his hand to speak into the aids ear. It was all quite formal in appearance. However, the discord was an underlying theme in a spirited overture. There was no half-step interval that could correct the low crescendo of dissonance that was building and adding complexity. It grew to resemble the sound of nighttime radio when one station begins to bleed into another signal then slowly fades in and out.

Drew looked at each member of the panel wondering whom they had angered to be assigned this job. The husbandry of all marine life in the Gulf of Mexico within 200 miles of the United States is a considerable burden. To consider all those affected by that task was inconceivable. How could this panel call a tune that all could dance to? All the dancers had a partner on the panel so it would never be a matter of consensus. The tune would be decided by consortium; democracy at its best and its worst, the majority rules.

The next several speakers were less cordial. One charter boat captain railed about his boat payment and the inability to make enough money in the shortened season. He finally uttered one too many oaths and was asked to step down. He uttered another, then stepped away continuing to offer unsuitable verbiage all the way back to his seat.

Another preservationist group spoke of closing all fishing and turning a huge portion of the gulf into a marine sanctuary. The buzz and jeers of the crowd quickly overwhelmed his input. The measured dose of tolerance had nearly expired. One of the sheriff officers stationed at the doors escorted him from the podium and out of the room for his own safety.

Christi had found a seat on the end near the exit door. She was attentive but it was hard to read what she was thinking. Mack was used to it. He steeled himself for these events, afraid that his input would eventually be shouted down. He remained confident of his reporting although the continued bashing by the charter boat captains often made it necessary to repeat his synopsis to the press at a later date. A prepared statement usually followed his delivery. The press loved the fact that they had first-hand input and could always call for a quick quote or to check a factoid.

The current speaker was a firebrand. He was a local angler that Drew recognized …Todd, Drew recalled. He had stopped him offshore in a 31-foot Ocean Master. His center-console open fisherman was one of the well-built competition style hulls with twin 350's on the back and customizing not typically found in manufacturing lines. The simple lines and incomparable ride made it a favorite of those that liked to stretch the boundaries of their offshore fishing region. He was known to stretch those limits frequently and was prone to stretch the size and quantity limits, as well. Drew didn't know his business but he was stirring up a sentiment that was not conducive to dialogue.

"These fish belong to the people. We are Americans and we have the right to catch what we want. It's time that we stood up for that right. It can be taken away!" he shouted pointing at the panel.

The murmur in the crowd had gotten louder and several stood and raised their fingers as well. A second fisherman joined him at the podium. It was his fishing buddy. Big guy, didn't remember a name. Their combined input was half to the panel and half to the audience. The press allowed the cameramen to step forward. This was what they came for.

"We don't need you to tell us what we can catch and what is too small! Who gives you the power to…."

The chairman stood and asked the two men to return to their seats. When they didn't acknowledge his request, the chairman stepped forward. Both sheriff officers left their stations and made their way toward the podium. In an unprecedented collaboration, the crowd moved to prevent the authorities from reaching the front. Drew recognized Captain Wayne and Toby from the *Reel Fun* and several other members of the commercial fleet moving to block their path. The sheriff officers continued through the crowd but it required that they physically move people out of the way. Meanwhile, the firebrand used the microphone to instigate even further.

When Mack stood, it was time to act.

Drew told Mack to go to the soundboard at the side of the panel and turn off the microphone. While he made his way, Drew stepped to the podium.

Drew arrived just before the microphone went silent. While the reverb dispersed, there were still loud voices and shouts and he approached from behind them, facing the audience. Drew tapped on both of their shoulders. His intent was to briefly discuss their future fishing prospects with the FWC inspecting their boat every time they entered the pass. Instead the big guy lunged at Drew with his right fist. Drew had approached them from behind and recognized the potential for a fist to be immediately presented, so he was able to side step the blow. Drew grabbed his wrist and pulled him forward tripping him over his foot as he passed. Before he could move, his boot was on his back and Drew leaned over to recommend that he stay there. Todd tackled Drew from behind. He rolled with the momentum and the pair slid toward the panel.

Parts of the audience now jumped to their feet and the noise grew several decibels. The press cameras moved forward and the sheriff officer's route became even more occluded.

As Drew jumped back up, he saw that Mack had gathered the panel and was moving them toward the exit. Christi held the door. Parts of the audience were on their feet but only a few had rushed to the front. The flash of press cameras and the shouts of men being forcibly moved from their position preceded the rush of additional sheriff officers into the room. The standby reinforcements had arrived.

Drew stood and wrenched Todd's right arm behind his back, pushing him gruffly toward the wall. The six to eight sheriff officers had nightsticks in hand and set up a perimeter in front of the table where the panel formerly sat. The perimeter surrounded the press and the area where Drew stood with Todd and his buddy, who was now on his feet. With his other arm, Todd reached into his sports jacket and retrieved a small pistol. Still somewhat off balance by Drew's grip, he inadvertently pointed the gun at his buddy who immediately dove for cover beneath the table. As he dove, Drew realized that this was about to take an appalling turn.

Subsequent actions were the result of considerable training in years past; training that was reactive and immediate. It had saved Drew's life before. His right leg came up between Todd's legs sharply with a blow to the groin as Drew reached and grabbed his left arm. Todd squeezed off a single shot into the ceiling as Drew pulled him backward into his knee and onto the floor, wresting the gun from his hand as he fell.

He lay next to his buddy who hid under the table. Todd doubled up in pain and Drew held the gun high by the barrel so that the sheriff squad could see it. The cameras flashed and the press surged forward, while exit doors on all sides flung open. Christi still stood at one exit door but she now ran into the room to avoid the mass of people storming out. She sat just one seat forward and to the right of Mr. Whear, who sat quietly.

The head of the sheriff contingent arrived at Drew's side, "Nice work. We'll take it from here." He moved toward Todd and his buddy with cuffs, followed by a second officer. Deputy Jason McBride stepped forward with a plastic evidence bag that he opened and Drew placed the weapon inside. He nodded and Drew returned the sentiment. Without a word spoken, acknowledgement, thanks, and respect were passed between enforcement officers who were trained to handle moments of distress and confusion.

Three of the reporters that had been too scared to flee came to ask Drew's name and rank. Only one asked what he was doing at this hearing.

Mr. Whear walked slowly toward Drew just in front of Christi. As he approached Drew asked, "So, Mr. Whear, what happened to the rules?"

The old man stopped for only a moment. He looked up directly at Drew and said slowly and without the hurry of everyone else in the room, "Monkey-boats don't follow the rules." He shook his head, pursed his lips and casually walked on toward the exit.

Christi walked up as the officers pushed Todd and his buddy through the press and out of the room.

"Are you okay?"

"I feel like I just drank three high-caffeine energy drinks."

"Nothing like an adrenaline rush."

"Did you get the panel out of here?" Drew asked.

"Mack ushered them out about the time the Sheriff's reinforcements arrived."

"Good."

There was an awkward silence as Drew looked around to see what was left of the public hearing. Some reporters were outside talking to the captains as they left. Some had hurried off with footage for the late news. Dr. Bentley stood in the far corner, his arms and hands in motion as he made a point to a disinterested commissioner. Sheriff radios squawked as the scene was cordoned off with wide yellow tape.

"You know what I heard?" Christi asked, breaking the silence.

Drew looked toward her without answering.

"I heard several of the captains sitting right behind me talking about how they are dealing with the dolphin. Apparently a number of them are trying different methods to discourage the dolphin from feeding near their boat."

"Anything about explosives?"

"No, but one of them was talking about using an acoustic generator to create a frequency that could jam the dolphin's bio-sonar. Another mentioned stuffing sleeping pills into a throwback. It seems there is a real cottage industry waiting for the right approach to emerge."

"I guess I need to do some recon. I haven't had much …." Drew started, but was interrupted.

"Officer Phillips, Drew, ...Drew!"

It was Rachel, with her camera man in pursuit, live and on the air. "I was hoping you could briefly tell our audience about your daring rescue?" She looked a bit disheveled and hustled along barefoot. But then the look fit the chaotic scene she just left; evidently she had been caught in the mass exodus.

Christi looked up and smiled, "We'll talk later. Your audience awaits," and she turned to leave.

Drew had several retorts come to mind, but none made it past the adrenalin surge. "See ya," was all that came out.

"Rachel Franco coming to you live from the Fisheries Open House where shots were fired just moments ago." Rachel swung the microphone toward Drew and the camera followed.

"Officer Phillips, I am told that you stopped the shooter before he was able to injure anyone. Are Wildlife officers trained in hand-to-hand combat? What can you tell us about the alleged shooter?"

She rattled off three to five questions without taking a breath or time to allow Drew to respond. This wasn't Rachel. This was a sensation that blinked on when the dull assignment was suddenly the hottest news in town. Drew turned to watch Christi leave through the exit. She looked back and waved. When he turned around the cameraman had engaged blinding lights and a microphone was thrust beneath his chin. All Drew could think of was that the boss was not going to be happy about his low profile.

"So was he trying to shoot you, Officer Phillips? Perhaps he was targeting one of the panel? Could you describe how you were able to disarm this assailant?

Has it really come to this in our fishing community?"

Chapter 17

Drew noticed the adrenaline had worn off as he left the building. He had answered all the Sheriff's questions. The news stations were wrapping up the news live from the scene as the sheriff's contingent escorted those arrested out of the building in handcuffs. He saw Rachel finishing her broadcast as he walked around the darkened side of the building in the same manner as he had entered, counting on going unseen this time. It didn't work.

"Drew! Hey Drew, got a second?" he heard Rachel shout from behind him.

He turned to see her jogging up without her microphone and leaving the bright glare of the camera lights.

She threw herself into him with a hug that he barely responded to out of sheer surprise.

"You big brute! You could have been killed. I can't believe you did that." She said loosening her grip and looking up at Drew.

Her smile was the one he remembered. Not the one used for the nightly news. Not the 'so-happy-to-see-you' holiday smile. This was the smile that warmed winter nights. This was the affectionate and lovely smile that was worth another seven years of labor under her biblical namesake's father. The smile that Drew had forgotten still existed. She reached up to his head and pulled it to her lips.

It was a kiss that stopped time. A kiss that immediately transported Drew back two years to a time when it all seemed easier to choose between fried or grilled, white or red, dark or light. There weren't so many gray's. Drew stayed there with his eyes closed until she released his head and backed away.

"I'm sorry, I... I shouldn't have done that," she said. "It's just that I saw what you did. I saw what... I was so proud of you and scared for you and...."

Drew looked at her and briefly saw a moment that they experienced some years ago. A moment when she was out of breath and looked up at him like the world had just shifted. A look that said he touched someplace she had never been. The look was fleeting. She quickly binned it and the face that returned was one he'd seen before.

"Thanks, Rachel. I miss you too." Drew said looking into her eyes, then turned to go.

There was that stirring in his gut. It was still there....the infectious physical and emotional response of her holding him affectionately. Drew could feel the symptoms returning. This time he could walk away. He didn't need to go back to that gray, muddled, in-between place wedged between commitment and her driven ambition. That's where she left him a year ago. Drew didn't look back.

Walking to the truck, Drew was lost in her. The what-if's, the also-could-have's, and the maybe-if-only's. Too many if's and all those gray's. The adrenaline withdrawal left him spent. Drew wasn't thinking so much as he was drifting-- drifting across a darkened parking lot that was just as deprived of that human warmth as he felt now. He was missing the cognitive awareness that he needed when three dark figures exited a van parked beneath the dark oak trees.

They approached quickly and a fourth exited from a nearby car.

Becoming aware of the situation, Drew dropped his backpack to the pavement, just as the two masked figures in front stepped into his space and hit him in the gut with what felt like a small baton. The third figure came from behind and struck the base of his skull. Drew felt himself falling as the three figures backed away, batons at the ready. He heard a voice say, "So what next, Harry?" as the dark night went black and Drew crumpled onto the pavement.

"You shouldn't have hit him that hard," a voice said.

Headlights turned sharply toward the parking lot and Drew heard the screech of tires. Car doors slammed and engines raced; tires squealed and vehicles sped off through a darkness Drew fought to avoid. The headlights were coming close and faster but he couldn't move. Drew lifted up on one arm then fell back to the pavement as the lights veered to one side and screeched to a stop.

#

Drew woke up in bed at the hospital. The back of his head hurt. A doctor lifted an eyelid and shined a light into his eye.

"He's coming around." Drew heard him say. "We'll want to keep him tonight to make sure there is no damage to the cerebrum or spine. What did you say they hit him with?"

Drew squinted to open both eyes and could see the doctor lift what appeared to be a short baton like the one he had seen only momentarily before he felt it vividly.

"Good thing they were slightly padded," he said handing it back to someone. "A hit like that with metal or wood could have cracked his skull."

He turned back around to see Drew's eyes opening.

"Officer Phillips, I'm Doctor Kalin. You are in the ER. Can you hear me?

Drew nodded but didn't say anything. He tried to lift his arm to feel the back of his head but the IV kept him from reaching it before the doctor pushed his arm back down.

"Officer Phillips, you have a rather big lump on the back of your skull. I've given you a sedative and you'll need to sleep. There are some people here that are responsible for your safe arrival. Would you like to see them?"

Drew nodded.

"Stay in bed. Ring the nurse if you need anything. I'll check back later."

Rachel was there listening to the doctor, then walked over to his bed. She took Drew's hand and leaned over.

"Told you that you could have been hurt, you big brute," she said.

"What happened?" he managed to say.

"I'm not sure exactly, but as we were pulling away, my camera man saw what he thought was a mugging in the parking lot. He turned the van, aiming the headlights at the scene, then a car and a van sped off. We were prepared to chase the van when I saw you lean up and we swerved to miss you and stopped. Drew, I couldn't believe it was you. I couldn't find a pulse and you were completely out. We put you in the van and drove you here."

She had been crying. Drew's head hurt. She held his hand and he closed his eyes trying to remember anything else.

"I thought you were dead."

Her face leaned against his hand that she still held.

"What'd dey hit me wiff?"

She let go of his hand and held up the baton. Drew reached for it but failed. He could see it well enough as she held it up. It wasn't a nightstick or a baton. It was the sawed off end of a deep-sea fishing rod. It was the fiberglass or wooden sort of handle covered with a thin layer of foam material.

"Coo you see a'nyone?"

"The sheriff has already asked all those questions and no. We got a partial license plate and the fact that it was a dark colored van but that's about it."

Drew lay back against the pillow and closed his eyes again.

He felt her lean forward and kiss his cheek.

"I need to go. I just had to know you would be okay."

Drew opened his eyes and saw her looking down at him. A little more disheveled than normal. A little red in the eyes but regaining her composure and reassembling that other face she wears. It's the face that puts those emotions back in the bin where they are kept, someplace other than the heart. The one that knows how to compartmentalize the wants and wishes and keeps them separated from the ambition and drive.

"Take care of yourself, Drew."

She reached the door and turned to leave.

"Rachel," he said and she turned around, "Bannacer?"

She looked at Drew as though he had thrown a knife. The knife hit a nerve like someone had a photo of a cousin she had been caught with under the bleachers.

"I needed something for a story and he could have helped. Unfortunately, Bannacer uses the brain cells attached to his male anatomy. He has a short little attention span, poor follow-through, and generally less than anticipated."

She didn't need to explain anymore. That was all Drew needed to know. Strike two.

"Look for a package from me coming to you at the office. I have some material I think will help you with the Bannacer problem."

"Coo' you call Mack fo' me?"

"Sure, I don't know that he'll answer when he sees it is my number, but I'll leave a message and let him know you're here."

"T'anks."

Drew closed his eyes and heard the door close.

He heard her heels click down the hall. He could see her leaving without opening his eyes. He had seen it before. She was gone again.

#

"So you saved the day and got beat up all in the same night?" Mack said with sarcasm.

It was mid-morning and apparently, Rachel's message had gotten through.

Drew was awake but only barely. The meds were doing a good job of keeping the pain suppressed. The trade-off was a loss of clarity that Drew found most distasteful at best and completely infuriating when the words get stuck. His brain could not assemble the words and consolidate a complete thought, much less a coherent sentence.

"Christi is out in the waiting room. She wanted to make sure you didn't mind her coming in. I'll get her if you only want to answer the same questions once."

Drew nodded and Mack stuck his head out the door and shouted. This was the quiet wing but he would never have noticed the sign.

Drew pressed the bed control to sit up a little straighter and ran his fingers through the front of his hair. He hadn't really noticed the pain in his ribs until the bed straightened his torso a bit. His head hurt enough that he had forgotten that the two guys busted him in the gut when it all started.

Christi was somewhat more subdued than Mack. She came to the foot of Drew's bed and quietly assessed his condition without the male bluster and buddy banter.

Mack picked up the nurse's chart and began perusing the entries.

Drew almost laughed and asked, "So what does a marine biologist know about medical diagnostics?"

"Well," Mack said, putting his hand up to push his glasses further up on his nose, "it says here you were brought into the ER non-responsive at 10:50. You had a suppressed pulse, not much bleeding but a large swelling on the back of the head consistent with a blow from a blunt instrument. Your doctor refused to allow the TV camera to enter the ER."

"Now that sounds like Rachel," Mack said looking down at Drew.

"Two more blows, both to the thorax, medication, mmhhhmm… prognosis, check for concussion, observe…. Hey buddy, don't get used to the oxycontin. They'll have you off that and walking around after lunch."

"So Rachel told me that three guys beat you up with small batons in the parking lot," Mack said.

Drew saw Christi look up when Mack mentioned Rachel again. She was still attempting to piece together a puzzle with only a corner and two matched pieces. Her face did not share anything and she didn't say anything either. Her usual extroverted mannerisms were shut down, like she was carrying a burden that couldn't be shared.

"Sounds like you know about everything I could tell you."

"How's that?" Mack asked.

"Well, I passed out there in the parking lot after I got hit in the head. I'm told that Rachel and her camera man chased off the bad guys, then brought me to the ER."

"I see what you mean. Not much chance you can fill in the details?"

"I saw the van that the three guys jumped out of. The other guy was in a car to the left of me. I could see that they weren't just there for an autograph but not much more. They wore dark masks. They hit me. I fell down and passed out."

"What did you hear?" Mack asked.

"I didn't hear anything, Mack. I fell down and passed out!"

"Open your eyes," Mack said, coming close to the bed and moving his hands around the edge of Drew's face. He looked like he was going to put his hands on his temples but instead his hands stayed just at the edge of Drew's peripheral vision and moved slowly around his face.

"So what's this, some kind of transcendental re-visitation or a hoodoo spell you learned in Haiti?"

"Just work with me Drew," Mack said. "Try to watch the movement of my fingers. See them moving right there on the edge of your vision. See how easy it is to watch that slow movement around the edges? That's it. Watch it moving right there on the edge of your periphery."

Mack continued the hand motions around Drew's face but made no sound. Drew didn't say anything but he did like Mack requested and continued to watch the chaos in the edge of his peripheral vision.

Drew closed his eyes and felt the pillow on the lump on the back his head. He felt Christi's eyes on him from the base of the bed. He felt both places where they hit him in the ribs but the pain was someplace else. It wasn't as acute and he had an awareness of all that he heard around him as though he was attached to the ceiling and looking down.

"So there you are in the parking lot." Drew heard Mack say. "You see three guys jump out of a van and you realize that you are the target. What do you hear next?"

"I hear a car door open and close beside me." Drew said and his head turned to look out at the parking lot. "Actually it's a little ahead and to the side because I can see another dark figure."

"Next you see the three guys spread out," Mack says.

"That's right. There are two in front with batons and one has moved out of my sight behind me."

"So what happens next?"

"I drop my backpack. Crap, all my stuff is in that backpack!" Drew said, opening his eyes and sitting forward abruptly, then grimacing in pain.

Mack leans over the bed so that he is all that Drew can see. He moves both hands to the left and right of Drew's face almost like a magician and says, "Drew, don't worry about the backpack. We have all your stuff. Now look at the movement of my hands."

Mack is right in Drew's face but his hands are moving on either side and it blurs the ceiling. Drew has seen him do this before but can't seem to remember when. Must mean the medication was kicking in. "Forget about your stuff, we have it," Mack repeats. His hands are still moving around either side of Drew's head and the edges of his vision, but his eyes are just inches away and his hands are moving in circles around his cheeks and ears.

Drew saw that Christi had moved to a chair in the far corner. She is quiet and watching Mack. Drew can see Mack and his eyes with his hands moving. The movement is just on the edge of what he can see. His hands are moving, undulating, rhythmic almost like seaweed in a fast moving tide. He can almost see them. There are crabs and jellyfish in the fast moving water. Now there are fish swimming in circles. They were all swimming around in circles.

"Close your eyes, Drew," he says quietly still moving his hands. "Relax and go back to the parking lot. You just dropped your backpack."

"So your backpack is on the pavement. It's dark and three guys have just surrounded you. When you drop your backpack, you hear your phone and other electronic components hit the pavement but that isn't what you pay attention to. What is it that has your attention?"

"...they have sticks and something over their faces."

"It's dark but you can see. Describe what you see."

"The van that they came out of is dark blue or brown, maybe black, with a light colored Florida tag."

"You're looking at the van. Why are you looking there?" Mack asks in a soothing manner.

"I want to see if anyone else comes out. That's when I heard the fourth guy come out of the vehicle to my left."

"Let's ignore the vehicles for a minute. What do the assailants look like? It's dark but you can see a little in the starlight and reflected streetlights. What do they look like?

"They are wearing masks and carry batons."

"Tell me about the masks. Are they western scarfs or T-shirts pulled up?"

"They aren't t-shirts or scarfs. They look like buffs, you know, like the fishermen wear. One is light and has black and gray sharks, the other looks like dark camouflage."

"What about the other one, what is he wearing?"

"He has a dark buff and dark hair, but he's moved behind me now and I can't see him."

"Keep your eyes closed and tell me about the guy that came out of the vehicle to your left," Mack says calmly, leading him through the entire scene behind Drew's eyes.

"He's standing there in the dark. I can't see his face but he is wearing a suit. A dark sport coat and tie."

"What else can you see? Does he have a hat? Is the car a sedan or an SUV?

"The car is a big sedan, not an SUV. Maybe a big Lexus or a Mercedes. He's leaning against the rear side panel with a cane."

"So what do you see next?"

"Both of the guys in front of me have a baton. The guy to my right lifts the baton."

"With his right hand or is he carrying the baton in his left?"

"He has it in his right hand but the guy to my left hits me first and he's a lefty. I can see both of them but the one to the left hits me first."

"So the lefty hits you?"

"Yeah and it hurts. The next guy hits me too but it's not as bad."

"So you are still standing but hit. What's next?"

"I grabbed my backpack to swing at them but I get hit from behind."

"So the third guy is behind you and hits you at the base of the skull."

"That's right. I'm not seeing so good now. I'm falling forward because the guys in front move out of the way."

"Nobody hits you anymore? Did the guys in front hit you again?

"No, they didn't hit me again. They stood back and let me fall to the pavement."

Can you see their shoes, their pants legs? What are they wearing?

"Tennis shoes, jeans, dark t-shirt. One has on sandals with straps."

"So what do you hear now?"

"There is traffic on US 98. I'm laying there and I'm breathing hard, fighting to stay conscious. Somebody asks, "So what next, Harry?"

"Who said that?"

"The guy behind me."

"So the two in front back off and the guy behind you says, "So what next, Harry? Any accent?"

"No, he sounds like a local."

"Who answers?"

"No answer. Wait, he does say something… the two guys in front of me are looking over at the guy leaning on the car. He said something like 'You didn't have to hit him that hard.' Then I heard the squeal of tires turning sharply and I can see headlights coming. They are both gone and the third guy is getting into the driver's seat of the van. I hear the car to my left start and leave lots of rubber on the pavement pulling away. Bad smell. Think the van is going to back over me but then it does the same."

"Okay," Mack says, "stay there in the parking lot for just one more minute and relax. You know they are taking you to the hospital. You know that you're going to be all right. Just relax. Hear the sound of the wind in the oaks at the edge of the parking lot and traffic nearby. Relax…now, when you hear me say "War Eagle" you will be back in the hospital bed, relaxed and among friends. You will remember that we discussed this incident but the details aren't important, so forget about them. You're back among friends, relaxed, and Christi is wearing a nice perfume that smells like fresh sage and citrus."

Christi looked at Mack like she was about to say something, but Mack held his hand up to stop her.

"War Eagle."

" …So, I'm pretty much done," Mack said, like they had just finished a conversation and turned toward Christi. "Not really much to work with unless the sheriff can come up with that license plate partial. Christi did you have a question?"

Drew opened his eyes and both Mack and Christi were staring down at him. The nurse behind them walked to the other side of the bed and offered a pill and some water.

"So who's Harry?" Christi asks.

"Beats me," Drew replied. "Harry who?"

"Harry, the guy that said they didn't need to hit you so hard."

"Sorry," Drew replied. "I must have drifted off. I don't remember a Harry."

"So you don't know anyone named Harry that wants you dead?" Mack asked with the bedside manor of a buzzard.

"Not that I know of," Drew replied. "If he wanted me dead, I think I wouldn't be here right now."

"Not much to go on with three guys that look like fishermen, one wearing a suit and drives a nice car," Mack says with the efficiency of a night nurse.

"It could have been a couple good-ol'-boys that didn't like your treatment of their buddies in the meeting earlier," Mack offered.

"What about P&P and all that conflict of interest stuff I dug up on their advisory board?" Christi asked.

"So you think Protect and Preserve has gone rogue. Now they intend to beat their ideas into you?" Mack asked. There was more than a hint of sarcasm in the question and Christi just put her hands on her hips and stared at him.

"What about Harold Gardey?" Drew said, out of the silence.

"Maybe that's it." Mack said smiling. "The Bar Association has decided to instigate confrontation to drum up some business." It was stated with an equal amount of sarcasm.

"Ok," Drew said, giving up.

"I'm not saying either of you are wrong! But work with me, one angle sounds just as far-fetched as the other, especially when all the circumstantial data we have points to fishermen."

Drew wasn't up for the debate. Thankfully that sedative was kicking in and he could get another nap before getting booted out.

Christi came close and picked up his hand in hers. Drew just barely opened his eyes.

"You get better," she said softly.

"Thanks. Nice perfume. Reminds me of something I remember from home, like fresh limes and sage."

"I'll come pick you up, just call when they toss you out of here," Mack said leaving.

Drew was drifting off again. "I told you that frikkin' Haitian hypnosis, hand-wavin' malarkey doesn't work on me." He was asleep before the door fully closed.

#

"So what was all that?" Christi asked Mack as they left the hospital room.

"All what?" Mack replied.

"The in-your-face eyes, the swirling hands. What was all that?"

"It's hypnotism. Something I learned in Haiti from a mambo. Not like the kind you see on late night TV or variety shows, but it's similar," Mack said.

Christi just stared at him waiting for him to finish.

"I volunteered to help in Haiti after the earthquake in 2010. I was still in school and it seemed like a good thing to do. Learned this technique while I was working with the Catholics in Léogâne. Interesting, huh? Catholics and voodoo, those sort of misalliances always intrigue me. My teacher, Lola, she was very strong in Vodou, as they call it, and taught Sunday school at St Theresa's. She could hypnotize people to help them with their pain or the loss of a loved one. There was so much of that after the earthquake.

That was the first time I've had a chance to use it in some time. It's particularly useful on impaired subjects. I could never do that with Drew normally. It's just that the medication made him susceptible and we needed that information before he forgot it."

"So you think he told you the truth?" Christi asked with some skepticism.

"Absolutely. Everything was just as he saw it. Now what can we do with it? ...That is an entirely different subject."

"What do you mean?" asked Christi. "With the research material I found we have several good candidates."

"Oh yeah, sorry about downplaying your research. Drew just does not need to know about all that yet."

"Apology accepted," she said.

"He doesn't need all that," Mack repeated, "and he probably won't remember it until the meds wear off."

The doors to the hospital opened and they walked into a bright afternoon.

"Even then," Mack said, "Drew can be a bit headstrong and more than a little assertive when necessary. So, please, keep that under wraps for a little bit."

"But what if he asks?" Christi said.

"He won't remember."

"What do you mean he won't remember? You asked him all those questions…."

"…but he was hypnotized," Mack interrupted, "and I left him with the suggestion that he just forget about them."

"Why?"

"We need some time."

Mack's vehicle chirped as they approached and they both climbed in the Prius.

"But we need to be a little more careful," Mack said.

"Why is that?"

Mack looked at Christi before shifting into gear.

"Drew had no reason to be careful, nor was he implicating or indicting anyone. He was just looking for a clue and chasing leads on the dolphin case. He stepped into something, or maybe stumbled into it and we need to know more about what that is before he steps into it again."

"Why do you say that?" Christi asked softly.

"They didn't take anything. They could have killed him, but they didn't. They could have taken him somewhere; in fact, the van suggests that taking him someplace was likely the original plan but the news team messed that up."

"So you think someone specifically targeted Drew?"

"Yes, …Drew, law enforcement, further investigation, all of the above. But there is no obvious reason why, no motive."

Christi turned toward the window thinking about the research she had prepared for Mack. No conclusions only markers, speculation and coincidence. She had pushed him into this. She knew it. It was her fault that Drew was targeted. The weight of the investigation moved onto her shoulders and she felt it. She leaned her head against the window. Quiet tears were hers to bear alone.

As they drove back over the bridge crossing St. Andrew Bay, Mack broke the silence, "They didn't leave a note; instead, they sent a message."

Chapter 18

 Drew is not much for taking personal leave just because he feels bad, so he showed up one day after the hospital released him despite a headache and a nasty bruise on two ribs and the back of his head. The captain did 'award' him with some light duty but that didn't mean desk duty. Just because he got his picture on the front page of the local paper and a nice letter from Representative Northland didn't mean he got special treatment.

 It was a still and sticky summer afternoon. With the humidity well into the 90s, the temperature made the salty air stick to that first layer of sweat. The docks at Captain Anderson's were busy with folk returning from a day of vacation outings. The sightseeing boat unloaded families with shells, cameras, and pink-skinned bodies after a trip to Shell Island. A troop of four-foot swashbuckling pirates charged the unwary, anxiously followed by attentive moms just returning from the Pirate Ship excursion. Tired fishermen moved their catch between the boat and the fish house while well-dressed diners arrived to board the Dinner Cruise.

 Drew was in his gray and green workboat watching for jet-ski infractions beneath the bridge at Grand Lagoon and checking boat registrations when he spotted Christi on the boardwalk. She was talking to some of the charter captains and crew behind Captain Anderson's restaurant where the deckhands were unloading a fair day's catch. A crowd was gathering to "Oooooo" as the deckhands tossed the bigger fish onto the boardwalk. Drew continued around the basin unnoticed and decided to dock near the Grand Marlin and walk over.

Fifteen minutes later, he rounded the corner on foot. The crowd still lingered but the dinner patrons were peeling off in their early evening attire with their colorful plastic cups with cut fruit and umbrellas. The locals were gravitating to the scene like it had nearly reached critical mass. Drew walked faster when the raised voices included that of a female he recognized.

The fish were put away and the boats were clean. That usually means the show is over. When Drew arrived, the crowd parted slightly to allow him through to the attraction. At the edge of the boardwalk, Christi stood toe-to-toe with one of the local deck hands. Drew looked to Captain Cory on the deck of the *Kelley Girl* then to Captain Wayne who was fishing something silver from his pocket. Captain Wayne flicked the Zippo open and lit a cigarette on the fly bridge of the *Reel Fun*. Always best to ensure that no one was taking sides before stepping into a dock fight.

"So what's up here?" Drew stated with authority and moved onto the boardwalk.

Neither Christi nor Toby moved. Toby was the deckhand on the *Reel Fun*. Drew had seen him at work offshore a few days before. He was a big kid. Kid is probably a misnomer; he was mid-twenties, at least. He had broad tan shoulders and the tough callused hands of someone who worked with lines, knots, hooks, and knives. They remained eye-to-eye with stern faces and tense muscles. They didn't hear the jibes from the locals or the sound of the Lady Anderson's horn as she pulled away from the dock.

"I'd like to have both of you stand down but it's not my business why you are fixing to fight," Drew stated clearly. "I'm here to conduct a safety check of both these vessels. Captain Wayne, can you come on down?"

"Aw'ight, Toby, thass enough," Captain Wayne stated with finality. "Man says we got work to do now, les' go."

Toby stepped back. His eyes remained fixed on Christi until he turned and stepped back aboard without looking at any of the crowd.

Toby was a little too old to be a deckhand but he was one of the best. Not a bad kid; he grew up on the boats. He got a little mean now and then when the fishing was bad or when he got one beer over the line but altogether a hardworking and loyal deckhand. Something had pissed him off.

"Miss, I need to have a word with you first," Drew said to Christi.

Christi had not even seen Drew yet. She looked up and nearly spoke but Drew's stare and raised hand encouraged her to remain silent, at least for the moment. Drew motioned that she should move over to a nearby table and he faced the restaurant windows with the boats behind him. Drew was far enough that they couldn't hear him with the ambient noise of a busy boardwalk.

"Keep looking that way and let me know if any one of them comes off the boat or picks up anything that looks like a weapon," Drew told her.

"Now, I'm going to go over and do an inspection. I would like you to sit on this box and wait for me so we can discuss this after I'm done. Can you do that?"

"But...."

"Don't!" Drew interrupted a bit more forcefully than he'd planned but it got the attention of the deck crews. She looked at them but then turned back toward me.

Drew continued, "I think at this point it would be safer for you and me if they don't know we're acquainted. So if you'll sit here for twenty minutes or so, we can leave and I'll buy dinner."

"Okay," she replied after a pause.

She was still getting past the adrenalin rush and Drew was rather pleased with himself. He turned and walked to the stern of the *Reel Fun* where Captain Wayne and Toby were placing all the safety gear on the dock. The crew of *Kelley Girl* had just finished laying everything out so he moved to the stern of their boat. Starting with them would allow Toby a little more time to rein in the attitude.

These boats had been through many inspections. Some crews get a little testy about routine checks after a long day but they know Drew is just doing his job. They would much rather do it here than out on the gulf.

Toby didn't say anything while Drew went through the checklist. He spotted Toby looking up once to where Christi sat. Drew could sense a bridled anger that he held in check. He thought by pulling this inspection he could shunt some of that antagonism but it didn't work. Drew decided not to pursue a line of questioning that would help him understand why Toby and Christi had nearly come to blows. That was their business. While pretty much his usual impetuous self, Toby remained professional as the inspection finished up. Drew asked Captain Wayne to step ashore while Toby returned the gear to its appropriate location.

"Captain Wayne, can you tell me a little about what happened here?" Drew asked handing him the paperwork to sign.

"Don't really think it's any of your business."

"It doesn't have to be."

"…just a little misunderstanding," he replied quickly, looking up to where she sat and avoiding eye contact.

"She do anything I need to talk to her about with your boat or gear?"

"No, nothin' like that. Just that she don't really understand that those of us out here on the fishing boats don't particularly care for the Marine Fisheries people snooping around."

Drew didn't say anything to indicate that he knew she worked there.

"She was just another pretty face at the dock 'til she started asking Toby questions about dolphins and stuff. Guess she must'a told him where she worked. I looked up once and he was flirting. Next time I look up they's about to go at it."

Drew took the signed paperwork from him and pulled off a copy for him to keep.

"All right. I'll have a word with her."

Captain Wayne grasped the paper, but Drew held onto it just a little and Wayne glanced up at him. He had something to hide. He quickly pulled the paper from Drew's hand and stepped back aboard.

"I had hoped to come over and continue the conversation we started the other day offshore," Drew said.

"Whatcha mean?" he replied, looking back before he opened the salon door.

"I mean how you are keeping the dolphin from eating your fish."

"Oh that, yeah. Come on back one afternoon and we'll talk about it," and he opened the salon door and disappeared inside.

Drew turned toward the table where Christi was still seated. He was pretty sure that he had her attention by now.

###

After returning to where Drew docked the boat, he changed out of the uniform at the Grand Marlin men's room and met Christi at the bar already finishing her first beer. Drew nodded to one of the local flats anglers then leaned against the barstool next to her. The Grand Marlin is a restaurant on Grand Lagoon built adjacent to an operating boat yard. The dinner crowd is mostly tourists but bar scene is local, upscale, and outdoors.

"So was that a bit of extracurricular research?" Drew asked, while getting the attention of the bartender.

"As a matter of fact it was," Christi answered, "I was just following up on the suggestion of a certain Wildlife Officer to check around with the fishermen and learn something about the fishing business."

Drew took a Dos Equis from the bartender, laid a twenty on the bar and replied, "What dumb-ass recommended something stupid as that?"

She wasn't expecting it. She nearly spewed the previous swallow while choking down a laugh.

"Don't do that. I'm still mad and I want to be mad at you too for keeping me from putting Toby on the deck and rubbing fish slime all over his 'Fish Fear Me' t-shirt."

Drew decided not to discuss her fighting credentials. She could be black-belt trained or raised in a house full of older brothers. No way to know. On the other hand, Toby was six-two, a good two hundred pounds, and strong enough to pull a seventy pound amberjack over the gunwale with one hand. Fighter or not, she was way under his weight class.

"So what did you find out?"

"They HATE dolphin!" she blurted. This was clearly not an objective opinion, so Drew waited for more.

"I've been completely enamored with dolphin since I was five …and they hate them! I just can't understand how someone could be so contemptuous of a creature as beautiful and magical as a dolphin," she said.

"Since my first trip to Sea World, I've wanted to learn about marine mammals. High school science projects, summer camps, all the way through Fisheries at Auburn, they were the object of my passion for the ocean and everything in it. I just don't think I can ever understand someone that harbors that much disdain for the creature I've dedicated so much of my life learning about."

"So did they give you some explanation for why they feel that way?" Drew asked.

"Yes, it's like you said …they eat their fish. They live in the ocean. Of course they eat fish. You don't need a degree in marine biology to understand that. What are they supposed to eat …sushi?"

Drew smiled at the intentional pun. She was through venting.

Her own derision spilled out of the sarcasm. She had let her passion affect her understanding. She may have asked the questions but didn't hear the real answers, just the words. She heard the absolute rejection of that object that propelled her marine vocation. There was no way to immediately reconcile the affection she had for these creatures and the dislike for them that the fishermen harbored.

"Do you still have the Shamu stuffed pillow?" Drew asked.

"Yes," she replied, giggling a little. "My Flipper doll fell apart though." She looked away with a little pout.

Drew took a sip and looked out over the lagoon as the sunset added reds and golds to the sky. The white gel coat of the boats along the boardwalk reflected the pastel colors. A pod of dolphins rolled just off the orange marker. Christi saw them too but nothing was said. She wasn't defeated. She had merely wallowed in that self-deprecation that follows adrenalin-fueled anger, and it was slowly dissipating.

"Let's go fishing tomorrow," Drew offered. "Call Mack and see if we can get the Boston Whaler for the day. I can take a day off. We could leave at first light and have fish for dinner tomorrow evening. What'd you think?"

She knew Drew was patronizing, but it would allow her to observe the problem personally.

"I'd like that, Drew." She looked up with a gracious smile. A smile with a follow through that even Drew could see. She initiated that eye contact, that momentary glimpse into possibility.

"Thanks," she said then looked back out over the lagoon reflecting an inferno of orange from the fading summer sky.

The TV over the bar had the channel 7 news wrap up. Rachel was on scene at Gulf reporting on the dolphin still in guarded condition in the quarantine tank. Christi glanced up briefly then back out across the lagoon. Drew took another sip of Dos Equis and noticed that most of the bar was talking about the story but he didn't look up.

Chapter 19

Stars were still visible in the early morning sky when Drew pulled into the parking lot at the National Marine Fisheries Lab. A pink glow over the bay to the east hinted that daylight approached. Mack and Christi were loading all sorts of gear aboard the boat, none of which appeared to be fishing related.

"What's all this?" Drew said approaching the dock, "I thought we were going fishing?"

He had four stout rods with Penn 4-0 reels in one hand, a lunch size cooler in the other, and a backpack.

Mack stated unequivocally, "If we're going fishing on a regular work day then we're going to get some data. This has to be official business to use a government owned vessel."

He had several devices aboard for weighing and measuring- a video camera, a digital camera, plus a bag that looked like medical gear. It included sample bottles, calipers, and assorted implements that a marine biologist might wish he had if he were to catch a coelacanth or happen across a whale shark that didn't mind him excising a skin sample. "Did you remember the bait?"

"Back of the truck, be right back," Drew replied, and walked over to retrieve the live pinfish and large bag of fresh shrimp.

"Those are some big shrimp to be fishing with. Get those at Half Hitch Bait and Tackle?" Mack asked.

"Nope, Tarpon Dock Seafood…if we don't catch fish, what's left will be dinner."

Christi looked up from stuffing the center console to see what Mack was laughing about. She looked like the morning itself. Bathing suit top tied at her neck with a War Eagle T-shirt and shorts. Drew's gaze lingered a bit too long and she smiled to accept the tacit compliment.

A little embarrassed, Drew turned back to the truck to get a thermos. "So we ready to go?"

"Help me get the ice chest aboard, then we're ready," Mack said, climbing onto the seawall. Drew helped him lower it to the deck, released the stern line, and climbed aboard.

Christi started the outboard and Mack released the bowline. He handed it to Drew as he walked forward. He moved port so Mack would have room to climb in, but he looked down and grinned.

"You guys have a good day and bring me back some meaningful data. I'll bet I could tell you a lot about a snapper filet on the grill this evening!"

Drew seemed to be the only one surprised when Mack pushed the bow away. Christi smiled again as Drew moved aft to fend off the stern. She brought the bow around to idle out. Drew looked back and Mack waved. He cupped his hands to yell, "Back before five or you'll have to cover her overtime!"

Drew poured half a cup of coffee from the thermos bottle and stood beside the console while Christi maneuvered out of the basin. The sun was approaching the eastern horizon. A bright clear morning was in the offing. This time of year it was anyone's guess what the afternoon might bring.

"Coming up" she said, breaking the silent moment so Drew would grab a handhold as she applied throttle. He looked over at her as she pushed the throttle forward. A quick glance and a smile followed. She liked the power too.

The salty wind in his face and that slow acceleration has such a pleasant feel; a sensation of freedom and a pleasure as real as the morning sunrise and tangible as a warm cup of coffee. So Drew held onto it. He didn't look at her again. Instead, he took a sip of coffee and held onto the console as they headed through the buoys and out the pass.

Drew entered the numbers into the GPS unit that would take them to one of the offshore bridge spans. He knew of a small, off site location nearby that could hold fish. With snapper season just getting started, the fish were still on the inshore artificial reefs so heading out 20 or 30 miles was not necessary. Once the course was established, Drew set the unit on the dash and Christi turned slightly to starboard to match the bearing. Just a twelve-mile run so it wouldn't take long. Drew busied himself with setting up tackle, rigging, and getting things ready to fish.

The site revealed itself on the second pass when the fathometer spiked from eighty to seventy feet. Drew threw a marker buoy. With a little wind and virtually no current there was no reason to anchor. The wind and the seas would build this afternoon, but right now it was not even hot. No other boats in sight yet.

"Nothing like getting here early!" Drew pointed out. "Look, sea turtle," and he pointed to the large brown head sticking out of the water about forty feet to port. Christi whipped around in time to see the turtle take a deep breath then disappear.

"Loggerhead! A big one too! Did you do that just for me?"

"You bet. I also made arrangements for some dolphin to join us later."

"Did you know Mack named the boat *'Squirt'*?"

"Squirt? No, where he get a name like that?"

"It's his favorite character in *'Finding Nemo'*."

She laughed and reached below the console for a small bag. "You know, 'Crush the Turtle;' his offspring was 'Squirt'." In a slow, drawn surfer slang, she said, "Duuu-de!"

"Did you have favorite?" she asked.

"Let me think. Probably the little crab with the Jamaican accent."

"Wrong movie, dude," she said, continuing the accent. "That's Sebastian from The Little Mermaid!"

"Oh, uh, you're right."

"Would you mind putting some sunscreen on my back before we fish?"

Handing Drew the lotion, she pulled the t-shirt over her head in a slow, single motion. She could not have missed the next breath Drew took but she gracefully ignored it and turned her back to him.

"I usually get this done before I leave the house. I didn't have it in me at that hour."

"How about *'Scar'*?" Drew asked.

"What scar?" she said, turning her head and trying to see her shoulder.

"No, I mean *'Scar,'* the fish in the aquarium. I liked him. Stuck in a small environment with big aspirations and dreaming of being free. Which was your favorite?"

Drew spread some lotion onto both hands and she lifted her soft brown hair. He knew she couldn't feel his heart beating, but it measured time rapidly while rubbing the lotion into both shoulders and her back.

"I liked the sharks, you know, the ones that were trying not to eat small fish. Bruce is probably my favorite-- he's the Great White-- but I liked the Hammerhead too, but just because he was the honest one."

Drew's heart kept time faster when he rubbed lotion into the small of her back. She was lovely, soft, and brown. He held his breath thinking it might keep from embarrassing him again. This was a moment not unlike that salty-wind-in-the-face freedom. It was a moment to appreciate and savor. Christi suddenly jumped and shouted, "Dolphin, right over there!"

"Looks like they're headed elsewhere," Drew said, as the pod of four or five broached then disappeared.

Under his breath, Drew acknowledged, regrettably, that they took the moment with them.

Chapter 20

Mack had taken the day off too. Only he spent the day at his office on a computer or on the phone. It was time to finish the research.

He started with the short package that Christi had prepared summarizing her findings. It included seven separate folders of backup data that he could use. It only took time. Something Mack had to carve out of a busy week. Today were hours he excised specifically for analytical work. No distractions, no management, no administrative trivia. He owed this time to his friend Drew.

Mack reviewed the material Christi had prepared on both the Charter Boat Captains Association and the environmental advocacy group, Protect and Preserve. He intentionally started with the Charter Boat Captains Association.

There were few surprises but he wanted to make certain that there were not stones unturned. There was a Franklin County fisherman, now a state representative, that probably should have let his bias be known before voting on several net ban concerns and offshore reef developments. The environmentalists had placed a 'shot across the bow' by showing photographs of his own charter vessel involved with the project. Maybe there was a conflict of interest but no laws broken, simply an appearance of impropriety that would never even occur to a fisherman helping his neighbors.

Not much there. Scanning several charter captains' data sheets and political contributions made it somewhat clear that the association had played by the rules and had little to hide in terms of legislative and judicial advocacy.

That is not to say that personally there weren't some eye-opening revelations. Fishing partners married eleven years who essentially just changed partners. One divorced, the other divorced, then within two years they each married the other's ex-wife. Mack tried to imagine the complications for only moments, then bailed. There were captains arrested for transporting everything from drugs, immigrants, money, even Haitian art works, but they had paid their debt to society and returned to catching fish. There were captains that had married people at sea who had been later sued to annul or question the legitimacy of their nuptials.

Mack moved on to the Protect and Preserve files.

He reviewed what Christi had found on the advisory board. She had found several of the interesting idiosyncrasies that he had spotted at the diner with Drew. In addition to the retail magnate in ladies' accessories and the second level Hollywood 'face,' there were some connections to this organization that didn't seem right. Mack could imagine a funding line from a major oil company as a good faith effort in supporting the gulf cleanup following a major oil spill but there was nothing that overt.

What interested him was that there were several other threads that led to other oil interests. Christi had found one member of the advisory board was the son-in-law of the CEO of a major trucking firm that specialized in the transport of oil products. That alone was not particularly alarming except that she found he was an official of the PTA of Liberty Texas High School, a deacon at the Baptist church, and head of the Houston Oil Industries consortium. Another on the advisory team was Ms. Evangeline Boudreaux, who had other environmental interests, including Friends of Lake Bourne and the St. Charles Parish Anti-Litter Campaign, but mostly her work was in south Louisiana where her husband was the head of the nearby oil and gas refinery.

Mack paged through the advisory board and the Board of Directors. It appeared that Protect and Preserve had originated along the white sand beaches of Bay, Walton, and Okaloosa counties. The origin was a local water-quality volunteer organization. Dr. Bentley was a charter member and carried the banner to academia with several papers he authored based on water sample data collected by the volunteers.

Mack found it interesting that the original charter did not target fishermen. In fact, fishing interests had very little to do with the wording. While watered down somewhat in how's and wherefore's, the primary focus was essentially to eliminate all usage of federal waters. They had specifically excluded the state waters that extended from land out nine miles but after that they advocated no fishing, commercial, or recreational activity at all. They were opposed to oil exploration, military operations, undersea mining, fish habitat development, all of it. A complete hands-off, let nature do the rebuilding. Basically, they were opposed to anything except the passage of commercial vessels in established sea-lanes.

Mack sat back with his eyes open and stared at the wall. That part didn't make any sense. What did eliminating all commercial, government, and recreational use of federal waters have to do with the oil industry?

Mack could see why they stayed clear of state waters. The Florida legislature has too many other areas of self-interest each with their own political action committee, call list, or lobbying effort. The horse-trading of favors in this area would be paid for with favors in other areas. Those interests were completely unmanageable and not important, apparently. Besides, Florida's tourist trade depends on the recreational use of state waters whether beaching, kayaking, fishing or swimming. There simply was no way to pursue their stated purpose along these beaches in particular.

He looked over several other folders of notes but kept coming back to the question at hand. Why pursue the elimination of all interests in federal waters? He could not establish a logical motive or even good rationale.

Mack started writing down the interests affected by this charter. It was more of a doodle or maybe a method to distract him from the central question, but Mack wrote down fishermen with commercial and recreational split off to one side. Then he added the oil industry on the opposite side; they were still deeply interested in exploring an area known as the Destin Dome, a potential oil formation found in the region years ago. He put the U.S. Military at the bottom of the page with a split for Air Force who conducted exercises over gulf waters, and the Navy, who conducted operations and offshore testing. He could think of a few more but they were small or other environmental interests like turtles and manatees that would welcome the help.

While doodling, he looked over the faces again thumbing through the notebook Christi assembled.

Nothing but fishing interests showed up on the Charter Boat Captains Association. The fingerprint of the oil industry showed up on Protect and Preserve. But the oil industry has nothing to gain from closing federal waters, it would make the Destin Dome inaccessible. Mack tapped his pencil fretfully on the desk while he stepped a little further into some of the material Christi had developed using on-line resources that he had access to.

He started a new doodle, this time with a small fish. Beside the fish, he wrote fishermen. He scanned the papers spread out across his desk and he drew a second fish. This one encompassed the first and he titled it Charter Boat Captain's Association. The group consisted of a conglomerate of fishing captains but all of them were small businessmen that made a living off the bounty of the sea. That meant there were a bunch of small fish, like the one he initially drew, included in the larger association. Next, he looked over the papers for Protect and Preserve. Their interests crossed, but Protect and Preserve was larger. They weren't really a lot larger, but they were much better funded. For this he drew a larger fish and because they had interests in common, the larger Protect and Preserve fish partially encompassed the Charter Captains Association. Without thinking much about it, he drew another fish that encompassed all of Protect and Preserve and most of the Charter Captains Association. He labeled this Big Oil. They were certainly much larger and had an interest in the same gulf waters. Their interests would be funded the best because of the profit motive. From a funding perspective, theirs would be a much bigger fish but it still encompassed the same geographical area.

"But they can't play," he said aloud. He looked at his diagram and realized that the biggest interest on his doodle by far was the Oil Industry but they couldn't play! Why? They were not permitted to drill in the area because of the Department of Defense interest in the same area where they conduct offshore Air Force training and Navy Mine Defense testing. Mack drew another fish with the same interest area and labeled it US Military.

He stood up and walked around his desk tapping the pencil on his chin, thinking.

There were lots of beach communities that opposed drilling because of the prospect of a spill. A spill could decimate entire towns by killing the tourist business. These also had an interest but they were not specifically organized as an opposing interest. He stopped at his doodle and drew a number of small fish representing the cities and sections of the big fish that included the Department of Defense, Big Oil, the Charter Captains and Protect and Preserve. There would be factions in each city that supported or objected to different elements of each.

Holding up his diagram he turned and held it in perspective at a map he had hanging on the wall. It was a Mercator projection of the Gulf and he could see from Tampa to Tampico, from Key West to Destin, from New Orleans to Cozumel. The interests he held in his hand were bigger than the broad expanse of saltwater. There were so many interests in this region that the graphic parsed out the segments and made the Gulf of Mexico look small. So many interests, so much money, and so many lives affected.

Starting again, Mack tried to draw the diagram on the white board adjacent to his desk. In the middle, at the very start, there was a fisherman depicted as a fish. This time he used fish and different colors. They were all fish. The smaller fish was eaten by the larger fish, which was eaten by the next fish up who was eaten by the fish that was still bigger. When he got to Big Oil and the Department of Defense, he couldn't decide which fish should be the biggest. The Department of Defense was a very large fish, comparatively, but it has only a small interest in the Gulf. On the other hand, Big Oil is made up of many large conglomerates all of which have some interest in the gulf.

They were all predators to some extent. Eating the smaller fish. Mack's eyes fell on the Department of Defense. Perhaps the Defense Department couldn't be considered predatory, but they guarded their interests in the same manner. They had a stake in the split and would defend their need. What else is there?

In the manner of a man steeped in methodology, the scientific process, and the skepticism that makes a scientist a true researcher, Mack mentally stepped away from his white board depiction and tried to see it as though it were incomplete. He physically backed away and stared at it from a distance. Are there any other fish?

Of course there were. While the Department of Defense was a large fish, their interest in the Gulf would be small compared to that of the Department of the Interior who leased all the underwater land and regulated the oil industry practices in the region. Mack drew a big fish that would encompass all the area around Big Oil leaving a small segment of the Department of Defense uncovered. He was just about to finish the mouth of the fish when he spotted the Charter Boat Captains Association. He added some more fish beside that one and labeled them Commercial Fisheries and Recreational Fisheries. Next, he drew a fish that encompassed all the fishermen and titled it the US Department of Commerce.

Now he had the big fish. They may not be predators in the same manner but they were for this purpose. They would fight for their jurisdiction. Whale Sharks perhaps. Not an actual predator but they looked like one. They swam in the same waters, and they were big enough to scatter the other predators.

Mack came back to Protect and Preserve and concentrated on Harold Gardey. He looked at the face in the bio as a board member. He had found a credible pattern of oil industry involvement that was embedded with legitimacy and academic credence. There were papers, doctoral theses, and studies from Auburn University, LSU, Mississippi State, and the University of Florida. It was all quite a front. It was a well-designed facade of respected academics, businesses, services, and persons interested in the welfare of the Gulf of Mexico. What was he missing?

Mack stood up and again looked at the picture of Harold Gardey and wondered if he had ever contacted Drew. He was sure there was more than just a casual interest. Even if it was a passionate obsession, something told him it was more than the welfare of an injured dolphin and ocean ecology that motivated Harold Gardey.

As a civil servant under Marine Fisheries, Mack was part of the Department of Commerce himself. He could make some calls. It was time to call in some markers he had earned. He looked again at his diagram on the board while he looked up an email contact. He could probably get all he needed from one source if he was lucky. Bob was a computer nerd when Mack was at grad school. He was now a branch head at the Department of Commerce Information Technology department. Mack made the call and tried unsuccessfully to come up with some common ground when Bob answered.

"Hey Bob, this is Mack down at Marine Fisheries in Florida. How's everything along the Potomac?" ... Don't be feeding me a fish story; you know I'll look it up! No, I haven't been, should have, but work and you know, in my profession you would think I could make time for fishing.... Listen, it's never a good time, but I need a favor. Could you look up a name for me? I need some hard data... I know, I know, but this is a bonafide, need-to-know, favor. Can you help me out?"

Bob said it would only take a few minutes. Mack stood back and absorbed the implications of his diagram.

"Yes, it is related to the dolphin deaths here, have you heard about them? Didn't think the story was that widespread. Yes... yes... It's all the news around here too and this information will be a big help. You have my email? This evening or tomorrow morning would be great. Thanks, Bob."

Mack looked the big fish on his wall-size diagram and mentally moved them around changing their relationships by placing other fish in their belly. The little fish were completely erased from view once they were grouped together and the larger fish were a bit more obvious. He could see that this was no longer a skirmish of opposite interests. Deals and agreements, allocations and understandings started to make relationships but ostensibly, there were none to be had... none that were obvious anyway.

The connections seemed to be at the macro level. There were interests at the policy level. Those were the big fish. The fishermen and the environmentalists were part of a diversion; a highly visible part of a distraction-- causes leading to predictable effects. This was the making of a feeding frenzy.

Chapter 21

Christi watched until the pod of dolphin moved east where the water brightly reflected the morning sun. She reached to the console for sunglasses.

When she looked up Drew was standing with rods in hand. "Ready to fish?" he asked.

"Yeah. What do I need?"

"You've never been fishing?"

"Not out here... on lakes and stuff in Alabama but not in the Gulf. This is my first time."

Drew set her up with a dropper rig, circle hook and a two-ounce weight on one of the rods he brought. He netted a pinfish from the live well and threaded it through the lips onto the hook. She watched the bait swim just beneath the surface while Drew explained how you don't have to jerk the rod when you feel a bite, just start reeling. It was an unrehearsed repeat of something he overheard from one of the deckhands, but who out here would know?

"What's that thing?" she asked looking at the fighting belt Drew was adjusting for her waist.

"You'll find out soon enough. Here, hold it on your hip and turn around"

He clipped the fighting belt and tightened it enough to stay in place.

Drew brought the boat back to the buoy and showed her how to set the drag while sending the shrimp to the bottom. She hooked up before Drew could get rigged and started reeling with a howl of excitement with a distinctive feminine flavor.

"I can't get it, I can't get it," she exclaimed as the rod bent over the rail, the reel turned sideways and the rod end pressed into her gut.

Picking the rod end up, Drew put it in the fighting belt and she immediately understood why that was important.

He loosened the drag a little and watched as the fish took line. She continued to reel and slowly started bringing the fish to the surface.

It was a snapper ...a keeper too! Drew held the gaff as she brought it alongside the boat where he could lip the fish and hoist it aboard.

She released a bellicose howl and thrust both fists in the air. Both arms clasped around Drew for an excited bear hug. He managed to keep from getting the fish on her and she retreated to do a little victory dance on the deck.

"Can we can keep it?" she asked.

Drew held the fish to the measuring tape along the port gunwale and announced, "twenty-two inches. You can keep it! Nice fish for your first one."

Christi grabbed the rod and watched as Drew put the red snapper into the cooler. When he stood up, she looked at him like the bait should already be on her hook.

"Don't you need to do some biological recording or something scientific?"

"I'll do that later. I want another fish!"

Drew got her set back up and dropped a live bait over the opposite gunwale himself. Almost immediately she had another nice fish coming to the boat. Drew set his reel down to provide assistance and something grabbed his bait and took it under the boat. By the time Christi got her fish to the surface it was hopelessly entangled. "We're all tangled up," she said.

"You've tangled with the law now," Drew told her.

She looked up rolling her eyes.

"Is that something I need to worry about?" she asked.

Drew brought her fish into the boat, then cut his line in order to extricate the snapper.

"Maybe, but not today. I wouldn't let just anybody off the hook this easily, you know," Drew said with his best western lawman and John Wayne parlance that he could muster.

"Is it because I'm National Marine Fisheries?"

"No, it's because you're cute."

She cocked her head sideways and flashed that smile. The smile she saves for the highway patrol when she gets pulled on the interstate. The same one she should have used with Toby on the boardwalk to end the confrontation. The smile that opens doors, launches ships, and reminds men that they are hopelessly destined to follow primitive instincts throughout all time.

She had a third fish on before Drew was able to rig up again, so he gave up.

"You'll have to stop catching those fish now," he told her.

With the enthusiasm of a young co-ed she smiled and said, "What do you mean, officer? This is only my third. I want to catch more!"

"But you are only allowed to keep two red snapper. That's the law."

"Aww ... I forgot! So I can't keep this one?"

Her dejected pout was probably typical of the look every deckhand gets on a party boat at this same point at the start of a good day offshore.

"Why don't you catch this one for me," and Drew looked over the gunwale as she excitedly reeled up a third snapper.

It looked about the same size as the previous fish but when he measured, it was only fifteen inches, "This one has to go back."

"Why?"

"It's not long enough"

"Isn't that an over used cliché?" she said laughing.

Drew held it back up to the measuring tape and showed her it missed the minimum length by less than an inch. She looked disappointed, but shrugged and set the rod aside. Drew showed her how to vent the fish then leaned over to release it alongside.

"I don't think I like having to let them go. Especially after bringing it all the way to the surface and seeing you vent them."

"I'm sure you share that feeling with many sportsmen. Looks like we've drifted off the site. Let me bring the boat back around."

Drew looked around before putting the boat in gear and noticed that other boats were in the vicinity.

"Looks like the rest of the fleet is arriving. There's a boat on the adjacent bridge span and a charter boat astern. Let's see if we can get one more before somebody else pulls up on our spot."

Drew pulled back up to the buoy and got her bait rigged before noticing that several dolphins were arriving as well. A pod was tracking in front of the charter boat.

In short order, she had another hooked up. She smiled, giggled, and grunted as she fought it to the surface. Drew watched, ready to bring the fish aboard, as a gray object rushed beneath the boat and Christi's rod tip bent hard toward the water. She unleashed a startled scream that she cut short when the rod went slack.

"What was that?" she yelled, and started reeling up quickly.

"We'll see in a second"

The snapper broached the surface nearly dead. Drew lipped the fish easily and raised it for her to see that the scales were literally falling from the fish about half way down to the tail.

Christi looked at it as though something were terribly wrong with the specimen, then reached for Mack's bag to retrieve a camera. Drew measured the snapper at nearly 15 inches and stated that it was another short. There was no need to vent this one but Drew hung it over the transom while she prepared for the photograph.

Christi assumed a biologists demeanor and stated, "This fish isn't sick. It was a good fight until just a moment ago. But look how half its scales are missing." She took several photos as Drew held the fish along the measured scale from Mack's bag. "This fish won't survive if we release it."

"That's another dilemma every fisherman has faced," Drew noted unapologetically. "The law says it has to be released. It can't stay on the boat without being in violation."

"I could keep it for study."

"Let's release it for study ...watch."

Rather than release the snapper alongside, Drew tossed it 10 or 12 feet off to starboard. Just as the snapper started to revive and turned slowly to head back down the water column, the large gray object swam beneath. The dolphin came to the surface with the fish in its mouth. It swallowed the fish as if to say "thanks," then turned to swim away.

Drew looked at Christi and she simply stared at the ripple where her snapper used to be. Then she watched the dolphin as it swam to join the pod. She retrieved the camera and put it and the measured scale back in Mack's bag before saying anything. Some of the puzzle pieces had just fallen into place.

"I need to catch another fish," she said.

Christi got ready while Drew pulled back up on the buoy. The loss of enthusiasm was almost as stifling as the humidity that fueled the hot mid-morning air.

"You want to try something different?" Drew asked matter-of-factly. "We could change rigging and move a little offshore to a spot that's holding some big amberjack."

"No. This is what I came to learn."

Chapter 22

This was the lesson Drew had planned. Unfortunately, he was rather enjoying her enthusiasm for fishing. For someone that has been fishing as long as Drew had, the enthusiasm is contagious. It rekindles the pleasure of the sport. It stimulates that same feeling as the salt air in your face and the slow acceleration of a powerful boat. These nuances spark an immediate exhilaration that connects to pleasure centers in the brain.

The excitement may have waned but the intent was genuine, so he let it ride and threaded another bait onto the circle hook.

"Uh oh. I think that's someone I know," Christi said.

Drew looked up to see *Reel Fun* about forty feet to starboard with a small party plus Toby and Captain Wayne. Captain Wayne's flagrant approach this close was aggravating because he was clearly attempting to see what sort of obstruction or bottom contours Drew and Christi were fishing over. Between charter captains there are unwritten rules. Rules they live by day after day. Rules Captain Wayne would never break in this town. Those same rules don't apply to 'monkey-boats.' The weekend warrior is not permitted the same gravitas. They're just monkey-boats and in the way of a man trying to make a living. Not all captains alter the rules but some do. At this point, anonymity was of more value, so Drew simply ignored his personal annoyance and threw the live bait over the gunwale.

"Let 'er rip."

The *Reel Fun* had three customers on deck with rods in hand and Toby was giving them the snapper pep talk as he baited the lines.

"…. so if you feel that bump…bump… bump, start reeling, you'll probably have him hooked. If not, you'll know soon enough; but keep on reeling and I'll get'cha a new bait." Toby had done this before. He hated to see when they just let them chew up the bait, spit it out, then chew it again and not bring it onto the boat. It was pride but it was also the sheer economics. That bait was a cost of doing business, which is another way of saying profit, already spent.

They had three lines going down in minutes on the bridge span just south of our location. .

Christi whooped and the rod bowed up as she started reeling up a fish. Drew could see the *Reel Fun* had one on too and Toby was trying to make sure the other lines didn't get tangled.

He watched as Captain Wayne stood and pointed from his perch in the fly bridge. Toby came to the port side and looked where he was pointing. Then Drew saw a sequence of fins broach.

"More dolphin," he muttered.

Just as Drew spoke, Christi released a howl and bent at the waist. The rod bowed sharply and she used both hands to hold on. "Same thing like last time-- it was coming up, then it started pulling really hard." Just as she got the words out, the rod went slack.

"Dolphin again. They are over at the *Reel Fun* too. Probably need to move to another site. But, that looks like a keeper," Drew said leaning over to net the snapper. This time, the dolphin turned alongside and rolled upright, waiting for Drew to throw it back.

"They learn quick," Drew said. "Since we have an enforced size limit, the dolphin have learned to simply wait and we'll throw the fish back. The fish are worn out from the fight; then we throw them back so they have to swim alone and unprotected through the barracuda, sharks, and dolphin. You gotta wonder how many of them, if any, make it back to the bottom?"

Drew flipped the snapper into a bucket to remove the hook. When he leaned over to measure the fish, something exploded on the wreck below.

Drew's head went into the gunwale and he fell to the deck. It was an automatic response from a previous lifetime. There was no concussion, just a loud report. It sounded as though a diver set off a grenade on the wreck somewhere below and the pressure wave expanded as it surfaced nearby. Drew's subconscious also registered the sound as a detonator going off in a nearby mountain, or a precise missile strike into a cave, or a mortar landing too close to the dirt where he had buried his head.

"Are you okay?" Christi said, seated on the leaning post.

"Just an automatic response learned in a country far from here. Otherwise I'm fine. Any idea what that was?"

"Sounded like somebody on the wreck just shot a cannon, but I didn't see anything."

Drew looked over at the *Reel Fun* and Toby was directing all three patrons to get their lines back on the bottom while he flipped a snapper into the cooler. Drew looked up thinking maybe a jet flew by and it was a sonic boom. He was unable to resolve that prospect and went aft to find the snapper now floundering around the rear bulkhead.

"Looks like we get to keep this one, plus," holding up the fish to show Christi. "It's almost already cleaned!"

Like the previous snapper, half the scales had been removed.

"What do you think removes the scales like that?" Christi asked. She wasn't in the scientific mode, just curious, but preparing her camera anyway.

"My guess ...the dolphin's teeth," Drew replied. "They are smart enough not to eat the fish coming up with a hook in it. But if they can pull the fish off the hook, then they get lunch. I'm told by charter captains that they have started targeting the larger fish on the way up, knowing that the smaller fish will be coming to them soon enough."

Wuh-bump!

Another explosion, this time on the wreck but closer to the *Reel Fun*.

They had to have noticed. Drew looked starboard and Captain Wayne was looking over at their Boston Whaler. Toby was tending to a patron obviously reeling up something while the others fished. Drew knew he needed to pay better attention.

"I'm going to set you up with another bait, but I'm going to be checking out the *Reel Fun* this time. You just keep fishing."

With Christi rigged, Drew pulled back to the buoy. This put them closer to *Reel Fun* and he attempted to hold up into a mixed wind and sea. Just as Drew pulled up, one of the rods on the port side of *Reel Fun*, bowed up, then let go just like Christi's had. His rig came up empty and Toby let out a string of profanities directed at the dolphin below. Captain Wayne glanced over but then goosed the port throttle forward to swing the boat a little further away.

"Okay, catch us one more," Drew said, and Christi let the weight take her bait to the wreck.

Looking over at the stern deck, the *Reel Fun* had two fish on and Toby had the gaff at the stern. Captain Wayne was facing forward but Drew could see him again stand and point forward and to starboard.

Toby moved forward and let both fishermen fight what appeared to be two sizeable fish. He nearly disappeared on the starboard side when Drew watched him throw a small object away from the boat. He walked aft and gave each patron a little encouragement to continue the fight. It appeared that they had good fish on.

WHUMP…another explosion on the wreck.

Again Drew hit the deck and Christi looked at him aghast. Almost immediately she started reeling, let out a whoop, and her rod loaded up too. Drew sat on the deck while Christi fought the fish and thought through what he had seen. There had to be a correlation to what Toby threw overboard and the explosion. Why would he do that?

Drew mentally revisited the situation as he remembered it. There were two fish on. Captain Wayne spotted dolphin. Toby walks forward and throws something; …two fish on, dolphin approaching. That has to be it; something that can scare the dolphin long enough that they can get the fish onboard. Drew needed to see him do it.

"Drew, help me here!" Christi yelled.

Drew looked up and Christi was doubled over holding onto a rod that was bent over the gunwale. As he stood up, the line went slack and she fell backwards into him.

"What happened? I had a good fish!"

"Looks like the dolphin decided he needed it more than you. I need your help with something. I apologize but I need to transition into a work mode. Since we're out here on assignment, I could really use your help."

"The dolphin case?"

"Yes. Certain of it, but not sure how to make it stick."

Chapter 23

Drew explained to Christi that he had seen Toby throw something over the side moments before the last explosion. He planned to watch closer this time and hopefully get it documented. This could be the break they were looking for. Drew wasn't sure it was all that simple but he had a good feeling.

Drew often relies on intuition. It is sometimes more trustworthy than hard facts. Facts have to be verified. Intuition is just a gut feeling that requires some arbitrary instinct. You don't have all the facts. Your intuition expects you to act on 'gut feel' and with that alone, approach truth. Drew knows that it fails him sometimes, but he's been down that path enough to know when the feeling is something that he has to trust.

When he pulled back up to the buoy ready to fish, Drew had Mack's small video camera on the console wrapped in a towel.

He could see Toby with a camera taking a picture on the stern. Two patrons were holding up a nice snapper and the third guy in the middle held up one he got out of the box. It was a man's moment, the type that makes for big tips and return customers. Toby was good at customer service. He knew it took more than just fishing. They were in the entertainment business. You could no longer call this a business of producing food for the family. This was how sportsmen preferred to spend their spare time, not to mention some of their disposable income. Captain Wayne looked down from the fly bridge and yelled to get ready. They were going to bring her back around.

When he pulled up, *Reel Fun* was forty feet to starboard. Drew turned the motor to port so the *Squirt* would drift astern of the *Reel Fun* then Christi sent the bait about halfway to the bottom. Halfway to the bottom would reduce the likelihood of catching a fish but would keep up appearances.

Toby had his customers at their stations and ready to fish when Captain Wayne signaled to let'em go. The starboard side loaded up first, followed by the guy fishing astern. Again, the third guy reeled up complaining but making room for his compatriots. The guy on the stern had a good fish and moved slowly to the port side while pumping the rod and reeling to keep the fish out of the structure. Drew saw Captain Wayne point to starboard where he must have seen dolphin. Toby reacted and stepped forward to a hatch where he grabbed something.

The Whaler was nearly astern when Drew asked Christi to reel up so he could check her bait. He reached to the console to check the video camera and then moved astern to get a fresh pinfish. Drew replaced her bait then put the rod and the steering wheel in a position that he could continue watching the rear deck of *Reel Fun*. Christi again let her bait drop until he told her to stop, well short of the bottom.

At the stern live well, Toby netted a baitfish. He hooked it onto the patron's rig then stepped up to his workstation to retrieve something. It was a small weight attached to monofilament. He hooked a small item then allowed the weight to fall away.

Christi let out a shriek as her line tightened and the rod bent over. He hadn't planned on that but it made a good diversion. She stood to fight the fish and Drew moved behind her and repositioned the camera a little. Moving to the starboard side with the gaff Drew could keep an eye on *Reel Fun* while appearing to be interested in what Christi was catching.

"Christi, play the fish, let it run a little. I need to watch what Toby is doing," Drew said. Captain Wayne leaned over from the fly bridge and handed Toby something shiny. It reflected in the overhead sun as Toby reached up to take it. Toby put it next to the weight he had in the other hand then threw the weight away from the boat. He handed the shiny item back to the fly bridge then went to attend his anglers.

In the bright sunlight, there was no way to determine exactly what Toby had done but Drew suspected he lit a fuse. The shiny object would be Captain Wayne's cigarette lighter and the explosive was attached to a weight. Not so much weight that the explosive would immediately fall to the bottom but enough that it would slowly sink. An M-80 or a cherry bomb fuse would continue to burn underwater. That kind of underwater explosion would likely discourage a dolphin.

"Wait for it," Drew told Christi, and grabbed her shoulder.

WHUMP.

"There it is," he said. The expectation at least left Drew the dignity of not diving for the deck.

"Can I reel the fish up now?"

"Oh yeah, sure ...sorry. Let me help." Drew reached over and turned off the video camera then leaned over the gunwale to retrieve their limit of snapper.

Christi was elated and inspected the fish like an investigator before it landed in the cooler. Drew reviewed the video still wrapped in a towel on the console.

"There is nothing rock solid here but harassing a marine mammal is a tough wrap for a charter captain, we still have work to do," Drew said turning off the camera and stowing it in the gear bag.

"Is that bad?"

"Could cost him his captain's license."

...WHUMP...

Chapter 24

The *Reel Fun* was pulling back around as Drew approached the marker buoy. Drew took off his hat and leaned over the bow to retrieve the buoy. Captain Wayne looked over from about thirty feet. Recognizing Drew, he yelled over the drone of diesels, "So what is this, a covert operation where the Wildlife Commission collaborates with the National Marine Fisheries?"

Drew was tempted to keep his mouth shut but a pent up discomfort would not let him.

"No, just something for the table, but I think you better head on in. We're going to need to talk."

Christi had nearly assembled the gear and had tried to phone Mack. Cell service is spotty offshore. She picked up the VHF and switched to 71. The Marine Fisheries office routinely monitored channel 71 when fieldwork was in progress. Someone in the office was finding Mack while Captain Wayne and Drew continued the boat-to-boat conversation.

"Why should I be heading on in? We still got snapper to catch and we ain't even started on the AJs yet."

"Wayne, I got video that shows you and Toby using an explosive while fishing. While that is a fishing infraction, it could also be harassment of marine mammals. As you know, that is a federal offense."

"Well I guess we could be shootin' em," he replied angrily. "Those dolphin followed me out! I wouldn't have one fish aboard without something to run the fish-stealin' bastards off."

"I don't get to make the rules," Drew told him.

"Don't you tell me anymore what you think out here disguised as a monkey-boat, checking up on a guy trying to make a livin'."

Drew recognized that use of monkey-boat as a derogatory term. When used by a captain that knows the score, it was meant to be provocative. Since recreational boats aren't being paid to be there, most are considered to be in the way and a nuisance to the purist out there earning a living, but this was a research vessel. There's a difference. While typically just a term used to reference non-commercial vessels, in this case it was not only disparaging, but accusatory.

Christi had Mack on the VHF but continued facing the other way in order to hear over the diesel noise. She leaned against the starboard gunwale next to the center console. Drew could not hear their conversation but she could surely see where this one was headed. *Reel Fun* had fallen off the fishing site a bit and Captain Wayne kicked the starboard throttle to position, his port side alongside the *Squirt*.

Drew watched as Toby encouraged the three patrons into the air-conditioned salon while he cleaned up the stern and got ready for the next fishing site.

"Now, Wayne, I'm just out here fishing today. We can discuss this later."

"No, by God, we gon' discuss it right now. I have three paying customers in there and I intend to take them to catch more fish. I don't need a patrol boat out here harassing me whilst I'm working hard to show these boys a good time."

Drew stopped what he was doing. He put his hat back on and stood at the starboard side looking up at Capt. Wayne.

"No. I'm taking this lady back in and we're going to discuss this officially tomorrow," Drew responded. "I do not intend to call this incident in now and spoil the rest of my day off… unless you insist. At that point, your day will be over and so will mine."

The intent was non-confrontational but the inflection was official. If he wanted to push it, Drew could have two maybe three boats alongside in less than 20 minutes.

"Well, what's your little fisheries girly doing right now?" Wayne asked with a snappish tone. Drew looked back to see Christi with the VHF microphone held to her cheek while she read numbers off the GPS.

Drew finished wrapping up the buoy and began heading to the stern when Wayne goosed the port engine in reverse. *Reel Fun* came directly along the port side and the hulls bumped sharply. Drew reached to grab the center console and missed. Missing the handhold, he fell against the port gunwale. His feet locked under the leaning post to keep him from going overboard. Christi dropped the microphone as she fell into the leaning post. Drew heard Mack still talking as she leaned over to retrieve it. When she stood back up, Toby appeared at the port gunwale of the *Reel Fun* directly behind Christi.

As Drew recovered his footing, he watched as Toby leaned over and wrapped his huge arm around Christi's neck. He held a gaff in the other hand. Toby slowly lifted her off the deck as the seas rolled the boat to port. She struggled but her feet found places to push off. Her hands went to his forearm and he simply continued to stand up as the *Reel Fun* listed to starboard. Her feet found the leaning post, she pushed then fell onto the gunwale of the *Reel Fun*. She attempted to push off the gunwale with her feet but Toby stepped back and her feet landed on the deck of the *Reel Fun* with the rest of her body in a compromising limbo position.

Toby stared at Drew. Drew stared back with the stern look of law enforcement. He couldn't let him see how helpless Drew felt right now. Toby simply held Christi but his look was one of someone hovering along the brink.

"Drew, I can't afford to lose this job. It's all I know. I'm not good at school but I can fish, and I can rig, and I can drive a boat. Wha' I'm goin' do if I don't work the charter boats?"

He was just standing there now. Christi looked scared but he wasn't hurting her. He simply wouldn't let go and she remained slightly off balance. Drew was disadvantaged standing below him on the deck of the Boston Whaler. It would take him three moves to get anywhere close, so he looked up at Captain Wayne.

Toby continued in a slow deliberate voice, "Captain Wayne got to pay the pump price when we fill up. I seen it; it takes thousands of dollars where it used to be four, maybe five hundred. These 'ol boys won't keep paying that if they don't catch fish. Tips suck this year. Hardly make a living this way anymore."

Toby nodded to the patrons in the galley drinking beer behind a glass window completely opaque with condensation. They had no idea what was going on. They were just waiting for the next time the captain said fish.

"Then the dolphin, they take the fish right in front of us and eat 'em. All we do with the little 'uns anymore is feed the dolphin by throwing them back, I 'spect thass illegal too. So you got me either way."

He was choked up now. The words Captain Wayne and Drew had tossed across the gunwales were cannonballs from opposing ships. In one ship, there was a law and a means of enforcement. In the other, was his way of life and all that he knew.

He could fight the predators that ate his livelihood. For the law, there was nothing on which to focus his rage. Christi wasn't his focus …Drew was. Drew was the face of the other predator. He was hurting Drew. Hurting the law because fishing was something he could do well. He had built his life around something he did well. He was hurting Drew because the law, the costs, and the dolphin threatened to take something from him that made him whole. All three collaborated to remove this piece of his life that he found fulfilling and he was good at. They progressively sliced away his ability to earn a living over a period of painful years. The years served to wither his dream of owning and operating his own charter boat. This disorderly process of conflicting philosophies, administrators, and laws sliced away his future and his opportunity to provide for his young family.

"Captain Wayne, tell Toby to let her go," Drew said with conviction and with the hope that he was the only one that detected the loss of authority.

Captain Wayne knew they were past the bar and heading for perilous waters. The cannonballs were no longer words; they were now actions that people live to regret.

"Toby, you heard what the man said…. You let her go, son," Wayne said softly, as captain, as his friend, and as his mentor. He had a fatherly tone. One that knew there would be ramifications. He couldn't take back the cannonballs but didn't need to fire anymore.

Toby looked slowly up at Captain Wayne then back at Drew. The rage was still there. It was too late to consider the consequences. His actions were giving way to sadness and remorse but combined they turned into a deep, gut-wrenching anger. This was a good kid, but the seams were breaking loose. Drew glanced down looking for anything, a paddle, a boat hook, something with some heft. But any movement he made could start a horrendous sequence of bad responses should Toby decide to use that gaff. With skills he had developed over years of fishing, the thought was too horrific to consider.

When Drew looked at Christi for reassurance, she no longer looked frightened. Instead, she wore a resigned face. Was it a look of defeat or resolve? Drew retreated to a helpless silence over the drone of diesels while his brain argued for action knowing that the next move could not be his.

Both boats rocked in the seas counter to one another; one side up, the other side down, both in a sinusoidal frequency but opposite one another.

Drew looked up to see defeat and a sad resolve that could not be consoled.

"TOBY!" Drew yelled and he looked up with defiance.

Christi's right leg came up in a swift, practiced maneuver. In a deft, clean stroke she smashed Toby's instep. He raised the gaff and leaned toward the pain, directly into Christi's well-aimed right elbow, powerfully cocked during the first action. The gaff clattered to the deck. She spun loose of his grip as he reeled backward reaching for his face. His nose was askew and the blood drooled from his lips and chin. With a feral grunt she jumped to swing her left foot in a half circle that landed across the outside of his ear and jaw and followed with a right foot thrust into his midsection. Christi landed in a crouched, low stance. Her practiced position left her ready to continue, if necessary. Toby crumpled unconscious on the deck.

The three patrons opened the salon door and heads poked out to see what was going on just as Christi slowly stood pressing her shoulders and elbows out while pressing her hands in front of her face. She closed her eyes and exhaled to regain her composure. They looked up and smiled to see Christi standing there in her bathing suit top and shorts, hands pressed together as if in prayer. Nearly in unison they looked down to see Toby sprawled on the deck blood oozing out of his nos and mouth. One hoisted his beer in an informal salute while another popped open a fresh can with an audible 'fssst.' Drew heard one of them say, "day-um....missed it!" as they closed the door to keep the cool air conditioning from escaping.

Chapter 25

Drew put a quick wrap on a stern cleat and jumped aboard and stood behind Christi. She was no longer the lean, gaunt defender. She tore her hands apart then turned and leaned against Drew. She shook as she pressed close.

"You okay?" Drew asked, putting an arm around her.

"I was so scared."

She started into a full body shake as the shock waned. The fear departed but the adrenalin remained, and Drew held her.

Captain Wayne climbed down from the fly bridge.

"Good God, what a mess!" he said from about half way down the ladder. "Looks like she gaffed a bonito and let it flop around over here."

The blood splattered all along the deck, across the starboard gunwale and started pooling along the seam where Toby lay. It wasn't really that much blood but his exaggeration was offered like a true fisherman and someone who had seen the bloody rendering of a gaffed bonito, hook released, and abandoned on the deck.

Drew grabbed a towel from Toby's workstation and wrapped it around Christi then set her against the port gunwale where it connected to the cabin.

"Let me check on Toby," Drew said.

She nodded and Drew turned to see Captain Wayne leaning over Toby with one knee on the deck.

"Grab that first aid kit off the bulkhead, would yuh?" Captain Wayne said pointing at a white plastic box mounted on one side of the doors.

Drew opened the box and set it on the deck next to Toby.

"I got some gauze in there somewhere and a bottle of peroxide. You see it?"

Drew shuffled through the box while Wayne retrieved a towel and wet it partially with salt water.

"I tol' him he should'a took some of them karate classes, but he'd have nothing of it. Just wanted to fish!"

Drew put two fingers on his neck and found a strong pulse.

"He's just out cold," Captain Wayne stated, ringing the bulk of the salt water onto the bloody deck. "Probably wake up with a bad headache, a busted nose, and a perfectly rotten disposition having been whupped by a little skinny girl."

He wiped the blood from Toby's face with the wet towel. Turning Toby's face sideways, Drew handed him the peroxide that he poured excessively over his nose and lower chin.

"Let me have some of that gauze. I really can't do much or he can't breathe, but if I tape a big wad of it over this side, it'll help stop the bleeding and he'll leave it alone."

Drew reached into the box for the tape while he folded a large piece of gauze along the lower side of his nose.

Ka-BOOM-aaaahh!

Christi yelled from across the deck, "What was that?"

Captain Wayne and Drew both looked up in recognition. Drew immediately jumped up, looking to starboard while Captain Wayne slipped a dry towel under Toby's head.

Christi reached into the Boston Whaler and retrieved the binoculars she was using before all this started.

There were two other boats to starboard, one trolling over the adjacent bridge span and another anchored at the other end.

Captain Wayne stood up next to Drew after he finished taping Toby's nose.

"That's the *Norma Jean* trolling. An' I seen that other boat out here before fairly regular, not sure who's running that. He's usually out here by hisself. Keeps his distance."

Christi moved to the starboard side looking through her binoculars.

"Just one guy, white boat, appears to be fishing."

"Let me see."

"Wait, what's that? Never mind. He just threw one back."

"Seems that's all I get to do anymore," Captain Wayne complained.

WHADUMMMP...*aaaaahhh!*

The explosion startled everyone and seemed louder or maybe closer than the previous one. Drew was immediately below the gunwale in a familiar position.

Christi jumped and was standing next to Drew with her hand on his elbow. The sound was in the decibel level of a sonic boom several miles away, only it was muffled by the water.

Captain Wayne turned immediately and watched as a small eruption evaporated on the surface just aft of the white boat. The sound dissipated with a hiss as the displaced water fell back into the gulf.

"That ain't M-80s," Captain Wayne said. "You don't get that from an M-80."

Christi stood next to Drew again looking through the binoculars. She groaned in disgust and handed him the binoculars.

"He killed one," she said. Her disdain punctuated the 'k'. Her look was one of contempt as she placed the binoculars in Drew's hand.

"Look behind the boat about thirty feet," she said, and walked to the stern placing both hands on the transom and looking up at the sky.

It was too far for Drew to be sure what she saw but something was floating astern of the white boat. The fisherman didn't seem to pay any attention and resumed his fishing charade, just another nice day on the gulf.

Chapter 26

There was blue sky with high white cirrus clouds. Pointed chevrons of white against cerulean blue that gave it the look of spears or teeth. Christi seemed to be studying them, staring motionless up into the blue, but her eyes were closed.

With the binoculars Drew focused on the white boat to starboard and the single fisherman. He wore a large straw hat, sunglasses, and a long-sleeved, light blue shirt. Even if Drew knew him, he wouldn't recognize him. Not from here. The boat was like any of hundreds in the area, just like the hat and the blue shirt.

"I'm going over there. Captain Wayne, I need Christi to stay here with you. That okay?"

"I want to go with you," she said, coming out of her trance.

"I'll be back to get you, but this just became official business."

"But..."

Drew didn't wait for her rebuttal. He stepped off the *Reel Fun* and back aboard the Marine Fisheries Whaler.

"*Squirt*. What a name," Drew thought. It made him smile as he checked the camera and pulled his backpack from beneath the console.

A lot could have been different if he had pulled this out before, Drew thought to himself as he unzipped the bag. In the front center pocket was his service weapon. He released the clip on the Glock 17 checked the chamber and reassembled the 9mm automatic. Drew reached behind him to place it in the small of his back but thought better of it and slipped it back into his backpack. Drew checked below but he already knew that he hadn't brought along a uniform. What could possibly go wrong? Drew smiled, but quickly focused back on the task at hand.

"What am I going to do? Run up there and shout, "Hey! You are under arrest!" Drew thought, no uniform, wrong boat...probably a bad idea.

"I'm just out fishing, just another fisherman pulling up to his favorite fishing hole. I'll have to be careful not to let him see the NMF block letters on the stern but that's doable," Drew thought.

"Be careful," a soft, feminine voice said from the side.

Drew looked up to see Christi standing at the rail, watching.

"Be back in just a few minutes. Throw that bowline for me, would you?"

Drew started the motor and released the stern line. Christi threw the bowline on the foredeck and he pulled away from the *Reel Fun,* intentionally using the large fishing boat to visually block his departure.

Idling away, Drew set the camera up in the towel on the console like he had successfully done previously. The Glock was positioned next to it and easily accessible. He checked the gear, set a fishing rod up in the stern and one leaning against the passenger seat. He just needed the look as he approached. After that, it was completely seat-of-the-pants.

Drew looked back once more and Christi waved. *Reel Fun* was far enough away that he would wonder where the boat came from but it wouldn't be immediately obvious. Drew pushed the throttle and jumped up on plane while turning to pass several hundred feet astern of the *Reel Fun*.

"Here we go," Drew said, as he raced behind *Reel Fun* and turned upwind toward the stern of the white boat.

Dropping off plane, he slowed and fiddled with the depth sounder as though he needed to adjust for the current site. Drew reached beneath the towel and pressed the record button on the camera, then checked to see that it was pointed forward. He needed it pointed just a little off to starboard at about where he intended to pull alongside.

When Drew looked up, there was a dead dolphin floating belly up on the surface. He had to steer hard to port to miss the carcass. He couldn't see the head at all, just the gray-white belly and pectorals. Drew made no effort to pay any further attention but he was certain that the port turn had put the dead mammal in view of the camera.

Drew approached from the rear and watched the fisherman put his rod down and go forward. Drew pulled back on the throttle and fiddled with the depth sounder a bit more at a slow speed. There was a boat name but he still couldn't read it. Pulling up, Drew fiddled with the depth sounder a bit more then looked up to read "*The Brink*" on the stern of the aging white Proline.

Drew had seen that boat. Who was it? Had he stopped the boat before? Fishing out here by himself... Where did he go? Drew knew he had best pay attention. It wouldn't be the first time an angler pulled a weapon on someone they thought was stealing the numbers of their fishing hole.

There he is. He's pulling the anchor.

Drew was just to his starboard and astern about twenty feet when he yelled, "Hey, you packing it up?"

The man didn't say anything as he bent over to cleat the anchor.

Drew asked again pulling alongside but still fifteen feet to one side. "You leaving? This is one of my good spots, ya' catch any?"

He nodded and made his way back to the cockpit area.

Drew knew that he'd seen this guy before. He pulled back to idle and looked at the depth sounder and allowed the boat to get a bit closer. Drew feigned a surprised look when he shouted, "Hey!"

For a big gulf, Drew was definitely crowding his space. He added some turns to the throttles to pull back upwind. This time the boats were no more than twelve or thirteen feet apart.

"I've been looking forward to fishing here but you were here first so I'll back off if you intend to keep at it," Drew shouted.

"No, I've had enough. It's all yours. Caught a few snapper but they were all too small and I threw them back."

Drew knew the voice. In the hat and sunglasses, he didn't recognize him but the voice was Dr. Tom Bentley, the biologist and leader of "Protect and Preserve." He was the guy that the reporter had cornered during the press conference.

"Man, did you see that big dead dolphin back there? Bet he won't be eating any by-catch anymore!" Drew said with North Florida conviction and local accent.

"Can't say I noticed. I've had a lot of them around here this morning."

Drew pulled back up alongside, this time even closer but slightly astern so that *The Brink* would be in view of the camera. The boat was drifting away from the wreck and he was getting the gear ready before he got underway and otherwise ignoring Drew.

"Think we'd be a lot better off if we just kept everything that came aboard regardless of the size," Drew said. "Least that way they wouldn't be hanging around waiting for throwbacks."

"Not sure what the answer is," he offered, but not willing to engage. Drew was beginning to wonder if he was suspicious, or maybe he recognized him.

"Dr. Bentley!" Drew yelled abruptly, and he looked up.

"Say what?"

"It's Dr. Bentley, right?"

"Sorry, must have me confused with somebody else." He stopped putting stuff away and moved to his console.

"Well, sir. I need to talk with you about that. I'm Drew Phillips, Florida Wildlife Conservation Commission."

He looked back when Drew said that.

"So what do you need? I'm about to head home."

"I think we need to talk for just a minute."

He walked to the stern, opened a hatch there and leaned on it looking at Drew like he was now paying attention.

"I just observed you throw an explosive over the side and it appears that resulted in the death of a dolphin. I think you and I need to discuss that before my associates arrive."

"Nothing to discuss," he said. "Don't know what you're talking about."

Drew knew it was time to play his hand.

"Dr. Bentley, I think you do. I think you intentionally threw an explosive overboard to kill that dolphin. Now I have no idea how that furthers the cause of Protect and Preserve, but it is a violation of federal law and it is something you'll need to discuss with a judge."

"...Furthers my cause! How dare you. You have no idea!" He was instantly furious. "These fishermen are indiscriminately overfishing every species here. The catch is unsustainable. My cause is the survival of the species and the ocean itself!"

He walked forward and started the outboard then returned to the stern hatch.

"Dr. Bentley, it's my job to catch the fishermen that keep unlawful fish."

"It's not enough! Not enough to catch thousands of pounds then to say that we're saving the smaller fish when dolphins eat them before they can get back to the reef!"

Without stopping the conversation, Drew maneuvered the boat where Dr Bentley would be looking into the camera. He placed the starboard side of the Marine Fisheries boat gently against the Proline where he could maintain the position without a threatening appearance.

"Sir, you'll have to present that to the judge. I'm just here to enforce existing laws."

"Even if you enforced the law to the letter, we're still depleting the stocks at a rate that can't be sustained. We did it to the cod, we did it to the shark, and to the redfish. We have a track record. One that clearly proves that you can't manage it!

His finger was pointing at Drew. He was not the professorial character with a bit of a high-brow edge; he was angry. He was quickly leaving the rational and moving to unreasonable. "The only way to MANAGE it is to STOP it. Stop it before it's too late!"

"Well, sir, I disagree, but then it's just my opinion. Why don't you discuss it with my friend Dr. Haymer at the National Marine Fisheries? He thinks there is another way."

"Haymer's a fool. We have discussed it. There is no other way. It has to be stopped!"

"But stop it completely? Wouldn't that start an economic war with the fishermen?"

"It already has," he said, without reservation and some arrogance.

Drew thought about it for a minute. This was the war. Dead dolphin. Charter fishermen blamed. Dead dolphin photos, indiscriminate explosives. It would be a public relations nightmare for the charter fishing industry.

He closed the stern hatch and Drew could see that he was holding what appeared to be a short stick of dynamite. It was about four inches long and the fuse that hung from one end was rapidly disappearing in a short trail of smoke, disbursed quickly by the wind. Dr. Bentley's eyes met Drew's and Drew could sense what he was about to do. Drew reached for for his backpack and stuffed the video camera inside as he slung it over his shoulder. Mentally, his intuitive alarms were sounding. Drew could see intent. He's not going to toss it overboard. It was there in his face.

Killing dolphin was a big jump for a man like this. A leap he took for a cause. The next step would not be nearly as big a jump.

Tom Bentley did not glance to the side or look at the fuse. He simply held it. The fuse shortened; then he looked casually back at Drew and tossed it into the bow of the NMF Boston Whaler.

Drew watched it bounce off the front platform and land on the forward hatch, still rolling. Drew spun off the console side rail and in two giant steps he was in the bow. He could see the explosive was nearly an inch and a half in diameter. If not for that, he would have thought it was an oversized firecracker, but the sound of it as it bumped against the ice chest gave it heft and bulk. As the driverless boat rolled to starboard, the small stick with a smoking tail rolled back across the deck and stopped against the starboard bulkhead. In less than a second, Drew determined that there were only moments before the fuse would be gone.

With little time to consider options, Drew stepped forward and then lunged off the gunwale in a desperate leap toward *The Brink* just as Dr. Bentley pressed the throttles forward. With the boat accelerating, he missed the stern deck and landed badly on the transom holding onto the stern rail. The explosion was a deafening blast behind him and Drew glanced back to see a gaping hole as pieces of fiberglass and foam splayed across the water.

One foot was still in the water dragging behind the accelerating boat but Drew had death grip on the rail. He pulled forward to get an elbow over the edge and from there vaulted over the stern where he tumbled headfirst into the boat.

###

Both Christi and Captain Wayne heard the blast. Since it wasn't muffled at all by water, even the charter patrons exited the air-conditioned salon to see what was going on. Toby was awake and leaning against the bulkhead when the door flew open and the patrons emerged. The door slammed into the right side of Toby's head where he was leaning back to slow the bleeding. Toby let out a curse that would normally have been followed by a string of oaths. This time he simply leaned his head forward and held it with his free hand and moaned.

Christi yelled, "Captain Wayne, he jumped!"

Wayne was at the top of the ladder climbing back to the fly bridge. His head whipped to starboard in time to see Drew hanging from the stern rail with one foot still dragging in the water as the white boat rapidly accelerated.

"Can you pull over to the Outrage and let me get aboard? I can follow them. That Boston Whaler won't sink," Christi yelled.

Captain Wayne stepped to the console and gunned both diesels. The *Reel Fun* isn't a fast boat but goosing both throttles was enough to throw all three fishermen into the transom. Captain Wayne looked down and smiled just a little as they cussed and untangled limbs from where they all landed in a heap. He winked at Toby.

"Listen," Captain Wayne yelled down to Christi, "I'll come alongside but the boat is going to move away as I get close. Use the boat hook or you'll have to jump for it."

Christi stood on the gunwale as Captain Wayne maneuvered alongside the Boston Whaler, now moving sideways with the wind and rocking side to side in the waves and boat wake.

"I'm going to jump for it," Christi yelled, and readied herself.

When the Outrage made its first movement away from the *Reel Fun*, Christi took two steps down the gunwale. She timed her leap to catch the boat before it rocked the opposite way, but her foot slipped on some fish slime. Her foot went down the side of the *Reel Fun* and sapped the energy from her jump. Her shin hit the starboard side gunwale and she went feet first into the water, her head barely missing the stern.

Captain Wayne immediately reversed the throttles and backed away so not to trap her between the boats. Christi surfaced, sputtering but otherwise unhurt. The Boston Whaler was now twenty feet away, but the wind was blowing it away from her. She was a good swimmer but knew she needed to get to the boat quickly or wait and let Wayne turn around and pick her up. Her shin hurt but she turned and started swimming toward the Boston Whaler.

Looking back, Dr. Bentley was surprised to see that Drew landed aboard. As Drew found his feet and stood, Bentley turned hard to port and Drew fell against the port side. He pushed hard against the port gunwale. He didn't have the luxury of thinking this through. He had to stop the boat.

Approaching full speed and blasting off each wave that thundered hard against the keel, Bentley turned the boat hard to starboard. When the boat crossed the plane that would be level, Drew launched off the port rail and the transom. Whether subliminal timing or fortuitous luck, his right arm caught Bentley's midriff and Drew grabbed him like a linebacker. His left elbow jabbed hard and caught Drew in the ear but Bentley held tight to the steering wheel. A bit stunned by the hit, Drew slipped down along Bentley's knees but managed to hold on. Bentley's left foot landed a glancing blow to Drew's rib cage but now Drew had him by the foot while landing flat on the deck.

With a twist, Drew found purchase on the starboard bulkhead with both feet. He pushed both legs straight and pulled Bentley's feet out from under him. His face hit the steering wheel but he hung on and the boat turned further to starboard as Bentley pulled on it for balance.

The momentum shift of a powerful boat is centripetal, but at this speed, it is also centrifugal. It's the force that keeps a racecar on a banked track thanks to speed and the momentum, while the centripetal force acts to continue the vehicle on the axis of its turn. On the water, it can take your legs out from under you but it's a power that can be harnessed by time spent on the water. Time in a boat-- that was Drew's advantage. He had to make use of that advantage and immediately.

Bentley fell away from Drew by the centripetal force of the turn. When Drew let go of his feet the momentum of his body weight slammed him back to starboard beneath the steering wheel.

Standing with one leg pressed against the starboard bulkhead, Drew used his arm to chop Bentley's forearms until he released the steering wheel. With his weight no longer holding the wheel into a permanent turn, Drew grabbed the wheel to level the craft.

Beneath Drew, Bentley pushed off the forward bulkhead lunging aft, then crawled to the stern.

With the boat level, Drew glanced aft to see him standing up. Forewarned by that blessed sensation, Drew turned around and sheer instinct provided the necessary motion to duck just as he stepped forward. The stainless steel hook of a gaff swished just over Drew's head.

Dr. Bentley stood amidships with the gaff behind his head like a baseball bat. The hook could pierce soft tissue and rip out organs in a well-timed swipe.

"Tom, stop this," Drew yelled.

He looked at Drew and there was more than rage. His face was flush, his forehead bleeding from his fall against the steering wheel. His eyes squinting in the bright sunlight betrayed his intent.

This was his war. Drew was the enemy.

Perhaps in a previous decade or some encounter with a wild animal Tom Bentley had stepped beyond the smooth demeanor of a biology professor and gentleman activist. Maybe a bad marriage or an unbridled temper, or something after years of corrosive missteps finally let go and allowed the man to step beyond his ability to be rational and to assume that barbaric mindset from which all humans evolved. Perhaps there were other forces involved that Drew would never know. Dr. Bentley had gone there. There was no one left to speak with rationally. There was only Bentley and his enemy. He intended that there would soon be one less impediment, one fewer in the ranks of those that opposed what he felt so fervently was right.

He swung again, lower this time, but Drew sucked in and pulled back to avoid the blow, but that placed him against the corner. With his back to the steering wheel, there was nowhere to go.

Bentley saw the opportunity and moved quickly to take one step forward. When Drew raised his right arm to deflect another attack, his left hand found the steering wheel.

Drew pulled up hard on the wheel as the gaff came from behind Bentley's head. The boat lurched to port and Bentley no longer had control of forward motion. Those forces were again Drew's advantage. The boat turned in a tight circle then he reversed its course. The gaff flew wildly and Dr. Bentley fell back and over the port gunwale into the water.

Chapter 27

Drew turned quickly to grab the steering wheel and level out. As he pulled the throttle back, he looked up to see Christi slip off the gunwale of the *Reel Fun* and land in the water too, just a hundred yards away. Between her and Drew was the carcass of the dolphin Bentley had killed. Sharks were moving toward the fresh kill. Drew could see several fins and Captain Wayne could see them as well, but Christi couldn't.

Drew looked back where Tom Bentley was thrashing on the surface. He knew what he had fallen into. It was where he intended to leave Drew. He would have left Drew there bleeding.

Just past Bentley, Drew saw where Christi had surfaced and was swimming toward the Boston Whaler. The sharks would not be discriminating. Once the frenzy began, both Christi and Dr. Bentley were in danger of becoming part of the menu.

Drew brought the throttle to dead slow. He could see that Captain Wayne was backing away to keep Christi out of the props. Behind Drew, the sharks had begun dismantling the dolphin. They had followed the trail of dolphin blood. They were starting to feed in the frenzied and brutal manner that is their nature. Swimming in tight circles and ripping off chunks with teeth designed specifically for that purpose. Drew saw a spectacle of teeth and fin, blood and tissue in a splash zone of thrashing intensity. The frenzy had begun.

Drew was Bentley's only chance.

Drew turned the wheel and pressed the throttle hard to whip the bow around and head back to where Bentley was treading water and looking frantically to either side. Just as Drew backed off to keep from running over him, Bentley went under. It was as though he knew it was coming.

Bentley resurfaced in moments just yards from the boat. Drew threw a life ring and he grabbed and held on with no effort to pull himself to the boat. With the engine at idle, Drew leaned hard into the gunwale and pulled him alongside.

"Can you reach my hand?" Drew asked.

He slowly lifted his hand up but there was no grip. He looked at Drew with a blank stare. No longer the enemy. The stare was resignation. Drew grabbed under his arm and lifted him onto the gunwale. He was too heavy to lift any further but he couldn't let him go back in. Half-in and bent over the gunwale, Drew grabbed both pockets of his shorts and pulled him into the boat.

There was blood everywhere.

Bentley crumpled and red blood flowed all over the deck. Now sprawled on the deck, Drew could see that a huge chunk of his leg was missing just below the groin. The shark had ripped away a section of the muscle and severed the femoral artery. What blood remained flowed onto the deck, thin and wispy where it mixed with saltwater.

Grabbing a towel, Drew pressed against the wound and looked to his face. The calm had returned. The barbarian was gone and the professor was back. There was nothing to be done. He had lost too much blood. He knew it. The fight was over.

"You knew the stakes would be high," Drew said.

His resigned look now included remorse. All that he had tried to do. Protect and Preserve. A noble cause, the intended outcome disappearing. As a biologist, his last thoughts would be of the irony. The sharks and the seagulls were against him.

WHUMP!

Someone had again thrown an explosive. Drew looked back toward the *Reel Fun.*

Christi!

Drew pushed away from Dr. Bentley and jumped to his feet. At the console, he slammed the throttles forward and spun the wheel to port. Tom Bentley slid to the stern and closed his eyes.

Christi was still in the water but had nearly made it to the Whaler where the bow of the *Reel Fun* was holding it into the sea. Captain Wayne lit another M-80 with his cigarette and threw it.

Drew watched incredulously at what appeared to be a cruel joke. The adrenaline that had kept him sharp for the fight with Bentley was changing and welling up as anger.

The M-80 landed about fifteen feet behind Christi. In just seconds, it exploded below the surface. Drew could see the surface erupt but the sound was muffled over the sound of the outboard running nearly at full speed.

Christi reached the boat just as a third explosive detonated, this one off to her side. Drew sped past the rapidly dwindling remains of the dolphin and focused on the side of the Boston Whaler where it met the bow of the *Reel Fun*. At full speed, Drew could put some distance between the two hulls quickly but that sudden impact would send him flying over the console.

Drew watched Christi pull herself up the gunwale in a single motion as yet another M-80 exploded twenty feet behind her.

Drew reached into his backpack to find his service weapon. He held the grip leaving the pistol inside the bag and slowly pulled the throttle back.

Captain Wayne held another four or five M-80s in his hand leaning against the fly bridge rail and smoking his cigarette.

The words were forming in anger when Drew looked at Christi who looked tired but didn't appear the least bit upset.

"Did you see that?" she asked. "I had sharks swimming all around, it was wild!"

Her look was sheer exhilaration. It was a look of wonder.

"Awesome!" she exclaimed. "I opened my eyes and could see ten, maybe fifteen sharks. There was at least one big hammerhead and several blacktips! Didn't we bring a mask and snorkel?"

Drew released the pistol grip and looked up at Captain Wayne while pulling his hand out of the bag. He shrugged and took the cigarette out of his mouth.

"I tossed these at the big'uns before they got too close," Captain Wayne said, holding out a couple M-80s still rigged with lead like Toby had used. Enough heft to toss them easily and enough weight to drop them eight to twelve feet below the surface before they exploded. Christi was lying on a towel and leaning over the hole blown in the starboard bow to see if she could spot more.

"There's a bull shark! Ooooo, a big one too! Drew, isn't there a mask in that gear Dr. Haymer loaded aboard?"

"So what about the dolphin killer there?" Captain Wayne asked.

It's a trait of all boat captains. No beating around the bush, no sensitive inquiry, plainly spoken with the emotional deference one might offer the widow of a suicide bomber.

"He didn't make it," Drew said looking back. "Shark cut his femoral just before I got to him. He bled out just after I got him aboard."

One of the fishermen aboard *Reel Fun* threw open the salon door and ran to the port side with his hand over his mouth and a look of nausea. His eyes opened wide and both cheeks filled. He leaned over the rail and proceeded to empty his guts. Captain Wayne looked down, took another draw on his cigarette, and a second member of the party staggered slowly along the gunwale holding onto the rail. He had the look of too many beers in conjunction with the slowly building seas. He looked to be in control and headed to the transom until he had to go around his buddy. Letting go of the rail, he leaned to starboard, then fell over his fishing partner and puked all over his back. The third fisherman appeared on deck with a fresh cold beer, laughing at his two buddies and ribbing them for their seamanship. He bypassed the other two, walking directly to the transom and looked over to see shark fins swimming among the rapidly dispersing chunks that his buddies had deposited over the side.

Looking up at Wayne, he asked, "Are those...?"

"Sharks, yep. Lots of them. They live here."

He looked over into the boat Drew was in. He saw the blood, looked at Drew, then looked aft to see Dr. Bentley.

"Is that...?" he pointed, looking up at Wayne taking a sip of beer.

"Yep, shark got him."

He looked back to the Whaler, his eyes got big and his cheeks filled. His head bobbed just a little just before the beer can hit the deck. He didn't make the rail, didn't try. His stomach contents departed in a stream that splattered over both his buddies.

Toby was up. He didn't look too good and held an icy cold, bloody rag over his nose. He turned on the water, lifted a spray nozzle, and then proceeded to spray off the deck and all three fishermen from a safe distance of about six feet. The fishermen raised their arms to fend off the water assault, but neither moved from their self-assigned position.

Captain Wayne looked over at Drew. "Guess it's time to go."

"Yeah, I need to call in and get the office working on having someone meet us at the dock."

"Drew! Come look at this Dusky! He must be twelve feet long. Just look at those teeth!"

Drew looked at Christi, kneeling at the bow rail of the Boston Whaler, her head under the rail and her face just a foot above the water as a dark gray dorsal fin swam slowly past.

Chapter 28

Toby was nearly finished cleaning the boat by the time Drew and Christi arrived at the dock. The fishermen had left, and it hadn't improved Captain Wayne's attitude that they refused to pay any more than the 60% deposit they used to reserve the trip.

A Wildlife Commission officer was standing by. Drew saw the truck in the parking lot. Mack had insisted that someone be there to take statements. He said he would call the office or we could tell it to the sheriff, Drew's choice. Mack planned to be there after closing up the office. No one had mentioned the damaged side of the boat. Drew decided that was a story that would be better told in person.

Drew secured both boats, *The Brink* and the *Squirt*, along the dock in an easy to find but out of the way location. The fish-gawking tourists were to be avoided at this point.

Toby walked to the ambulance and sat down. It didn't appear that he would be going to the hospital but Captain Wayne would not be talked out of having somebody check him for a concussion. After what happened on the boat today, Drew suspected he was hoping they would find something.

The Wildlife Officer walked over and Drew introduced Christi to Javier Rodriquez.

"Encantata, Christi," Javier said. He had a genuine smile and was not ragging Drew like usual. Drew thought that there was a remote chance that he could be a sensitive soul.

"I have video footage that we will want to review. I'll bring it in tomorrow," Drew said.

"It's probably best if I get it now, amigo. You know the captain will want to look it over before anything gets to the press."

"You're right," Drew replied, after he thought about it for a second. "Be right back," and Drew stepped back aboard *The Brink,* to retrieve his pack.

"So Christi," Drew heard as he climbed aboard, "how is it you came to know my somewhat secretive partner, Drew?"

Christi looked at Drew and he knew she was watching.

"I'm the sister of a girl he knew in college. I'm here working with NMF for the summer," she replied, so that Drew could hear her.

While he was aboard, a deputy sheriff and the coroner arrived. With the arrogant, somewhat indifferent manner of a man too accustomed to death, the coroner stepped aboard *The Brink.* He nodded, then stepped to the rear and lifted the towels Drew had used to cover Dr. Bentley.

Jason McBride took off his sunglasses and reached his hand out as a greeting and to help Drew step back onto the dock.

"Tough day," he said.

Jason was still being the 'tough guy,' but he said it with empathy.

"Guess there aren't too many things you can say when you're following up the coroner," Drew said.

"Is she okay?" Jason asked, with a nod toward Christi.

Drew looked him in the eye and said, "She'll be fine."

He nodded. He didn't move but glanced over at Christi. Drew could feel her eyes staring at his back. Once again, without words, there were volumes unspoken.

Jason must have heard an unspoken book, maybe two. He looked back at Drew and nodded. He turned to face the stern of *The Brink* where the coroner was recording verbal notes into his phone.

While they worked, Christi and Drew provided statements to Javier.

"The method he used is consistent with what Christi identified in the death of the dolphin we found last week. The methodology fits. He was using an explosive designed for underwater seismic exploration so he simply attached it or inserted it directly in the fish and lit the fuse before throwing it overboard. It also explains how some of the dolphin victims received much worse injuries depending on how much of the fish had been ingested," Drew explained.

Christi provided some details on the findings that she and Mack had reported. The explosive was consistent with what they found during the necropsy of the beached dolphin. She told him that the office had a copy of the report and the commission was welcome to use it in any way required by law enforcement or the courts, but it was not suitable for public release.

Javier explained that he didn't intend to arrest Captain Wayne. Javier was to assemble material over the next few days. In the meantime, Wayne needed to prepare a statement. As captain of the vessel, he was personally responsible for the actions of his deckhand. However, Toby may have separate charges depending on whether assault charges were filed.

Christi looked down as the topic was discussed. This was the first time she had thought about the fact that she had been forcibly abducted. That event seemed so out of context and removed from what had occurred since then. Javier left to advise Captain Wayne as Christi stepped away. She was mentally dealing with all that transpired this afternoon. Drew didn't need to be a factor, but chose to remain close. She sat on the dock, dangling her legs over the edge.

When Jason McBride looked over and nodded, Drew walked to him to discuss the altercation with Dr. Bentley. Javier joined the two of them so that he could hear the events at the same time. Both would have to submit a report.

"Where do you think he got the explosive?" Jason asked.

"I think we need to have a talk with Chuck Whear," Drew answered. "He tells me that he was paid to pick up a crate in New Orleans along the river and drive it back. It's only circumstantial but this sort of explosive is used in the offshore oil business."

When Drew had finished, Jason walked back to the coroner scribbling in his notebook, leaving Javier and Drew standing on the dock. Javier looked up and told Drew that the captain had received the package.

"What package?" Drew asked.

"You know, amigo, the package that the captain asked for."

"No, I don't know, Javier, …what package?"

"It's the package from the television station. Oh, let me tell you, he was hot when he saw it was from the media."

"So what was in the package?" Drew asked patiently.

"I'm told that it was just what he needed. Lt. Bannacer will be moving on after his brief probation period."

"…. and he got that from me?"

"Oh yeah. He was most impressed that you were able to keep the information outside the office. While he was surprised that it came from the media, I explained to him that you and Rachel have some 'history' and that seemed to smooth it over. You know the captain; he can be quite a difficult man when he thinks someone has overstepped his bounds. I made it very clear that using an outside source was all part of your plan not to have it affect office morale."

"So can you tell me about this package?"

"Oh yeah, I can tell you the captain was impressed. He was very impressed. He told me to tell you that he had all that was required and that he appreciated your prompt follow-up."

"The captain said that?"

"Well, ...yes, something like that," Javier replied. "I was telling him that we work together on these sensitive things, so I knew that the Bannacer thing was something you were working.

"You told the captain that?"

"Of course I did, compadre. I was afraid you would get in further trouble if I did not ...er....cubre tu culo."

"You?.. cover my ass? So tell me, who delivered the package?"

"It came from Rachel, of course. I did not see the contents, amigo, but I'm told that it included details of a boat cleaning business he supposedly operated as a side business in Pensacola. Evidently his oil spill claim was somewhat unscrupulous. The captain was quite happy that it had come from an outside source you know, things get so messy when incriminating data comes from a fellow officer. By the way, you must have learned some appalling things about this man. The captain, he was ...he was not happy about what you had learned. I do not know how you do these things."

Drew smacked Javier on the shoulder and laughed, walking back to where he had left Christi on the dock.

"How is that you do these things and I do not know? Am I not your partner, amigo?"

Drew kept walking and laughing. Interesting that he should hear of his exploits from a partner. Equally surprising was the source. Whatever Bannacer said that night at Schooners must have really pissed her off. Been there before, Drew thought to himself, still laughing.

Javier moved back to where Captain Wayne and Toby were working with the ambulance team. Mack arrived at about the same time, and Drew waited as he walked up.

"So what do you think happened out there, Drew?" Mack asked openly.

"In my opinion," Drew offered, "Dr. Bentley was using the method to place culpability on the charter boat industry. He was aware of the tactics that the fishermen were using to scare the dolphin away from the catch. He simply decided that the public would be easily directed to his cause if dolphin started dying. It may have happened that way eventually because of the increasing tension between the fishermen and the protectionists --and the law. He just decided to push up the timetable… and the stakes."

Drew looked up at Mack to finish the thought, "He went all in."

Mack stayed with the deputy sheriff. Dr. Bentley was a comrade in academia. Even if they weren't friends, he owed it to him to be there. It would be up to the sheriff's office to determine how far to pursue the issue. Not much of a criminal case to be made against a dead man accused of a hideous felony.

Chapter 29

With Christi still contemplative, Drew picked a convenient dock box and sat nearby. Looking back, he saw Toby join Captain Wayne and Javier as the ambulance pulled away slowly. Toby's face was white with all the gauze and tape. It looked as if they had taped a new nose in place where the old one used to be. The summer heat was palpable, as the afternoon rays of sun broke free of the cumulus clouds now drifting out over the gulf. Shafts of orange and gold light vectored across the horizon in wheeled directions.

Gulls and pelicans argued over a school of menhaden trapped against the seawall. Drew had watched as the school had been effectively maneuvered against the rock hard wall by a persistent unseen predator. Luck or learned response, the process played one predator against another until the prey had been properly placed. The pelicans don't say much whereas the gulls argue incessantly. A lone pelican stuck his head below the surface and caught dinner; there was a shrinking supply of food and the gulls just don't get it. A moment later, the menhaden jumped clear of the water to avoid another predator, probably a trout or a redfish. Perhaps it was the unseen predator; there are a lot more bad guys down there if you are on the menu.

Watching the predator and the prey, Drew mentally outlined parallels based on perspective. The rules of this engagement were much clearer, particularly to the menhaden. On the bridge above them all stood a lone man with a cast net poised to toss at any time. To the right was a squadron of pelicans in wait. In the water or from above, the growing list of predators would slowly reduce the school until it simply disbursed or the predators were satisfied. The gulls seemed to be content in arguing about it.

After several minutes, Christi noticed that Drew was nearby and joined him leaning against the dock box.

"You want to press charges? I'll get Jason."

"Don't want to press charges," she said.

"You sure?" Drew asked, turning to look at her face.

"Yeah. He's the one that's hurt, not me."

"You could have been. He stepped over the line; Toby can be held accountable…."

"He already is. It's his world that's changing. You showed me that."

Drew looked at her with an understanding eye. "Sometimes the line between predator and prey is not so black and white as it is gray." He meant it to be insightful but it came over a bit trite and he knew it.

Christi looked up, "I'm not a predator; in fact, I'm absolutely certain that I'm right and unbiased, but my being right doesn't make his life any less changed."

Drew thought about her comment for a moment. Perceptive, that's an attractive attribute …so is forgiveness.

"It's humbling to recognize that the work you do profoundly affects others," Mack said from behind Drew. "It's some of that same salty bitter medicine. Guess it's good that it gets spread around, because nobody seems to like it."

"Dr. Bentley wasn't a friend in as much as he was a colleague," Mack continued. "He was certainly passionate about his cause."

"Passionate to a fault," Drew added.

"Yeah, he was. On the other hand, he wasn't wrong about the end game. He was wrong in his methods-- but we will collapse the species."

Christi looked up interested. "New data? What's changed?"

Mack shook his head and looked down. "No. Nothing new...just history. Look what we did to the whales, to the cod, to the salmon, to the redfish-- there are seven billion people on this earth. That number hasn't stopped getting bigger. Do the math."

"You really think so?" Drew asked, "Has it already passed us?" It was quiet for just a moment after he asked the question.

"Couldn't do this job if I really thought so," Mack said, shaking his head. "What do you think it would have been like to have been a biologist for the Kansas Pacific Railroad while the train tracks moved west and Bill Cody was killing buffalo. The buffalo had roamed the plains for hundreds, maybe thousands of years. We practically wiped out the entire species in the nineteenth century to feed our progress to the west. They had to know." He looked down into the water and pursed his lips. "...they had to know."

Christi and Drew were silent while Mack took a moment to look out across the gulf toward the light fading in the west.

A voice in the parking lot behind Mack yelled, "So what next, Harry?"

A spike of anxiety, fear, and anger flashed up Drew's spine. He heard that voice like it was something out a distant past. It hung there like a bad dream but he couldn't connect it to recent memory. Drew felt a nauseous panic, the same as the click of an improvised explosive device or the smell of a burning fuse.

Chapter 30

Christi looked past Mack as he whipped around in the direction of the voice. They had both seen the look when Drew recognized the voice.

A man with a cane walking up the dock from *The Brink* dismissed the voice with a wave of his hand. He walked slowly toward the dock box, backed by the orange glow of twilight. Drew squinted in the light. The man was dressed in a suit but walked casually from the scene where the coroner and his team were removing the body of Dr. Bentley from the boat with the assistance of several deputies.

There was a loud explosion from across the lagoon and Drew dove behind the dock box. Before he hit the planks, brain patterns had connected the sound to the cannon at Schooners announcing the sunset. The cannon marks the daily celebration that occurs just as the sun disappears below the horizon. He felt foolish but recognized the rush of adrenalin and heightened awareness that he had experienced earlier that day. It was that sensitivity, that instinctive reaction, that odd premonition, that kept Drew and other soldiers alive as they patrolled the streets of Kandahar. He could feel that sensation coursing through his extremities when the man spoke.

"Good evening, Dr. Haymer," the man said.

Christi knelt beside Drew and put her hand on his shoulder.

Again, Drew recognized the voice. He pushed to stand but Christi leaned against his shoulder with both hands and he stayed down. They both turned to sit on the dock leaning against the dock box while Drew took several deep breaths.

"Mr. Gardey?" Mack said, as the man stepped out from behind the sunset, now a disappearing glow. "What brings you out this evening?"

"The loss of a dear friend, Dr. Haymer." Gardey said. "A dear friend, however tormented or confused he may have been. He was still a friend and distinguished colleague. Dr. Bentley was a man I've admired for years for his work and for his environmental passion."

Drew slowly stood back up with Christi holding one arm. He wasn't injured so much as embarrassed. He moved at a reserved speed, intentionally slow in trying to keep the adrenalin suppressed. He was keenly aware that this new knowledge kept that heightened sensitivity engaged. The connection to this man was still being assembled and a false impression or bad reaction could easily finish the prospect of learning any more. Besides, Drew knew that he had to maintain firm control or he might kill him.

"Officer Phillips," Gardey said with a nod in Drew's direction. He lifted his cane slightly and Drew saw that it was distinctive. Gardey noticed that his cane had captured Drew's attention.

"Ah, you see my unique accessory," Gardey said, lifting the cane as an object to behold. "I'm quite taken by its distinguished, and yet colloquial look."

"A gift from a client," Gardey continued. "A commercial fisherman appreciative of some money I was able to wrench from a negligent oil company. You see that it is made from a commercial fishing rod." Gardey held it up, then to the side like he was going to fish off the edge of the dock.

"It is an excellent conversation piece and serves me from time to time when the lumbago pains me. It's stout enough to be a fairly useful defensive tool as well," he said looking at Mack and holding it out like a foil, one hand raised behind him, knees bent, his foil slightly down and forward at the ready.

He set the end back on the dock and leaned forward with one arm pressing the weight of one side onto the cane.

"My condolences to your client, Mr. Gardey," Mack said. "But I'm afraid he stepped way out of bounds. He attempted to kill Mr. Phillips today so you won't find us terribly sympathetic."

"That is what I have heard," Gardey replied, and he looked over at Drew. "Do you anticipate the need for legal council Mr. Phillips? While I would be somewhat compromised, we have a competent legal staff and could find excellent representation. Here's my card."

Gardey leaned toward the dock box where Drew stood but he made no move to retrieve it. After an awkward moment, Christi stepped forward and took it from his hand.

"The same applies to you, miss...."

"Miller," Mack said. "She works with me."

"I see," Gardey replied to Mack, but glancing back as the brain impulses connected. He nodded in Christi's direction with a knowing smile and turned his attention back to Mack.

"Mr. Gardey, I understand you represent Protect and Preserve in addition to serving on its board of directors," Mack said.

"Why, yes, Dr. Haymer. I offer that service pro bono. As you must know, I've been associated with that organization for years."

"I have recently learned that the advisory board has some rather complicated and diverse interests as well," Mack stood up straight and crossed his arms, "some that may even seem somewhat counter intuitive."

Gardey assumed a defensive pose holding one hand out while the other leaned against the cane.

"Why, I'm sure I don't know what you mean, sir. Both the advisory board and the directors are intentionally selected to represent a broad sector of society. This makes us stronger and broadens our appeal."

"Even to special interests promoting the further expansion of oil drilling off the coast?" Mack countered. "That seems well outside the bounds of the organization's charter."

A dock light overhead switched on as the last red glow of sunset faded. Mack stepped forward into the light and stood facing Harold Gardey with his arms crossed. Gardey was easily eight inches taller than Mack and made an imposing figure in the light with his suit and cane. Mack did not seem to notice at all.

"As stated before, we intentionally look for opportunities to broaden our appeal, and I don't think I like the tone of your inquiry, Dr. Haymer."

"Tone is the least of your problems with my inquiry, Mr. Gardey."

Mack had just moved from defense to offense, but Gardey had not yet switched over. There was now a tension beneath the dock light that seemed to exclude everything around it. At this point, Drew stepped from behind the dock box and leaned against the side of it just behind Mack. Christi turned around and sat on the box next to him.

"Mr. Gardey," Mack said. "Can you tell me who would it serve, in such a notable organization and environmental guardian like Protect and Preserve, to maintain a distinguished list of oil interests in Alabama, Louisiana, and Texas on the advisory board?"

Gardey leaned against his cane without answering for a moment.

"Dr. Haymer, it appears you have been investigating my affairs. You know I consider those client relationships as valuable investments. I tend to consider investigations of that depth a challenge to my personal and professional wellbeing. I suspect the loss of a government grant or a funding snafu could refocus your attention to the marine fishery you are paid to evaluate. I am somewhat certain a lesson of that nature could be arranged."

So the first salvo had been fired. Gardey was countering Mack's offense with an offensive move of his own. Mack stepped forward again and was now face-to-face with Harold Gardey, invading what most southern gentlemen would consider their personal space.

"I believe my friend, Mr. Phillips, is already aware of your ability to convey a message. He was on the receiving end of one of your lessons in the college parking lot after the open forum several nights ago."

The affront caught Harold Gardey off guard but it was barely perceptible. He leaned into his cane staring into Mack's face with a stern, resolute, but confident look. Drew took a step forward. In Drew's face he saw a steely reserve pressed by an adrenalin rush that still coursed through every muscle. Drew's arms were not crossed; they hung on taut tendons with veins that were visible. A thin line of sweat coursed down each arm. His neck pulsed but his eyes focused steadily on Gardey's without blinking. Drew pulled back into a state that he had left in Kandahar. It was anger. It was disdain. It was violence held in abeyance only by a will that was determined to hear him out.

With a simple motion, Gardey adjusted the position of his cane and three figures appeared out of the dark behind him each carrying what appeared to be a baton and wearing a fisherman's buff that covered their faces.

Gardey's eyes moved back to Mack. His face and demeanor had not changed except that he had played the card that he previously held up his sleeve. His ante was in and his position was no longer inconspicuous. He was no longer threatened. The coroner had left. The sheriff deputies were not to be seen. The dock was strangely devoid of tourists or other passersby. Gardey spoke with a relaxed but serious voice.

"Dr. Haymer, I am a predator…."

"I've resolved that internally. I make money simply doing what I do well. I assemble the prey. Once they are assembled, feeding is a much simpler and natural process. In my experience, it is sometimes easier to first reduce the number of predators before the prey are assembled. It's not complicated. That way there is more for me. That's how I make money. It's never personal."

He was strangely matter of fact. Drew heard a car alarm beep three times to the left when a car door was locked. Gardey shifted his cane to the other hand and looked to the parking lot for a moment. Drew heard Christi stand and take a position nearby. Drew remained taut and ready, but motionless. The three men dressed in dark clothing behind Gardey stayed just on the edge of the dock light perimeter. Drew assessed each of them separately, the lower part of their faces covered with a fisherman's buff, pulled tightly from their neck up over their mouth and nose.

After the long silence Mack said, "It appears that you first remove the Department of Commerce. That takes out the fishermen. Next you take out the Department of Defense by eliminating testing and flight training. With those predators out of the way, there's only the Department of Interior… the devil you know. Since they control oil leases in all federal waters, I can only presume that there are, shall we say, …opportunities, to ensure that your interests are considered when it comes to leasable areas like the Destin Dome."

There was a palatable silence. Two resolute adversaries face-to-face in the sultry summer heat battling with accusation and countering with supposition and possibility.

"Very astute, Dr. Haymer! You have been doing your homework."

Harold Gardey blinked.

"So you know these aren't predators that can be removed without considerable resources," Gardey continued. "I needed a juggernaut. I needed a roundhouse punch. I needed something that could remove the really big fish from the water. The simplicity of our grassroots ocean guardian was my own invention. Dr. Bentley was a vain, ambitious man and it was easy to persuade him to participate. As I said before, it was his passion! His sort of drive and dedication to cause is hard to find. It has to be cultivated over years. It's always easier to buy a little additional passion when the cause is so just, ...so right. I simply fed the flame and afforded him opportunity. It is a shame. His belief was always there."

The stakes were on the table. The hands were played. Mack's gambit had smoked out a motive, a rationale, a definitive intent. He found something that connected the dots.

"I think its time I should leave," Gardey said, finishing. "I do apologize for dominating the conversation, Dr. Haymer. No doubt, you'll hear from the NOAA office later this week. Mr. Phillips, I suspect you will not want to find out how well these gentlemen follow orders when I'm not present to supervise."

Gardey turned and Drew grabbed Mack's arm to keep him from swinging. Gardey's men stepped back into the dark outside the dock light perimeter.

"Christi, get beside me," Drew said quietly as he stood facing the darkness next to Mack.

Gardey continued down the pier then turned at the edge of the next dock light. Drew, Christi and Mack stood fully in the light, just one dock light away, and awaited the onslaught of three dark dressed men carrying sawed off fiberglass weapons, and who knows what else. There was no need for a lesson anymore. Gardey had no reason to hold back.

Chapter 31

The docks were strangely quiet. Drew heard a mullet leap from the water followed by a long silence then the familiar slap as it hit the water after a brief moment outside its normal boundaries. He could feel the darkness creep in and again he felt that sensation, that premonition of something about to happen.

Christi looked up toward the sound of tires screeching into a fast turn in the parking lot and could see the headlights racing toward the docks. Each of the three men dressed in dark clothing with partially covered faces slowly stepped back into the lighted circle. Drew stood at the ready with nothing but fists and determination with Mack and Christi in formation behind him. Christi moved up, Mack followed closing ranks; pressing against each other, like a school of bait pressed to the point where the only option was to turn and fight. Each man slowly emerged from the dark, each holding a baton with hands above their heads, and followed by a uniformed sheriff officer who held a gun to their backs. Deputy Jason McBride stepped into the light.

"Everybody okay?" he asked.

Drew felt the adrenalin flow out through his feet. His palms were sweaty and there was a rush of tension release that left him a bit lightheaded. He turned and Christi's hands were placed one on the other in front of her waist and her eyes were closed as she stood on one leg, the other at a 90-degree angle and her foot at her knee. Then in a slow, deliberate maneuver both hands reached above her head then came together in front of her chest in a prayerful position, eyes closed and feet together. She had been prepared to fight and now released that tension with a practiced breathing technique that exemplified years of training.

Jason stepped up to where Mack and Drew stood, just as the Channel 7 news van screeched to a stop with its headlights only yards from Harold Gardey. Both doors bolted open and the cameraman spilled into the parking lot with lights on and camera rolling. Rachel grabbed a brush from the front seat, took one swipe, then stepped into the light next to Harold Gardey.

Jason said, "I saw him walking down here while the coroner was finishing up. Mack had called me ahead of time, so we kind of knew to expect something."

Drew looked at Mack and he smiled back raising one hand. You're just full of surprises tonight," Drew said.

"What about Gardey?" Mack asked.

"I heard it all. Not much to charge him with, unfortunately. We could arrest him but he would be out tomorrow before noon. On the other hand, we will all probably enjoy the 10 o'clock news...."

Jason turned and looked toward the bright camera lights with even more of the surroundings lighted by the van's high beams.

Drew could not hear the conversation but Rachel held the microphone close and Harold Gardey appeared to back away slightly. The cameraman's lights beamed into the dark and Mr. Gardey wiped his brow with the sleeve of his suit.

"It appears he's getting all of Rachel's vicious attention tonight," Drew said.

Mack smiled and said, "I called her too," and he pulled his cell phone out of his pocket and pressed the end call button. She and her crew had been parked across the street and heard it all as well.

Drew's laugh was only partly tension relief. Mack's smug, self-satisfied look was priceless. Harold Gardey sweating in the bright lights under a relentless investigative reporter was nearly as good. Gardey knew better than to back away from a chance to trade rhetorical barbs and quips with the local news media. They could destroy all he had started with less than innuendo.

"I also sent her a media release ...in advance."

Mack looked back at Drew with a knowing smile, "You know, there's more to Rachel than meets the eye."

Drew looked at Mack with a quizzical look. "So where's that coming from?" he asked.

Mack shrugged and looked back at Rachel who was working the issue.

"I'm just saying...." Mack replied.

Drew thanked Jason as the other officers moved the three cuffed men toward squad cars.

Jason held one individual by the black and gray buff that still covered his face. He intentionally pulled back and held his head while pressing forward.

"Don't you want to say it again?" Jason asked.

"So what next, Deputy?" the man asked.

Drew recognized the voice, but it was only partly connected. It was not just the vocal utterance, it was the sentence construct. Drew knew that voice but he couldn't make it out clearly until he closed his eyes.

"Say it again. This time, say it soft and slow, and call me Harry" Jason said.

"So what next, Harry?"

Drew heard "So what next" again with his eyes closed and he could see him grabbing the dolphin fin with a boat hook. The lieutenant's face was clear. Drew knew that voice, and opened his eyes.

"Bannacer!" Drew said.

Deputy McBride stood with his charge in cuffs and smiled. He pulled down on his buff exposing more of his face in the dock light, then pushed him toward the waiting squad car.

Drew pictured Javier with his 'career crash and burn' finger play. Bannacer had done the one thing law enforcement can't afford to do. He took sides. The metaphorical rocket spun out and returned to earth, crashing unseen in a brief, intense fireball.

In the next car, Drew saw Chuck Whear's face looking at him. The buff was around his neck and his hands were cuffed in front of him. His face was no longer defiant; it was resigned. Now that it had come to this, it was no longer about finances or family or fishing. This was about choices.

"Deputy, I suspect Chuck will help with your investigation," Drew said. "The kid may not deserve another break but his family could use one. Call me if you need to. I'll help."

McBride looked toward the car then back at Drew.

"I'll keep that in mind," Jason replied.

Turning to Mack, Drew watched Christi walk toward Deputy McBride, but he turned to avoid the encounter.

"Don't you want to see what happens?" Mack asked.

"No. I want to know what you found out about Rachel?"

Mack looked at Drew with a dimwit's eye.

"She's on the mound, two men on, no outs," Mack was doing the play-by-play using a nasal voice like AM radio as Christi spoke to Jason. "She winds up, the pitch, it's a curve ball…"

"Mack, let it go."

"She plays in the big leagues," Mack said looking back toward Drew.

"Christi?" Drew asked.

"No, Rachel," he said, "you always knew she was ambitious; she's undercover but I believe she moved up to the pros," and he turned and walked back down to where the NMF Boston Whaler was docked.

Drew turned around and could see Rachel still in the hot lights quizzing Harold Gardey leaving links and a trail of incomplete bread crumbs leading to local fishing leaders, oil spills, and fake ecology groups. There was none better at attacking credibility, exposing and breaching gaps in logic or timelines. She could dodge and weave like a prizefighter with a microphone. What better cover could there be than a face in the limelight, a household name that was dedicated to fleshing out a story and driving home a message? Drew wondered, CIA? FBI? …maybe EPA? Where would he start? The pieces fit. They slid into place like boats backed into a pier. Even when there were gaps, Drew knew something belonged there. In their past there were disappearances, phone calls, long assignments with poorly defined intentions, even mysterious other men. Drew had already learned not to argue with truths once they manifested themselves.

Drew felt a preeminent presence.

He wondered if maybe it was associated with understanding, but then, it was the same feeling he gets when something big is about to happen. He remembered that same feeling when he pulled the corporal into the wadi. It was that same perception that moved him out of the NMF Boston Whaler and made him jump for the stern of *The Brink*. It was that same premonition that ….

"Hey! Are you going to just stand there or what?"

The drama, the inquiry, the focus of the evening… Drew felt it move. The earth, the waters of the gulf, and the weight of the world shifted and he turned away from the camera lights.

"Do you think you could walk a lady back to her boat?"

Christi smiled and entered from the darkness to his left. Drew turned toward her and extended his elbow.

"Perhaps you would be so kind to allow me to escort you, M'Lady," Drew said with the best renaissance brogue he could produce.

Chapter 32

"So which one of you was going to tell me about what happened to *Squirt*?" Christi and Drew stammered over the er's and uh's.... Mack let it hang for a bit.

"I should have said something about that name. A Boston Whaler named *Squirt*." Mack shook his head, smiling and looking through the hole blasted out of the starboard bulkhead.

"Think you can get her home, Drew?" Mack inquired, putting a hand on his shoulder as he turned and walked toward the car. "See you on Monday, Christi," he said without turning back.

Christi sat next to Drew as they idled away from the marina and headed toward the mouth of Grand Lagoon in the damaged boat.

"You know, dolphin would likely be injured and not just annoyed by an explosive that close," Christi said as the lights of the marina dimmed behind. "The sound would create an acoustic signal that could be painful to something as sensitive as the sonar melon. There are studies that indicate the melon is a complex connection of incredibly unique sound-producing and sound-receiving cells. They even have a means of communication using those clicks that are detectable at great distances. Did you know that each eye functions separately? While foraging...."

Drew let her continue and mentally stepped away as Christi told him the potential biological ramifications associated with acoustic membranes, low frequency sound waves, and explosives, until she asked, "What do you think?"

"I think I've had a day."

"Me too."

She laughed as she said it and snuggled up a little closer.

"Did you talk to Mack earlier while we were coming in?" Drew asked.

"Yes, he was worried sick, especially after I told him about you and Dr. Bentley. Oh …," she said, sitting up, "and he wanted to make sure we had a snapper for him to take home tonight. Ms. Haymer was expecting fresh fish! I guess I blew it."

"What about you? Was he worried about you?"

She leaned back toward Drew and put her arm around his back.

"Only because I was out here with you and no supervision."

Drew looked ahead in the dark to see two dolphins playing in the bow wave in front of the boat. They were visible through the hole where the explosive had removed a section of the starboard side. The navigation lights reflected red and green on their dorsal fins as they romped just ahead. The moon sketched a broken silver path across the bay from the old fishing community of St. Andrews. The dolphin crossed under the bow, then emerged riding the wave as though they had nothing else to do except enjoy the moment. With the cool breeze, moonlight, a slow pace, and Christi nestled up comfortably, Drew could appreciate that concept.

"Should I be worried?" Drew asked.

"Maybe."

###

Drew awoke to the aroma of fresh coffee. The newspaper was on the back porch where the local section had a spread on the injured dolphin at Gulf. The injured mammal was swimming and eating on its own but was not likely to be returned to the gulf because of irreparable damage to its mouth. It had learned to eat, but needed the assistance of trained professionals, or really slow fish. Gulf had a contest to name him. He had become quite a local celebrity.

Drew sat down at the table with a fresh cup of coffee and scanned the sports page. Looking out across the backyard, a familiar silhouette with a broad brim hat cast a top water lure walking out from the beach at the end of Michigan Ave. He stood on the flat adjacent to a drop-off of several feet. The water beyond him was dark blue but he stood in a clear, light green sandy flat. The precipice made all the difference. It was in that transition water where the fish would wait for prey to swim off the flat, or for the tide to move something along the steep drop off, or a current to push food along the ascending water trough. With these changing conditions, he knew where the fish would likely be. He was fishing the brink. That's where the magic happens, at the edge where the light green flat drops off into the dark blue. Where currents and tides mix the salt water with the fresh. Where the predator finds the prey. Where you can never know what will happen or when, but it's more likely to happen there.

Just as Mr. Whear lifted his rod tip, the still water erupted some thirty feet in front of him. Drew watched as the rod bent sharply and he deftly lowered the tip slightly to allow the fish to rip line off the spool in the opposite direction.

Drew watched intently as he let the fish play, swirl, and run, then slowly succumb to a persistent but superior force. Bigger fish have been lost because of impatience. Mr. Whear demonstrated how easy it could be to apply the fishing tactics of gentle but firm pressure, agile but strong equipment, and a practiced, hard-earned persistence. A confident fisherman doesn't employ the wait-then-attack behavior of a predator, but neither is it the instinctive school-and-run response of the prey. Smaller forces willing to engage his tactics and maintain a slow, determined pressure have vanquished entire armies. Persistence is the strategy of a survivor.

While Drew took a sip of coffee, he saw Mr. Whear hoist the redfish up by the lip, knowing that Drew could see him. It was a big fish, well over the size limit. He slipped the fish gently back into the water and moved him back and forth for a moment to get water across his gill plates.

"Did you see that?" Drew said. Something had just clicked. Christi stepped into the room stirring a cup of coffee and wearing a long, white button down shirt of Drew's.

"The old man knew...," he said, staring into the bay waters at the fish and fisherman. "Tried and true methods, patience, and persistence. He knew all along... it was simply a matter of time."

These fundamentals were an intrinsic part of the original pioneers that fished these waters. They would still be a part of those that remained... the survivors.

In a flash, the redfish was gone. Mr. Whear slowly stood up and watched the crease in the shallow water behind the fish as it raced across the shallow flats and disappeared at the edge of the dark blue. He checked the top-water lure at the rod tip, then looked up toward the house and tipped his hat. A pod of dolphin rolled in the bay out beyond the markers.

Christi and Drew waved back.

THE END

Made in the USA
Monee, IL
13 September 2021